I0522501

He thought he was doing the right thing, sending his daughter off to a brighter future, until he saw this…

What came next was much, much worse. As an unidentified male voice spoke, pictures of Nadia—being manhandled and made to strip by a pudgy little man whose face was blotted out, then her head shoved brutally between the legs of another woman—flashed on the screen.

Mikhail turned away in despair and disgust, and listened to a deep voice make, in an even tone, the following terrible statement: "Mikhail Petrovich, you must listen carefully, if you ever want to see your daughter alive again. Unless you do exactly as I tell you, she will be sold as a sex slave or made to do things much worse than what you have seen here. She has suffered relatively little so far, and if you obey, and if our mission is successful, you will get her back intact. If not, as I said, you will be giving her a future filled with horrors.

"Now, Mikhail Petrovich, you must listen very carefully: we know that you have the day shift this coming Tuesday, May twenty-third, so exactly at four p.m., a white Ford Focus will be driven by a chauffeur to the East Gate where you are scheduled to work. There will be a woman named Julia Saparova in the back seat. You will let this car go through with its passenger and whatever it is carrying, after only a very superficial inspection. If you do this, as I said, your daughter will not be harmed and will be brought back to you. If you do not, or if at any time, you tell the police, your bosses, or anyone else—even your wife—about this approach, as I said earlier, your daughter will suffer the consequences."

The sound track ended with Nadia's unearthly screams in the background, as the screen went blank.

Greg Martens and his wife, former Interpol agent Anne Rossiter, are called back to Vienna by Anne's former boss at Interpol, since their beautiful Russian friend, Julia Saparova, who is now responsible for monitoring nuclear material at various sites in Russia, has disappeared. Afraid that the "merchants of evil" from the former Soviet Union, who are deeply involved in human trafficking, are behind her disappearance, Greg and Anne embark on an international search for Julia, getting drawn into a messy and disturbing web of human and arms trafficking that takes them first to Hungary and then to Montenegro in a desperate bid to rescue, not only Julia, but a group of girls trafficked from Chelyabinsk oblast as well—girls held hostage to facilitate a nuclear heist…

and Greg search for Julia, they fear she has been taken by a human trafficking ring in Russia. The search takes them from Vienna to Hungary, Russia, and Montenegro, and from human trafficking to nuclear heists and the deep dark criminal underworld, where they will be lucky to escape with their lives. *Twisted Traffick* is not an easy read. While the writing is excellent, the characters well developed, and the action fast paced, Tatrallyay exposes the harsh reality of a crime that is all too common, and one we know too little about. Blending a captivating mystery with a page-turning thriller, *Twisted Traffick* is a story you won't soon forget. ~ *Regan Murphy, The Review Team of Taylor Jones & Regan Murphy*

ACKNOWLEDGMENTS

I would like to thank Lauri Wellington, the Acquisitions Editor at Black Opal Books, for seeing the merit of publishing this book, and for assembling a professional team to make that happen. The editorial suggestions of Faith C. were all very appropriate and helpful, and the cover design by Jack Jackson is catchy and captures a key aspect of the book. Many thanks to them and the others who worked on this book.

Twisted Traffick

Geza Tatrallyay

A Black Opal Books Publication

GENRE: CRIME THRILLER/SUSPENSE

This is a work of fiction. Names, places, characters and incidents are either the product of the author's imagination or are used fictitiously, and any resemblance to any actual persons, living or dead, businesses, organizations, events or locales is entirely coincidental. All trademarks, service marks, registered trademarks, and registered service marks are the property of their respective owners and are used herein for identification purposes only. The publisher does not have any control over or assume any responsibility for author or third-party websites or their contents.

DEDICATION

For all the victims of human trafficking

"Our lives begin to end the day we become silent
about the things that matter."
~ Martin Luther King, Jr.

"Slowly, I'm beginning to realize that
what happened to me wasn't my fault,
that I was taken advantage of
by a group of vile, twisted men."
~ Girl A

February, 1950

Chapter 1

Under the dim halo of the rusting streetlamp, Katerina quickly hugged her friend. Natasha congratulated her again as she took her leave outside the grim apartment block where she lived with her parents and brother. Turning into the biting wind, Katerina picked up the pace and shivered with each thick snowflake that managed to land on bare skin inside her hood and the red scarf she had wrapped several times around her face.

Trying to warm herself, she thought of the praise lavished on her that morning in front of the entire class by Gospodja Yevchenkova for the prize she had won in the physics competition. Not only had her project been the best in the class, but it had also been judged the winner among those submitted by students in their last year at school in all of Chelyabinsk-40. That meant that she would stand a good chance of being accepted at the VUZ of her dreams, the celebrated Moscow Institute of Physics and Technology, where her father had studied. He would be proud of her. He might even open a bottle of that sweet Nazdrovia bubbly they all liked so much and let her have a small glass. After all, she had turned sixteen last summer.

The street was deserted in the frigid darkness of the Siberian afternoon: it was hard work trudging through the layers of snow, but Katerina knew that she only had a couple of hundred meters to go, just around the corner, to her building. With the elements howling around her, through all the protective layers she did not hear the purr of the Packard's motor until the car pulled up right next to her. Wondering why the sleek black limo was stopping, she slowed her steps and, turning, saw two men in black leather coats jump out and move quickly in her direction.

It was only when they grabbed her roughly from either side and lifted her toward the car, that a sudden rush of panic overwhelmed her. They shoved her inside, the doors slammed shut and she heard the click of the lock. A confusing feeling of gratitude for the warmth and comfort of the back seat helped blunt the fear. The Packard took off, spinning its wheels around the corner, and she felt it accelerate again as she forlornly looked out to see her apartment block whizz by through the sheet of falling snow and wondered what her parents would think when she didn't come home on time.

"Well, you're a pretty one." Katerina heard a voice penetrate the darkness. Looking across the backseat, she saw a diminutive, balding man sporting frameless glasses, enveloped in an oversized black leather coat. He looked vaguely familiar. "Aren't you, my dear?"

She sat unmoving as he reached over to unwrap the scarf around her face and pull back her hood. Only when the man reached inside her coat and started to unbutton it, did she recoil and move closer to the door.

∾∾∾

The Packard came to a halt on the other side of the town—by the lake, where Katerina knew all the main party officials lived—outside a huge wrought iron gate behind which loomed a luxurious looking dacha. Their family had been honored last summer by being invited to a party near here somewhere, she remembered—a gala event hosted by the exalted Igor Kurchatov, the head of the entire atomic program and, therefore, the most important person who resided in all of Chelyabinsk-40.

"Bring her in quickly," the balding man ordered gruffly, slamming the limo door behind him.

His two henchmen pulled her out of the back seat, taking pleasure from roughly manhandling her, and it was only then that it came to Katerina where he had seen the man. Yes, it had been at that very party: Kurchatov had introduced the family to Lavrenti Beria, and she remembered how uncomfortable she had felt when the man had looked her up and down, stroked her hair and then her chin, and said to her father, "You shouldn't keep this flower hidden, Pleshkov."

And even more so, when on the way home her father explained who Beria was: the most important Deputy Premier of the Soviet Union, Stalin's de facto number two. The former head of the dreaded NKVD, the secret police, of which he was still in charge despite his more exalted position. Stalin had also put the sensitive nuclear program centered at Chelyabinsk-40 into Beria's trusted hands, so he now spent several days a month here to oversee it. Kurchatov reported directly to him, and all the scientists, engineers, everyone—her father included—were there for only one purpose: to develop the Soviet atomic bomb.

But it was the even more frightening discussion that she had with Natasha and Irina at recess one day last spring, a couple of days after their friend Tanya had vanished, that now came flooding back to panic Katerina. Irina reported that she had overheard her father say to her mother that, "no doubt it was that pervert Beria who was behind it all." And the girls were old enough to know that a "pervert" was not a good person, even if he was the second most powerful man in the entire Soviet Union. In fact, that just made it much, much worse.

Katerina was roughly propelled by the two big men through the gate, along the shoveled walk, and around the big house to a side-door. Once inside, one of the men quickly stripped her of her coat and scarf and, grabbing her by the elbow, pulled her through another heavy door, down some dimly lit steps, through yet another entrance, and into a big room. Here, the thug addressed some words that Katerina did not catch to a man in a uniform with a pistol at his side. The official guffawed and looked at her lasciviously as he produced a set of handcuffs and handed them to the big man, who forced Katerina's hands behind her back and clipped the shackles around her wrists. The guy then shoved her through another door and into a dark corridor lit only by the light creeping in through the crack from the room they had just left. Katerina saw bars along the side, and her heart raced with fear as she was pushed into a narrow little cage. As she stumbled to the hard earthen floor, she heard the iron-barred gate close with a creak and a key turn in the lock.

Lying there, in total darkness, bruised and sore, Katerina could not hold back the tears. She was deathly cold and terrified, wondering what was going to happen to her and wanting nothing but the warmth and comfort of home with her mother and father and little sister.

❧❦❧

Although it seemed like an eternity passed, during

which she did not stop crying as she conjured up all kinds of terrors, it was maybe only half an hour later that the door at the end of the corridor opened, allowing light to seep through the crack again. Katerina heard the key inserted in the lock turn and the iron barrier scrape open.

"Don't touch me!" she screamed, as she felt the rough hands of the guard grope her before tugging her to her feet in one motion.

"Come!" the brute commanded. "The boss wants you."

She tried to resist, but she had no choice, since the man was strong and moved her swiftly along, through the large room, up the back steps to the main floor, into the hall, then climbing the grand central stairway and along an opulent corridor to the end, where the guard knocked on some big wooden double doors. Katerina heard a voice from inside say "Enter," as the door opened and she was shoved through. She blinked and wanted to rub the sore arm the thug had gripped so hard to manipulate her, but realized that she was still shackled.

She looked around the luxurious room and saw that the voice must have come from the balding little man from the car with no neck and frameless glasses, standing over by a sideboard pouring a glass of what looked like champagne. Yes. Lavrenti Beria. She was now certain. The face was the same as the unsmiling framed picture in her school, right next to, but slightly below Stalin's, and the panic she had felt earlier overcame her being again with a vengeance.

In the middle of the room, a table was beautifully set for two, she remarked: embroidered tablecloth and carefully folded matching napkins, steaming hot food on porcelain plates, wine filling crystal glasses. From a gramophone on a chest, she heard the strains of her favorite Rachmaninoff piano concerto.

"Here, my pretty little flower," Beria said, coming toward her, "how about a glass of French champagne? Bolinger Grand Réserve, 1928."

It was only then that Katerina noticed that her host had changed into a burgundy silk dressing gown, loosely tied over some more casual clothes.

"Oh, but we must take those off, my dear, mustn't we…Katerina?" He produced a key and opened the handcuffs, rubbing her sore wrists with his sweaty hands. "What a lovely name! Here, now let's drink—and here's to you, my beautiful little one," he continued, handing her a full *flûte* and downing the other one himself. "Come on now, dear, drink up. Our food is waiting for us."

Beria put his arm around Katerina's waist and led her over to the table, pulling out one of the chairs for her, and when she didn't sit down, he pushed her onto it. He took the chair opposite and picked up his napkin. "You must be hungry, my little flower. *Bon appétit!* Eat."

And Katerina could not deny that she was famished, so, after hesitating a moment, she lit into the artistically prepared fish and steamed beets and potatoes in front of her. As she ate in silence and sipped on the delicious wine that her captor kept insisting she consume, her hunger was gradually replaced, first by a leaden lassitude, and then by an irresistible sleepiness. She soon found that she could scarcely keep her eyes open, and the voice of Beria saying, "Here, have a little more wine," seemed to come from ever farther away. She vaguely wondered why she was feeling so tired. Was there perhaps a drug in the champagne or wine?

Katerina hardly understood what she was being ordered to do when, after her first bite of the delicious dessert of *Ptichie Moloko* or birds' milk cake—every young girl's favorite—Beria pulled her to her feet and maneuvered her into a neighboring room with a big bed in it, saying in a harsh voice, "Come, lie down, my dear."

She obeyed, knowing somehow that maybe this wasn't what she should be doing, but by now, her entire being craved the prone position and blissful rest so, so much.

Katerina barely felt the now-spectacle-less and naked man rip her clothes off, but she did scream involuntarily as he squeezed her nipples hard and forced himself inside her.

And then it was all darkness…

❦

The world around was still black when Katerina came to, and she shivered as she felt the coldness of the earthen floor beneath her seep through the blanket that now encased her bruised and naked body. When she tried to sit up, she couldn't. She realized she was sore all over, and especially between her legs. Reaching down there, she felt the wetness still and, bringing her finger to her mouth, she tasted her own blood.

"Oh God, what did that beast do? What did he do to me?"

The questions only brought the panic back, and, as she confronted the hopelessness of her situation, she let the tears flow, yearning for the gentle embrace of her mother, the comforting words of her father…

2018

Chapter 2

Mikhail Glinkov was glad it was Friday, and that it was time to clock out. He liked his work as a security guard at the Mayak Production Facility, but as always by the end of the week, he could not help looking forward to a day or two to rest up and spend time with the family. Though it was now already eight o'clock and starting to get dark, the late May Siberian sun had been warmer than usual, and the weekend promised to be equally nice. He smiled as he thought of the long walk they liked to take on Sunday mornings with his wife, Galina, daughter, Nadia, and son, Yuri, along the shores of beautiful Lake Kyshtym.

As he made his way out of the locker room, where he had taken off his holster and changed out of his work clothes and into his own much more comfortable casuals, he glanced at a notice on the bulletin board. He remarked on it only because the bright pink paper it was written on stood out from the usual drab adverts offering second-hand stoves or fridges for sale, or piano or English classes for the wife and children. The big bold black letters announced a meeting on Saturday afternoon at three p.m.

in Room B of the Ozersk Community Hall, where someone from the European Placement Agency would discuss
job placement possibilities in the west for children just
finishing school.

Just then, his boyhood friend, Pavel, who regularly
worked with him on the shift, came up behind Mikhail to
remind him of his wife, Svetlana's birthday party Saturday evening. Glancing at the notice Mikhail was looking
at, he added, "Yes, I saw that earlier. I was also thinking
of going to that presentation. It could be good for the
girls to get away from here, finally." And he looked
around, as if to see if there was anybody within hearing
range before he continued. "We both know that this is no
place to bring up a child, with all the contamination
around."

Mikhail knew, like everyone else knew. And,
although he had not thought about it much before,
because he didn't think it possible, Pavel was absolutely
right, Mikhail told himself in the minibus that ferried the
workers from the site to Lenin Park in the middle of
Ozersk. It would be best for Nadia to get away from here.

In the last few years, a few reports had appeared in
the press about the still dangerous levels of radioactive
pollution in and around Mayak. And the serious effects
on the health and morbidity of the population that resided
in the region. Several of these articles were clear that the
average life span here was more than five years less than
elsewhere in Russia. And there was that report a few
years ago circulating clandestinely among his friends,
claiming that over the last thirty-five or so years, there
had been a twenty-one per cent increase in the incidences
of cancer and a twenty-five per cent increase in birth de-
fects, and that fully fifty per cent of the population of
child bearing age was sterile.

The figures had stuck in his mind. They were staggering, if true.

Indeed, several of Nadia's classmates had been diagnosed with cancer already, and Svetlana, Pavel's wife—whose fortieth birthday it would be Saturday—was being treated for breast cancer. Many of their friends were ill. Some, like Galina's father, a former colleague—who actually had worked in one of the reactors—had passed away, he with pancreatic cancer. And there were many more. Although they were not supposed to talk about it openly, when they and their friends got together, the deaths, sicknesses, birth deformities often ended up being the subject of conversation.

So why not have Nadia go to the west, if a good job opportunity, that would allow her to have a better, healthier life, presented itself? In any case, it was unlikely that she would be accepted at the Institute of Physics and Technology in Moscow—even though she was an honors student, and her marks were possibly good enough, Mikhail was sufficiently pragmatic to know that politically he was a nothing. And what was the alternative? Marriage to her boyfriend, Gennady—Pavel's and Svetlana's two-year-older son? Who would no doubt also end up working at Mayak. And the standard boxy apartment in one of the Communist era apartment blocks that still housed most of the workers—other than, of course, the bigwigs who lived in the villas by the lake. Maybe two children if she was lucky—and not one of the sterile fifty per cent—hopefully, not deformed or plagued with illnesses. And pray, not an early death.

He would talk to Galina about this tonight, and perhaps Nadia as well. No, maybe he would go to the meeting first with Pavel, and then discuss it with his wife and daughter afterward. Better to get all the facts and make sure this was indeed a real opportunity. Yes, better that, than just to get their hopes up and then have to dash them.

⌇⌇⌇

When Mikhail and Pavel got to the Ozersk Town Hall, the meeting had already started. Mikhail had hemmed and hawed during his entire lunch over what he should tell Galina about where he was going. Finally, he decided a little white lie would not hurt, and he would just say it was a meeting concerning some new opportunities at work, and that Pavel was also going. That way, if there really was something worthwhile for Nadia, he could always just say he had misunderstood—and that, in any case, he was really glad that he went. Besides, then telling the falsehood wouldn't matter anyway since the women would be all full of excitement and anticipation. And if nothing came of the whole thing, they would never need to know the truth.

A slightly paunchy, well-dressed man sporting what to Mikhail looked like obviously dyed blond hair was speaking as he and Pavel sat down in the back row.

"We fly the young ladies and young men in a charter plane to our headquarters in Hungary, where our placement experts interview and select them for jobs we have specially identified throughout Europe. In this brochure—" And he started handing around a pile of glossy handouts. "—we have a list of some of the recent job placements we have made, as well as an insert showing the specific employment opportunities now waiting for your sons and daughters.

"As you will see, these are all well paying positions with strong, bona fide companies. We, at the European Placement Agency, will take care of all the necessary paperwork to make this a reality for the families that place their trust in us. We will work with the companies to secure working visas and make sure your children are eligible for health and other benefits.

"Of course, I am happy to answer any questions you may have."

Mikhail put his hand up. "Please, I would like to know how we can make ourselves and our wives absolutely comfortable with the idea of sending our sons and daughters to a foreign country to work in a strange environment. How do we know they will not be exploited? And even if you do succeed in getting them good jobs, where and how will they live? It's not just about the jobs—"

"Yes, I am glad you asked that question, sir, and of course that is all explained in the brochure. On page four there are testimonials from parents around Russia whose children we have placed. Also, on the page inside the cover, you will note that Deputy Prime Minister Malensky has given a glowing endorsement to this project to place Russia's young adults in meaningful jobs in the West where they can learn about capitalism first hand. With respect to where your sons and daughters will live, that is also treated in the brochure: arrangements will be made for them to be housed with families that are trusted by the program and have worked with us before. You can rest assured your loved ones will be in good hands."

"How do I secure a place for my daughter?" a reedy voiced, bespectacled man, whom Mikhail recognized as one of the doctors in the hospital facility at Mayak, stood up and asked without seeing the need to raise his hand and wait his turn.

"I was just getting to that." The man on the podium maintained his composure. "Now I know most of you will want to talk this over with your wives and children. It is not an easy decision for you to part with your young loved ones. But this will be a terrific experience for them in great surroundings, I can assure you. The loose page in the brochure is a form you and your teenager will have to fill out and get back to me before the end of next week. Full names of you and your wife, occupations, dates of birth, a photo of the loved one being sent, highest grade completed in school, any special trades or training, languages, etcetera—you will see on the form. I am at the Ozersk Hotel until next Sunday and happy to meet at your convenience. My cell number and email are at the bottom of the page."

෬෯෬෯

"So, Pavel, what do you think?" Mikhail asked his friend and colleague as they went out onto the sunny sidewalk.

"Well, I am convinced it's a worthwhile opportunity for Sasha. Anything, to get her away from here."

"I don't know…" Mikhail was pensive. "The guy—Kalinsky or whatever his name is—seemed a little sleazy to me. I just don't know if I am ready to trust Nadia to him and his outfit."

"But, Mikhail, the Deputy Prime Minister is behind them. And there are all those families who gave this European Placement Agency a very favorable endorsement. What else do you want?"

"Yeah, but—"

"And that doctor, you know from the hospital, he is jumping at the chance. He, if anyone, would know that it's best to get his children away from here. And the sooner, the better."

"Yes, I guess you are right."

"In fact, I am concerned there may not be enough places. I think I will contact this Kalinsky today, right after we talk it over with Svetlana. I wouldn't want Sasha to miss out."

ᴄ∕ᴊᴄ∕ᴐ

Galina received the news of the opportunity for her daughter with mixed feelings. She agreed with Mikhail that they needed to jump on it for Nadia's sake—anything, anywhere to get her away from this godforsaken contaminated place, she told herself—but all the same, she was not too happy about having her little girl go so far from home and her motherly love. She would just have to bear it, she told her husband, but the reality and the suddenness of it made it all that much more painful.

Nadia, of course, was ecstatic. She had been wanting to travel, to get away from the parental home, and see and experience the big wide world. Although, she assured her parents, she would miss them and her little brother, Yuri, and all her friends.

Mikhail tried to do some more checking on the European Placement Agency on various internet search engines, but there was not much on them. He did see some contact details for them in Hungary, and copied down the phone number with the intention of trying it on Monday.

The last hurdle Mikhail brought up with Galina that night was the money. It would not be cheap: right there in the brochure it said they would have to pay the representative of the European Placement Agency 250,000 rubles.

That was more than six months of his salary, and, in fact, almost all of their savings.

"We will just dip into our emergency fund," Galina answered, not hesitating an instant. "This is why we have been putting that money away all these years. So that we can provide a better future for our children. Mikhail, you know very well this is no place for them, especially our daughter. We do want to have grandchildren after all, don't we?"

☙❧

So the next morning, even though it was Sunday, before they went on their walk, Mikhail called the Ozersk Hotel and asked for Gospodin Kalinsky.

"Delighted, Gospodin Glinkov, that you are giving this serious thought. We are only doing this here in Ozersk now, and I don't know when we might be back."

"Of course. Of course." Mikhail did not know what to make of the implied pressure. "I will bring the form all filled out."

"Good. And, ahem, please, half the money—without that, we cannot reserve a place for your…is it son or daughter?"

"Daughter."

"Splendid. The rest is payable before departure. Oh yes, and a full body picture please, as it says in the form."

"What time?"

"Shall we say…five o'clock? Here in the hotel bar, Gospodin Glinkov. I would be pleased to invite you for a drink."

"Good." *That's the least you can do, you slimy bugger. With my money!*

Mikhail was still not certain that he was doing the right thing.

☙❧

"She is a very pretty girl, your daughter, Gospodin Glinkov," the dyed-blond-haired man who called himself Kalinsky observed as he studied the picture Mikhail had handed him. "We shouldn't have any problems placing her. The job at first may be…umm…secretarial, but judging from her marks, she will have no difficulties moving into something more challenging."

Downing his second shot of Putinka vodka, Mikhail felt a little comforted, but he still did not like this man. "Where will you take her?" he asked, again seeking reassurance.

"We fly to Hungary, as I said. But we don't know yet where we will place her. The employment experts in our office there will look through the list of opportunities and weigh what is best for her. Maybe something in Germany or Austria would be appropriate, since I see she is learning the language."

"Good. At least her German will get better."

"Well, Gospodin Glinkov, you will be pleased at the opportunity we will provide for your daughter. We do not put this in writing, but we know that for children, the odds of growing up healthy here in Chelyabinsk province are much reduced. And for girls, it is much worse, I am sure you are aware."

"Of course."

"That is one of the reasons I try to come to Ozersk, at least once every couple of years. To help the families here. After all, part of my family, too, was originally from Chelyabinsk Oblast, so I do try to make a point of coming here. But the demand for our services throughout Russia is so big that we can only take a small number from this region. So, I am pleased to say that Nadia will be one of the few…ahem…provided, of course the finances are in order."

Mikhail reached inside his jacket and pulled out an envelope. "Here, Gospodin Kalinsky. The money is all here. Half, that is, as agreed. The rest will come with Nadia."

"Thank you. You will not regret this, Gospodin Glinkov." Kalinsky put the envelope away without opening it. He knew that his clients were not in a position to cheat him. Since they would be handing over their most prized possessions: their daughters and sons.

(hapter 3

"Can you get the phone, Greg?" Anne Martens yelled to her husband, as—still dripping after her morning shower—she reached for her towel, exasperated that he had already let the phone ring four or five times.

"Hello! Martens residence." She heard his voice in the neighboring bedroom, where, still lounging in bed, he had finally lowered the volume of the Liszt Second Piano Concerto he was listening to on Vermont Public Radio. "Anne? You want to speak to my wife? Of course, she's here. May I tell her who is calling?" A pause. "John? John who?"

Then much louder, as Greg's well-toned naked form loomed in the bathroom door, and he reached the cell phone toward her: "For you, dear. John Demeter." And putting his other hand over the microphone, he added, "Geez, I never thought you would hear from him again."

She finished tying the towel around her body and, took the mobile. "Hello, John. What a surprise! Are you coming to visit?"

Her former boss at Interpol was the last person she

expected to be calling her on a beautiful Sunday morning in Vermont.

"Anne, I am glad I finally found you. Sorry, but I will get right to it. We need you to help us out. You must come back to Vienna."

"Why, John? I quit my job when I married Greg. I no longer work for Interpol—"

"I know, Anne. But you are the only one who might be able to get to the bottom of this. You, and Greg, of course."

"What do you mean?"

"Julia Saparova has disappeared. Your friend from that Russian uranium heist business a few years back."

"What?"

"She hasn't shown up at work for almost a week now. No trace at all, no clues whatsoever. The head of security at the International Atomic Energy Agency called a little while ago. They are extremely concerned over there."

"That is really weird, John. So—just like Adam—Kallay, who had the same job before her—"

"Yeah, I remember. The guy from the IAEA told me she was the one now in charge of monitoring nuclear security in the successor states of the former Soviet Union. Disappearing is an occupational hazard, it would seem."

"Hmm." This was too much, too fast. Anne needed time to process all this information.

"But come to think of it, didn't Kallay feign his death?"

"Yes, that's right, John. But I can't see Julia doing that. Do you think, though, that this could be related? Or could there be another heist in the making?"

"Don't know, sweetheart. But that is what the IAEA is worried about. And not just them. We at Interpol, too, are very concerned. That is why I need you here, with your charming husband. Pronto. You guys got to the bottom of that Kallay disappearance act, so I am hoping you will be able to figure this one out as well. And find the lovely Miss Saparova."

"John, I am no longer—"

"She's your friend, Anne." In fact, she had been Adam's friend, and Greg's, but Anne too, had become friends with the Russian girl through that ordeal. "And don't worry, I will make sure it is worth your while."

"Well, I'll talk to Greg."

She knew he would not be happy. They had made plans to go on a big hike up near Smuggler's Notch. And now that classes were over at Middlebury, he had wanted to catch up on his writing. He had shown her the synopsis of the next thriller in his trilogy, and he was keen to get going on it. There was also the vegetable garden they needed to plant, and the dinner party at the Gladstone's…Anne's mind wandered.

"We've booked you two on a KLM flight from Boston via Amsterdam, then Vienna. Tonight. I think it's around nine p.m. Hope you can make it."

"John—"

"Let me know in two hours. I'll arrange a car to drive you to Logan. Four p.m., how is that? And someone will pick you up at Schwechat. Bye for now."

Chapter 4

Nadia finally opened her eyes. She had not wanted to talk to anybody since saying goodbye to her parents and Yuri at Balandino Airport and being ushered out through a side gate to the unmarked Yak-40 waiting ominously on the tarmac. She watched the lights of the terminal whiz by as the plane accelerated, and then, when it lifted off, she closed her eyes. She just wanted to block everything out, empty her mind.

But now she had to go to the toilet. She looked back along the plane and saw that the single washroom was unoccupied, so she undid her seatbelt and got up. As she made her way along the aisle, she remarked that all the passengers were more or less her age, some just a little older. Twenty or so girls, maybe a couple more. No boys. Which was strange, because her father had implied that both males and females were being recruited by the European Placement Agency. And in fact, there was only one girl from her school, other than her friend Sasha who was five rows in front of her. Nadia could tell from the red eyes that most had been crying.

As had she, for a good part of the trip, despite her

shut eyes. It had not been easy to leave her parents and little brother. But she was sure that this was the right thing to do. Although she was not happy that her father had to pay such a huge amount of money—she had overheard her parents discuss it several evenings earlier—to that sleazy guy sitting up there in the front row, all by himself. Kalinsky was his name, if she remembered correctly, from when she was introduced to him as her father handed her over in the terminal along with the envelope.

Coming out of the bathroom, she was surprised to see a big man, head shaved and dressed all in black, just outside the door. He addressed her gruffly and told her to get back to her seat immediately. The plane would be landing soon. Was this how flight attendants behaved? And weren't most of them supposed to be pretty women, and not scary looking thugs? This guy sure was not dressed like what she had seen on TV.

Back at her seat, Nadia looked out the window, trying to glimpse the lights of the city where they would be landing. But she only saw a few glimmering specks, far in the distance. Other than that, it was pitch dark out there. She closed her eyes again, wondering what awaited her and her companions. What kind of new life, away from family and friends? What kind of adventures?

⁊ఎఎ⁊

Nadia stood, blinking, for a few seconds at the top of the staircase, trying to adjust her eyes to the darkness outside. Only two strings of landing lights on either side of the makeshift runway and the lights of a car and a truck penetrated the gloom.

It seemed that the plane had come to a halt on a dirt strip in the middle of some fields—no, in the middle of nowhere, she told herself.

Was this Hungary, where her father had said they would first land?

She looked down the stairs, and at the bottom saw six big men arrayed in two rows that led to the back of a covered truck.

"Come on, honey, move along there," the giant with one hand on the railing below yelled, as he waved a flashlight to illuminate the steps, "We haven't got all night!"

Slowly, Nadia took the stairs one by one, as she saw Kalinsky glance at her and calmly light a cigarette next to the guy waving the flashlight. Keeping her eyes glued ahead, she glimpsed Sasha being pushed roughly up into the back of the vehicle.

"Hmm, this is a pretty good crop, from what I've seen so far," the thug at Kalinsky's side said, shining his light into Nadia's bewildered face as she passed.

And then, when she reached the vehicle, a man grabbed her under the arms and shoved her up, patting her on the backside, "Get up there now, babe. Time to get going."

Inside, she sat down beside Sasha on the wooden bench along one side of the truck. Nadia put her arm around her friend and whispered into her ear, "This is not what I expected. I am scared."

"Me too," came Sasha's answer as she hugged her back. "Let's try to stay together."

"No talking there, you two!" The man all the way in the front shouted, as the doors of the truck closed shut, and the girls were left in pitch darkness. Several started sobbing, and Nadia heard the girl on her right whisper, "I want to go home. I want my mother."

"Shut up, you bitches!" The command penetrated the black space.

The adventure was not starting well.

◈◈◈

The truck bumped along what must have been a dirt road for several minutes and then, after it veered onto a smoother surface, increased speed. Another twenty minutes or so, and it must have turned off the tarmac road again because the ride became rougher. Then another change in direction, and it came to a screeching halt. Nadia could hear some muffled words exchanged outside, followed by what must have been the squeaking of an opening gate, before the vehicle started up again.

Finally, they came to a stop and Nadia heard the doors on the cab slam shut, some yelling, then the clang of the bolt and the doors of their compartment opening. The same gruff voice that had told them earlier to shut up now yelled at them to get out.

Standing at the very back of the truck before dismounting, Nadia was shocked by the well-lit scene that greeted her eyes: the girls who had already clambered down, huddled in a circle, frightened and clinging to each other, surrounded by ten or twelve armed guards dressed in black with black baseball caps. Kalinsky, off to the side, chatting and laughing with the giant thug and a square, balding man, smoking a cigarette. In the background, a complex of lit-up buildings to which a walkway led from where they had disembarked. As she jumped down, the guards were already ushering the assembled girls toward the door of the main structure.

Kalinsky came up behind her, just as she was trying to catch up to the others. "Come, my dear, you come with me. I want to show you something special. This way."

Nadia hesitated, looking after the receding line of girls, wanting to stay with Sasha, but then the man grabbed her by the arm, and literally lifted her along the path that led to the doorway of a smaller house over at

the side of the complex. There was no question of resist-
ing.

She did not like this Kalinsky, nor how the European
Placement Agency was treating its new charges.

Chapter 5

Demeter had a chauffeur with a sign that had *Anne Rossiter* written on it in big bold letters waiting for them at Arrivals at Schwechat Airport. Her maiden name, by which she had been known at Interpol.

A slight hint?

It was a beautiful May midday in Vienna, as the car sped along the Autobahn on its way to the center of town, taking them to the Sacher Hotel where Demeter had decided to have Interpol put them up.

"I know your husband stayed there during that infernal Kallay affair," he had said when Anne called back to tell him that Greg and she agreed to come, "so since you are doing me and Interpol a big favor, that's where we'll have you stay. Even though that'll blow my entertainment budget for the entire year."

Anne chuckled at her former boss's niggardliness, but was glad that he was willing to go all out, since that showed how much they were really needed.

Demeter had been clear though in his instructions that he wanted them to come to the office as soon as they had checked in and washed up. However, Anne indulged

Greg's insistence on first celebrating being back in Vienna by having a *Steinpilz* Omelet and a glass of Zweigelt, followed by a slice of the famous Sacher Torte and a *kleiner Brauner* Viennese coffee for a quick lunch in the Sacher Stube before going to help out the international intelligence agency *ex officio*.

They walked over to where Anne had spent three and a half years working in the Interpol offices behind the Börse, the old stock exchange building, and she was overcome with the exuberance of a little child as she remembered the Aida *Confiserie* where she would pick up the yummy marzipan-filled croissant that was her usual weekday breakfast, or the Tabak where she would get her newspaper each evening on the way home. And she was positively glowing when they arrived at the fifth-story offices in the turn-of-the-last-century building, and Frau Huth, the secretary she had shared with her French colleague, Nicholas Labrecque, welcomed her warmly with a double-cheeked kiss.

Demeter though, was his usual grumpy self, checking his watch and greeting them with a "What took you so long? I thought your plane landed at eleven-twenty-five a.m. It's now two-forty-seven p.m. Christ, the day is almost over."

"So—" Anne ignored the comment from her former boss, and started straight into the business, once the three men—Greg, Demeter and Labrecque—had joined her at the table in the Conference room where Frau Huth had placed her steaming *Mélange,* "—tell me, John, what do we have?"

"Not a lot more than what I've told you already," said Demeter, sitting at the head of the table. "The simple fact is that Julia Saparova has disappeared without a trace. As I said, I received a very worried call yesterday from Jean Timmermans, the Head of Security at the International Atomic Energy Agency—I think you know him, Anne—saying that she had not come to work for three days. And when they tried to track her down, she did not respond to any calls on her home phone or on her mobile. Nor to any emails. They also looked on the usual social media sites—you know, Facebook, Twitter, Linked-In. But nothing."

"Anybody talk to her secretary?"

"Yes," Labrecque answered. "I went by to check things out in her office right after the call. Her Peruvian assistant was there."

"Still the same one Adam had?" Anne remembered quizzing the Peruvian woman after Kallay's disappearance. "The little square lady? She's Inca I think, Adam once told me."

"Yes, it would seem. Well, anyway, she told me that Julia was supposed to fly to Chelyabinsk last Thursday and then go up to Mayak on business. But her unused ticket was still sitting right there, on her desk."

"Passport?"

"That she must have had with her or back at home. We need to check on that."

"What about her hotel out there? Probably the Meridian Chelyabinsk, which is the only semi-decent place in Chelyabinsk," Greg interjected, remembering from the time he had followed Adam. "And where would she stay in Ozersk, do we have an idea? Did anybody call to see if by any chance she checked in somewhere? Unlikely, I know, but…"

"I had the Peruvian woman call both the Meridian Chelyabinsk and the Hotel Ozersk, and although the Meridian confirmed that Ms. Saparova is a regular customer, they have not seen her in the last three weeks," Labrecque answered. "The Ozersk did not know her at all."

"Come to think of it, she must stay with her mother, who has an apartment there," Greg observed.

"Anything else, Nicholas, you were able to glean from the secretary?" This from Anne.

"Nothing. She, too, confirmed that your Julia just disappeared as if into thin air. Nothing out of the ordinary, before or after. No weird happenings, absolutely nothing. She just did not come to work on Monday, did not call in, and has not responded to any calls or attempts to get in touch with her."

"Did anybody go to her apartment?" Greg asked.

"Yes, in fact, I went by yesterday, straight from the IAEA. I rang and rang the bell downstairs, to no avail. Eventually I raised the concierge, who took me up to the second floor where her flat is. I pushed the bell there several times too, and knocked loudly, but no one came to the door. Although I did have the strange sensation that there might have been someone on the other side. I thought I heard some movement in there—in the apartment. And breathing."

"Very strange." This from Greg.

"Well, maybe there was someone inside," Labrecque mused. "It might even have been Julia."

"Possible, but not likely," Anne said, contradicting her former colleague. "She would have no reason to go underground like that. Unless she was pulling another Kallay. But that would not be her style. And hiding in her apartment would not achieve anything."

"You're right, Anne." Labrecque agreed.

"Well, let's go by there as soon as we can get a warrant," Anne continued. "John, can we get Frau Huth to organize Lieutenant Haffner—he's still around, I'm sure—to procure one as soon as possible and meet us there?"

"Yeah, we were going to get a warrant already but

we thought we'd get the whole team here first. Haffner, you said?" Demeter picked up the intercom and passed on Anne's request to Frau Huth. "She'll let us know as soon as she hears back from the Austrian police," he added grumpily as he hung up.

∾✃∾

"Rudolf, thanks for your help, yet again," Anne said, expressing her gratitude to Lieutenant Haffner, who had been her contact at the Vienna police during her years with Interpol, stationed in the Austrian capital, with special responsibilities for matters relating to the International Atomic Energy Agency. He had been good support during that terrible Kallay affair that Greg and she had managed to get to the bottom of, and was now waiting for them downstairs in his car with a warrant to search Julia's residence, which was where they headed next.

"I can't believe we have another IAEA staff disappearance on our hands. And as it happens, it is one of your friends again," Haffner said, smiling at Greg from the front seat. "You must be jinxed."

"Well, it was Adam Kallay who was really Julia's friend," Greg corrected, "and he was trying to get her a job at the IAEA before he got himself involved in that terrible heist affair."

"Yes, I remember. We came very close to deporting her as an illegal alien. She was working without papers. As an exotic dancer, of all things. But wow—"

"That was just meant to be temporary. So she could earn a living until Adam came through with the IAEA position," Greg said, taking the Russian girl's side. "For a beautiful girl like Julia here illegally, it was easier to get a job in that business, even though she has a PhD in nuclear physics."

"But then she cooperated with us to help find Adam, so you were kind enough to expedite her papers, Rudolf," Anne remarked.

"No, she actually did not need Austrian work papers once she was employed by the IAEA," Haffner corrected her. "They got her an international organizations visa, and the Austrian authorities just rubberstamped it. That is the normal procedure."

"So it was Adam then in the end who helped her stay!" Greg said, as Anne surmised that her husband was happy that his erstwhile friend had managed to do at least this one good deed.

☙❧

Once the doorman let them into the building on Momsengasse, in the Fourth District, Haffner rang the bell several times at the second floor apartment, but no one answered. Anne, who put her ear to the door as he was doing this, thought she heard some noises from inside. But in the end, she could not be certain that she was not just being influenced by what Labrecque had told them earlier.

With warrant in hand, however, Lieutenant Haffner had no problem in getting the housekeeper to open the door of the compact one bedroom apartment. Standing in the middle of the sparsely furnished combined living room, dining room and kitchen, and seeing that the door leading presumably to what was the bedroom was closed, Anne said to the other two, "You guys stay here and cover me. I will go inside." But she did pull out the Glock 26 Demeter had insisted she reequip herself with, just in case.

All the precaution, though, was unnecessary. No Julia, but sitting on the bed was a haggard looking, rather anxious, elderly lady. "Who are you? What are you doing here?" Anne addressed the stranger.

Greg came in just as his wife lowered her gun and moved closer to the woman. "Ah, Gospodja Saparova! What a pleasant surprise to find you here." He recognized Julia's mother from the time he and Adam had paid her a visit in Ozersk.

Julia's mother stared at the intruders with a blank look.

Was she not dying of cancer?

"You are here to visit your daughter?"

The look on the old lady's face suddenly changed, lighting up with what seemed to be the hint of a smile of recognition. "Mr. Martens, is it? I remember you from the time you and Julia's friend, Adam Kallay, came to see me. How nice. Yes, my daughter invited me to come to Vienna. The care is better here, and she wanted me with her. For the last few months, before this terrible sickness takes me. But now it is she who has gone. And I am all alone. My dear daughter, please—"

"Well, that is why we are here, Gospodja Saparova," Greg interrupted her. "To help find Julia. We know she has not been seen at work for over a week now. Do you have any idea where she might be?"

"Mr. Martens, I know you are a good man. Julia gave me your book, *András and Lily*, and I really like how you told the story of you parents. You have a lot of love in you, I can tell, and respect for my generation. Maybe you can help me, just as Mr. Kallay helped my daughter with the job."

"But of course."

"Yes, it was he who called six days ago when Julia was working late—"

Greg blinked, stunned. "Kallay?"

"Yes, your friend told me to tell Julia to meet him

that night at the Revuebar Rasputin. Where she used to work, he said. At ten p.m. He insisted she would know what it was about. By the way, what kind of place is this…this Revuebar?"

"No! That is impossible. Kallay—Adam Kallay—is dead! And Julia knew that." Greg was still too shocked by the revelation to focus on Gospodja Saparova's question.

"Dead? He can't be. Certainly not when I talked to him on the telephone a week or so ago, as I just told you. The man who called introduced himself as Adam Kallay—yes, definitely—and said he wanted to meet her. At that Revuebar place."

"So, you told Julia?" Anne asked.

"Yes, I gave her the message as soon as she came home from work that night. She too, was puzzled, but went off to meet your friend. At the Revuebar Rasputin. And I haven't seen her since."

"Hmm. The Rasputin has changed ownership," Haffner said. "Last year. It was bought by some Russian oligarch backed outfit, apparently. But there may be some criminal connection, we think. We are still trying to get to the bottom of it."

"Oh no—"

Anne could see that Julia's mother was on the verge of tears, as Greg moved closer and put his arms around her. "Gospodja Saparova, it's all right. We will find your daughter, rest assured."

"Well, my young friend—" The old lady looked up at Greg, wiping her eyes with a tissue. "—I hope you are right. My experience is that such things usually do not end well. Certainly, not with Russian—"

"But this is Austria. The West…"

"Never mind. Russians are involved. They are meeting at that Revuebar, which you said is now owned by some oligarchs. Maybe criminals. It's just like—"

"Yes, I guess if you are talking of my friend Adam. He went missing for a while. And you don't know this, but some Russian arms merchants ended up corrupting him."

"I see. But no, I don't mean just him. Also, my older sister, Katerina. She disappeared like this many years ago, and was never found again."

"What are you saying?" Anne asked.

"Wait, I show you. If you have a moment."

Not waiting for an answer, Gospodja Saparova got up from the bed, and went over to the chest of drawers. She pulled out the same battered old rusty tin box from where she had extracted the letter Greg's grandfather, András Bányai—who died after the war at Mayak, as human fodder forced to go inside the reactor to clean up a horrific nuclear accident—had asked her father to safeguard, and she had given to Adam and Greg on their visit in Ozersk.

"Here, I brought these family letters for Julia." She could not stop the tears streaming down her cheeks. "My father wrote this one, and left it for my mother. You see, carefully marked with big black letters: 'To open only after my death.' You read it. The others in here, too, go ahead. They tell of the terrible degeneracy of the Stalin years. And how my family was affected." She took out a few yellowing pieces of paper from a tattered envelope and handed them to Greg then went over to the counter to get another tissue.

Julia's mother wiped the tears from her eyes. "I cannot even look at this without crying. Sorry. Especially now that Julia is missing too. That makes it much, much worse. You take them all, these letters—here, take the box—and read what is in there. And Greg, since you are a writer, make this horrifying story public, like you did with your family's story, so that the world can know what depravity took place in the Soviet Union. For my sake. And Julia's."

"Sure, but—"

"I already showed these letters to Julia a few years ago, but if you find her, give them to her. After you read them. I don't want them anymore."

"Thank you, Gospodja Saparova. We will find Julia," Greg said, carefully taking the letter and the box from the old lady's hands. "And we will read these later, back at the hotel."

"They have cursed my life, these letters," the old lady said, crumbling back onto the sofa.

"I will go to the Revuebar Rasputin where Julia was supposed to meet this Kallay—or whoever is masquerading as him. That is the next step."

"Don't worry, Gospodja Saparova, we will find Julia," Anne added. "She is our friend."

"Thank you. You are good people, both of you."

"If this Kallay gets in touch again, let us know. Here, let me write down our mobile numbers."

"Thank you. I have no one else I can ask to help find my daughter."

Chapter 6

The heavy-set man with the dyed-blond hair her father had paid the large sum of money to unlocked the door and pushed Nadia inside the building, just as a guard came to see what all the noise was about.

"Hello, boss. I thought it would be you. Back with the new merchandise?" the thug asked as he leered at Nadia.

Kalinsky ignored the man's question. "Everything all right here, Ivan?"

"Yes. No problems. She is still here."

"Good. Take this one upstairs." The boss shoved Nadia toward the guard, nodding in the direction of an elevator with his chin. "Back where she is. I'll be there soon."

Ivan grabbed Nadia's arm, squeezing it really hard. "You come with me. I don't want no trouble." He shoved Nadia into a spacious lift, then pushed a button with his free hand. Nadia glanced into the mirror that formed the back wall of the cubicle, and she saw a pale, frightened face looking back at her. The elevator rumbled to a stop.

The guard tugged her out and along a long corridor at the end of which was another door. "Okay, honey. This is where I want you to stay put. For the boss. And no funny stuff," Ivan said as he manhandled her into a spacious room, flicking the lights on and closing the door behind her.

Nadia rubbed her arm where the guard had gripped her and looked around in the dimly lit, sparsely furnished room: there was just one chair and a big iron-framed king-size bed with a small table beside it, on which was the only lamp that illuminated the entire space. She blinked several times as she saw that the silk sheet on the bed was all rumpled and there seemed to be someone underneath. Unsure of what to do, and very frightened, she stepped closer, saying, in barely a whisper, "Hello. Hello?"

The teenager saw that the person sleeping under the sheet was a woman, perhaps a little older than she, very beautiful, with her disheveled blonde hair spread across the pillow and long slender legs and arms protruding from under the cover. To her horror, Nadia then noticed that the blonde's left wrist was handcuffed to one of the metal posts at the back of the bed and her face was all bruised. "Oh no," she said to herself. "Oh my God, no!"

A sense of panic overcame her. Nadia slumped down on the chair and rested her face in her hands. She needed to take stock of her situation, figure out what she should do. Should she just tell that man Kalinsky that he could keep all the money her father had given him, but that he should let her go home? That would be a really good deal for the creep. He wouldn't have to place her in a job, or do anything for the money. Her parents would have lost all their savings, but at least she would be free. But this was just too scary, not at all what she—or, she was sure, for that matter, her parents—had expected, and she had a bad feeling that it would not end well. Yes, definitely when Kalinsky came back, she would suggest this to him.

And then the door opened, and in walked the man himself, dressed in a comfortable jogging suit and thongs. He came straight over to where Nadia was sitting and, grabbing her under the chin, roughly pulled her to her feet, even as with his other hand he pulled a pistol out from somewhere in his attire and, pointing it at her temple, said with a smile, "Okay, my pretty one. It is now time for you to perform."

Kalinsky stepped back as Nadia started to cry, "Please, please, just let me go home. Please!"

The brute bashed her in the chest with the pistol. "Stop that whimpering, you stupid bitch. And take your fucking clothes off. I want you naked. You should consider yourself lucky that I did not send you off with the others. We will just have a little fun here, you and me. The two of us—" Then waving the pistol and looking over at the stirring blonde, he added, "No, the three of us," before he let out a Mephistophelean laugh.

When Nadia, who was in complete shock, remained motionless, he grabbed her by the front of her blouse and, twisting it, ripped it off her. Dropping the pistol, he pulled her against his fat body and undid her bra, throwing it on the floor, then shoved her against the wall. "Take the rest off yourself, bitch, or you will regret it."

Trying hard to stop crying, she was terrified that this monster would kill her or hurt her even more if she did not obey. So Nadia slowly started to unbutton her skirt. She stepped out of it, as the monster yanked the sheet off the blonde girl in the bed. Nadia saw that her beautiful body was naked with several bruises and whip marks defacing it.

"Panties off."

Nadia heard Kalinsky's voice as if from very far

away, and knew she had no choice but to do as she was told.

"Very good—" He picked the pistol up, as he looked her over. "—very nice, indeed." Then prodding the blonde in the crotch with the gun, the creep commanded, "You, you wake up." The semi-conscious woman uttered a groan and a whimper. Kalinsky pulled back and waved the piece at Nadia, saying, "Okay, now my dear, I want you to make love to this gorgeous wench. You know, with your tongue—down there." He made a slurping noise with his tongue and lips as he grabbed Nadia's hair and pushed her face between the blonde's legs. Pistol-whipping Nadia on the buttocks, he ordered, "Lick, yes, baby, lick inside there." And again, that Mephistophelian laugh.

Kalinsky stepped back, put the gun on the chair, then got undressed and fondled himself as he watched the teenager struggle with herself to do his bidding. When he was fully hard, he grabbed Nadia by the hair once more and shoved her aside, as he mounted the fettered blonde and had sex with her.

All Nadia could think of, was that she had to get away from here. She was beyond crying, disgusted, drained, and terrified as she slowly started to move toward her clothes, and yes, there was the gun. Could she dare? But Kalinsky was already spent and did not like what he saw as he glanced over at her. He quickly got up and grabbed the Russian teenager with his right hand, twisting her arm behind her back and pulling her into his disgusting fat stomach, as he toyed with her breast with his left.

"You sure are a looker, my dear, but you're totally useless. We will need to teach you a few tricks." And he laughed as he pushed her down on top of the pile of clothes, pulling his out from under her. "Now get dressed, bitch." Kalinsky proceeded to put his jogging pants back on, and then watched with arms folded and a leer on his face as Nadia got up to put her torn clothes back on.

"On second thought, don't. You just stay naked," the brute said, emitting a dirty little laugh as he looked her up and down one more time and kicked her clothes under the bed. "I like you that way."

Kalinsky grabbed her arm and dragged her over to the door, opened it, and yelled down the corridor. "Hey, Ivan, where the fuck are you, when I need you?" And as the guard approached, he shouted, "Here, take this slut and put her into the special room. I want her kept over here, separate from the others. And don't you dare touch her, or I will castrate you myself, Ivan. We will break her in over the next few days." He pushed Nadia toward the thug and went back in the room, closing the door behind him.

❦❦❦

Ivan had a firm grip on Nadia's wrist as they stood outside the door Kalinsky had just slammed shut. Traumatized by what she had just been through, Nadia tried to use her other hand to hide her private parts.

Ivan must have realized that she was close to a breakdown, so he let go of her. "Come on, now, the boss can be a little rough sometimes. But you'll be all right. Anyways, what's your name?"

Of course, this just made it all that much worse, and the tears came. Nadia's knees started to buckle under her, so Ivan grabbed her under the arms and started leading her down the corridor.

"Come on now, sweetheart. We can't just stay here. I gotta get you into that room, like the boss said, and then go downstairs to my post."

The guard slowly led Nadia along the hall and stopped outside two doors, one on either side. He took some keys out of his pocket and unlocked the door on the left, switching a light on. "Now, don't worry, you'll be all right in here."

But when Nadia finally blinked her eyes clear of the tears, she recoiled in horror at what she saw. A low cage in the far corner. A bloodstained table in the center of the room, and various whips and chains and other implements of torture hanging from the ceiling and the walls.

"Please, please—don't hurt me," was all she could say.

"It's okay. You'll be fine in here. Come on, I gotta put you in this—" Ivan said, guiding her toward the cage. He pushed her inside, closing the bars shut and then securing the lock, as Nadia collapsed on the floor, and involuntarily folded her body into the fetal position. Through her tears she could see that the man called Ivan stood there for a while, shaking his head, watching her tremble and listening to the strange sounds she was emitting, punctuated by her sobs.

She did hear him murmur to himself, as if very far away, "Poor girl. Gosh, the same age as my sister. Tamara. Horrible." And then, as he turned off the light and shut the door, " Oh well…"

Chapter 7

Back in their room at the Sacher, sitting on the bed beside Greg, Anne carefully opened the folded, stuck together pages of the letter pulled from the box by Gospodja Saparova, and started translating.

My dearest Ludmilla!

Now that I am no longer with you, I want to unburden myself of the terrible secret I have kept to myself all these years since our eldest daughter, Katerina, vanished into thin air. I know, in some ways, I have wronged you by keeping what I knew from you, but I only did so because I thought that knowing the truth would have killed you, and I could not stand losing you as well. Sometimes, living with uncertainty is better than knowing a horrible certainty.

Remember, Ludmilla, after Katerina did not come home from school that fateful February afternoon in 1950, we were at our wits end, and went to great lengths to try to discover what had happened to her. The next day, when, totally despond-

ent, we went to her school, they knew nothing, and no one there wanted to talk about her disappearance. The last person who saw her was Natasha, who had hugged her outside their apartment bloc, her friend said, as Katerina continued on her way. The authorities were also no help, claiming they had no clues, no trace of her. They tried to dismiss us by telling us that, no doubt, she just ran away, but would be back in a few days. This often was the case with teenage girls, they said. As if they would know!

It was her other good friend, Irina, who sought me out several days later. She felt terrible, she said, and was very nervous. Irina told me that there had been a similar disappearance at the end of the previous scholastic year that the school had tried to hush up. But she knew, because she had been friends with the girl, Tanya. After Tanya vanished without a trace, Irina had overheard her parents say one night that "no doubt it was that pervert Beria who was behind it all," and she told me that that she and Katerina had talked about this. Why her parents had surmised this, she did not know, and why Katerina did not tell us about Tanya is also a mystery to me, since she told us about most things in her life. And certainly the important things at school.

I went to talk to Irina's parents, but either because they were good party loyalists, or just very afraid, they claimed they had never intimated such a thing about the exalted man. And, that they would punish their daughter for spreading false rumors. In fact, they were shocked that I would repeat something like that, and I had better watch out because they might very well report me. I knew this was not an avenue that would lead me anywhere.

I made an appointment to see the boss, Kurchatov, and asked him if he might know anything of Katerina's disappearance, or at the least, if he could help us by asking around. Of course, he said he was very sorry that our daughter was gone, but he knew nothing. He also repeated the platitude that teenage girls often run away, and it usually takes some time to find them. Again, I did not take this for an answer, and pressed him for more. But when I broached the subject of whether Beria might know, Kurchatov became angry and defensive, and said to me never to dare suggest anything like that, or we would all be killed or sent to the gulag.

I was sure though, that I was on the right track. I was certain that Beria was somehow the key to Katerina's disappearance. So I spent most evenings after work—when, I told you that year, 1950, that I had to stay late almost every night—outside Beria's villa waiting and watching to see if I could catch a glimpse of our daughter. Or, if not, at least to see who was going in and out of the villa. But no sign of Katerina.

Eventually, I figured that my best approach might be to single out one of the guards who came and went—the one that seemed most sympathetic—and ask them if they knew anything of our daughter. I was in luck, though, because a few months after I started my watch, Andrei—you know, Andrei Siderov, my friend at work—bragged to me that his sister had just been promoted to head cook at the Beria house, and that her husband was chief of Beria's security there.

So that made things a bit easier. I met with

Andrei's sister and implored her to help a poor distraught father. I showed her pictures, and described Katerina to her in detail. I tried to get this Gospodja Lenkova to put herself in your position, my dearest—the mother of a daughter who had vanished without a trace. It was this sister of Andrei who finally took pity on me and told me that she might have seen a girl who looked like Katerina in one of the many corridors inside the house, but she would say no more. I pleaded with her to try and find out what she could.

Fortunately, there is still a modicum of human decency left in a few Russians. Five evenings later I collared her again on her way home from work, asking, "Gospodja Lenkova, do you have anything, anything for me?" She became ashen-faced when she saw me, and looked around furtively. "Gospodin Pleshkov, please, not now. I cannot talk to you. But meet me in Lenin Park on Sunday at three p.m. I will be there, sitting on a bench reading a newspaper, waiting for you. Just sit down on the other side of the bench and I will tell you all that I know."

So I did meet her in Lenin Park. And between heartfelt sobs, Gospodja Lenkova told me the horrid tale of what befell our daughter.

"Gospodin Pleshkov," she started, "I am really sorry for you and your wife. I am sorry I am the one who has to tell you this, but you must know the truth. I have shamed my husband to tell me everything he knows about what the monster we work for does in his spare time when he is here. And he, too, is very, very sorry, and will try to make amends. But he does not have the courage to look you in the face. Not now. It is too horrible."

"*What? Please, please—*" *I wanted to know, but I also did not.*

"*Gospodin Pleshkov, brace yourself. My husband told me that your daughter and at least one other girl—maybe more—are kept in cells somewhere in the basement of the house. And that Comrade Beria uses the girls for his pleasure whenever he is here. My husband knows from the sounds that come from the boss's bedroom where he sees him take them, and—and—*"

"*What? Tell me, please.*" *I was distraught, about to come out of my skin.*

"*No, Gospodin Pleshkov. I am sorry, but that is all I will say.*"

My worst fears had been realized. Until then, I had held out hope that this was not what our maker had intended for our daughter. But it had been hope against all hope, because deep down, I had known that the rumors about Lavrenti Beria I had heard during the last several months must have been true.

And I could not help but imagine the most terrible things, with our beautiful daughter in the clutches of this devil.

"*Oh God, no! Not my Katerina.*" *I remember sinking my face into my hand. I could not hold back the tears.*

"*Yes. Poor, poor girl,*" *was all the woman could say to try to console me.*

"*But—she is alive, no?*" *I asked. Knowing, though, that death would at least have given her peace. And us, too.*

"*Yes, she is alive.*" *Gospodja Lenkova's voice was barely a whisper.* "*I wish I could do more—something to help, Gospodin Pleshkov. But I have my children too, and I cannot risk their lives."*

"Thank you. You have already done a lot. But if there is anything, anything more you know or find out, please, please, tell me. Promise you will, please."

I kept that secret for several more months, and maintained my vigil hoping to spot our dear daughter, or find some way to help her. Then one evening in September—just the time when Katerina would have been going off to the VUZ that she had always dreamt of—Gospodja Lenkova collared me again on the sidewalk, and pulled me behind the trunk of a tree.

"Gospodin Pleshkov, I have something to tell you," she said, clearly agitated.

"Yes, please, please tell me," I pleaded with trepidation, fearing the worst. "I pray it is good news."

"Gospodin Pleshkov, the news is not good, but at least this terrible ordeal of your daughter has ended."

For sure, she was dead. "What do you mean?"

"Gospodin Pleshkov, that monster asked my husband—to—terrible as it is—to finish your daughter off. To get rid of her. And to leave no traces."

"God, no!"

"But my husband could not do it. We have a daughter that age ourselves. So, after confiding in me, and at great risk to both of us, he secretly arranged for your Katerina to be sent off to a gulag. He would not tell me where, because your searching for her would further endanger us. But at least your daughter, Gospodin Pleshkov, is alive, and that is all I can tell you. There is nothing more we

can do for you," was what the woman said, and she got up to leave. "Good bye, Gospodin Pleshkov."

I racked my brain every day and night after that to try to figure out where Katerina might be, made lists of the gulags I knew about, and, in spite of Gospodja Lenkova's admonitions, made discreet enquiries.

But nothing. I made no progress.

Until one day in 1953—several months after Stalin had died, and Malenkov and Beria had surprised the entire country by starting to dismantle the gulag system and giving amnesty to one and a half million prisoners, and then the monster Beria was arrested and executed, and my hopes were running really high—Andrei handed me an envelope at work. My heart skipped a beat when I saw that it was from Gospodja Lenkova, and I could barely restrain myself from opening it then and there.

I finally did, after work, when I was able to stop in the park and sit on a bench by myself. My hands trembled as they tore open the envelope, and pulled out the short note, which I incorporate to follow this page.

My dear Sir:

I am writing to you at the request of my husband, who—now that it seems that there is less depravity and more sanity and security in our country—wanted to pass on the little more he knows about your eldest daughter's whereabouts. I trust, Gospodin Pleshkov, that you have not forgotten our conversations in Ozersk just over three years ago. My husband, as you may know, was the Head of Security at Lavrenti Beria's villa, and he remains forever ashamed of having served this monster. He had no choice. Thank God, that the villain has finally been executed. It is partly to expiate his guilt that my husband asked me to write to you among others about the terrible wrongs that Beria inflicted on your daughter and other young ladies.

As I think I mentioned to you when we last met, dear sir, my husband was finally asked by Beria to dispose of your daughter. He couldn't carry out this vile act. Our daughters were of a similar age at the time, and we could not bear the thought. Moreover, what he did not tell me then, was that he suspected your daughter of being with child. Was this why Beria wanted to get rid of her, or had the monster just grown tired of your daughter and wanted to get on to the next pretty little thing? We will never know, but in the end, it doesn't really matter.

So, as I mentioned then, my husband, instead of having your daughter killed, as he had been ordered to, took it upon himself, in great secret, to put her in a gulag of which the commandant was a childhood friend of his. Back then, my husband was too afraid to tell even me which camp it was, because if anyone had known that he had not carried out Beria's orders, it would have gotten back to him for sure, and we would have been finished. However, now that Beria is by all reports in hell, and conditions in our country have improved somewhat, it may be possible to make some enquiries about your daughter. And maybe your grandchild, although it is difficult to imagine that a newborn would have been able to survive the horrors of a gulag. It is with this in mind that he has asked me to tell you that he personally took your daughter to a corrective labor camp at Gulag Chelyablag which you may know as the iron and steel works, Chelyabmetallurgstroy. But that, Gospodin Pleshkov, was in 1950, and as you know, much has happened since then. We are not even sure if that gulag still exits and what may have happened to the prisoners there, let alone your pregnant daughter.

We nevertheless both wish that you and your wife will be reunited with your loved one(s) soon and that you find her (them) in good health. You, like many others in this country, have suffered far too much already.

May God (if there is one) be with you.
Magda Lenkova
Moscow, July 28, 1953

My dearest Ludmilla, you can imagine that I was elated to have at least some clue to help me try and find our Katerina. And, hoping against all hope, her baby, our grandchild. You may not remember now, but one day in August of that year, I told you I needed to go to Chelyabinsk on business. Well, it was really to try to track down our dear daughter or any information I could about her.

But as we know, Beria terminated many of the gulags right after Stalin's death, when most of the prisoners were supposed to have been given amnesty and allowed to return home. In fact though, the few people I was able to talk to who worked at Chelyabmetallurgstroy, told me that the gulag there had been closed in October of 1951, with any prisoners still in the corrective labor camps transferred to other gulags in the system. So either our dear Katerina was already dead by then, or she was sent to another camp somewhere else in the Soviet Union, without any trace. And sadly, as you know, she did not come home in 1953 when amnesty was finally granted to many convicts in the camps, so the likelihood is that she is no longer with us. Any files on the occupants of Gulag Chelyablag, if they exist, must be in Moscow and remain top secret, so I was unable to trace any of them.

I have lived with this terrible tale of what befell our daughter, and despite continuing to try over the next few years, I was never able to find her, nor what became of her and her baby, if indeed she lived to give birth. Oh God help us!

Maybe she is still alive somewhere, our dear Katerina with her child, but I would think she would have tried to get in touch with us somehow. At least, though, she was able to stay alive long enough to get away from the clutches of that depraved gangster, Beria, thanks to that Lenkov and his wife. That is all I have to console myself with as I write this letter. Perhaps, in the new world that is sure to follow this horrific one we have been living, you will be able to have someone tell the story of our daughter's fate to the world. The depravation of the world Stalin and his henchman, Beria, created here in the Soviet Union must be made public, so that mankind will never let such monsters take charge again.

I still pray too, that our dearest Katerina is alive somewhere with her child, and that you will be reunited with them in a better future. If not, we will all find our rest and peace in the next world.

Your ever loving
Efim.
December 14, 1967

Chapter 8

So that was Julia's aunt?" Greg asked, more to confirm it for himself. "Katerina, Ludmilla's sister. Who vanished without a trace way back then? And pregnant, at that." He went over to the mini-bar and poured two full glasses from the screw-top bottle of Zweigelt, bringing them back to the bed.

"And the eldest daughter of the same Efim Pleshkov who was your grandfather's friend. To whom he trusted his letter, the one that Ludmilla gave you and Adam in Ozersk."

"Didn't Ludmilla say there are other letters in the box she gave us?"

"Yes, but she said we should give them all to Julia."

"They could be relevant though."

"Maybe to Katerina's disappearance. But we are looking for Julia now, Greg. Let's wait till we find her," Anne said. "Let's stay focused."

"You're right. I'll put them all in my backpack. We'll give them to Julia when we find her."

"Good idea. But—"

"It is a small world." Greg took a sip of the wine, not

allowing himself to engage in any discussion of the possibility of failing at their mission.

"Yes. These disappearances seem to be a regular event in Russia. But two women, related, years apart—very weird, don't you think? Then your grandfather, and your best friend at the time—Kallay—also really strange. And of course those journalists, and many more we don't ever hear of, no doubt."

"Though we did discover what happened with the last two. My grandfather and my friend, I mean. And speaking of Adam, there is something very wrong with Ludmilla saying that he called just a few days ago, wanting to see Julia at the Revuebar Rasputin. He cannot be alive. He just cannot. I was there when he died on that fishing boat in Poti. As I told you, I shot him when he was trying to escape with the uranium. I still don't quite understand how he became so…so evil. To the core."

"Yes, and I know how hard it was for you to get over that. And now we have this…this reappearance. Really puzzling, isn't it? But you're right. It cannot be Adam. Resurrected from the dead. Haa!"

"Who then?"

"It must be identity theft. Someone masquerading as Adam. It has to be somebody who knew he and Julia were close. Someone who wanted to get to Julia."

"Could it be Polyakov? He was the ringleader of the crooks in the 'Adam affair.' He could have done it. Or maybe one of his men." Greg regretted saying the name. He saw on Anne's face that it conjured up her horrific experience with the man. "Maybe the arms merchant wanted access to more of that highly enriched uranium from Mayak. And he saw kidnapping Julia as a means to achieve this."

"Or your friend, Billy. Could it be him? That Brother Peter, from the Sons of Jesus. He got away with half the uranium, didn't he? Maybe he's trying to use Julia—who has taken Adam's job—now to get more, so he'll have enough for a bomb. Bypassing Polyakov and all the intermediaries."

Greg had not thought of Billy Crawford—or Brother Peter, as he was known in police circles—for quite a while. He and Adam had known Billy as teenage campers at the Odd Fellows Youth Camp run by the Piarist Fathers in Prestonburg, Kentucky, where Billy had provoked Greg by writing *Greg masturbates. He will go to hell*, on the outhouse wall in red paint. This insult to his friend had so incensed Adam, that he stuffed Billy's head as far down into the shithole as he could, and then the two cornered him and landed a few solid punches on his fat stomach, all this resulting in their ignominious dismissal from the camp. During the "Kallay affair," to Greg's great surprise, Billy had resurfaced as Brother Peter, second-in-command of a home-grown American terrorist group that called themselves the Sons of Jesus, who was trying to buy some HEU from Polyakov and his gang. He managed to get away with the Russian arms merchant and others when Anne and Greg had closed in on them, just as the transaction was being consummated. This group that Billy Crawford had become one of the leaders of, was a fanatical evangelist band that vowed to combat the hedonistic, atheist, consumer society that prevailed in the USA and the western world.

"Well, as I told Gospodja Saparova, I will go to the Revuebar Rasputin tonight and see what I can find out. At least, that will be a start."

"I am coming with you."

"It's not a place for a woman, Anne."

"On the contrary, my dear," Anne said, giving her husband a kiss. "It's full of ladies, as I am sure you are aware. Of the night, of course."

"Yes, but—"

"Now, Greg, I do want to make sure you don't misbehave. I want to see what you guys do at a place like that." And she gave a coy little laugh.

"Come on, Anne, don't be ridiculous."

"Besides, this is my case. I am coming. That's that."

"Okay, then, dear," Greg finally acquiesced. "Have it your way. But maybe we should go downstairs and have a bite to eat before we go over. I am quite hungry."

"So am I."

"The Rote Bar?" Greg asked, glancing at the hotel's binder on services and amenities.

"That sounds good to me."

☙❧

They made their way down to the comfortable bar, all decorated in red, where the *maître d'* seated them in the conservatory, with a view across to the opera.

Greg ordered a bottle of Zweigelt, the *Wienerschnitzel* for himself and the *Tafelspitzsuppe* for Anne, after which he settled back in the plush red brocade armchair and said, "Isn't it great to be back here, in Vienna, my dear? Our old stomping grounds."

"Yes, it feels like home for me in many ways," Anne agreed. "Strange, but I guess I did live here for a few years."

"Until I enticed you away to beautiful Vermont."

"Well, it certainly is a different life there, Herr Professor."

The waiter brought the bottle and two glasses, pouring some for Greg to taste, then a glass for Anne.

"I love the way you have adapted, Anne," Greg said. "You have taken up some great activities at Middlebury. Teaching that course in forensics is brilliant. And of course, it is so much fun to go on those long hikes in the summer with you. Or skiing in the winter."

"I do miss city life though. And Vienna was particularly amazing with all the cultural activities—you name it: music, art, theater. It has so much to offer."

"You're right. And that's not even talking of the food and wine scene—" Greg stopped mid-sentence as he was pouring the wine, almost spilling it and continuing with a tremor in his voice, "What the—What the hell?"

"What, Greg? What do you mean?"

"Don't turn around, don't. Not now. But speaking of the devil, Billy Crawford just came in. He's over by the bar."

"You've got to be kidding! Brother Peter? Are you sure? Isn't he a fugitive?" Anne couldn't believe what Greg was saying. Was he hallucinating?

"No longer, it seems. I am absolutely positive it is he."

"We did just mention him as the possible Kallay impostor, but—it can't be. We've got to alert Demeter."

"Not now, because he saw me. Shit, he's on his way over."

"Well, well, if it ain't my favorite author of smutty crime books!" The big man, easily recognizable by his red hair and freckles, towered over them. "Although in the end you did write a pretty good one about your grandparents, I must admit. *András and Lily*, no?" And when Greg did not answer immediately, Billy continued, "But, Greg Martens, what the fuck are you doing back here in Vienna?"

"More importantly, Billy—or should I say Brother Peter—what are you up to here? Buying some more highly enriched uranium?"

"Now, now. No need to get nasty. I am jus' mindin' my own business," came the answer. "But tell me, who is this lovely lady?" The creep looked Anne up and down lasciviously, before faking sudden recognition. "By Jove, is this the former Interpol agent, Anne Rossiter? She is now your wife, isn't she, Gregie? Why, you lucky feller, you."

"Anne, meet Billy Crawford." Greg racked his brain and remembered they had not met during the entire Kallay affair. But how did this guy know that they were married?

"Ah, yes, I have a friend who only has the best things to say about you, Anne," the big Southerner continued with a big smirk, touching her on the shoulder. "He's darn right, baby, you sure are a looker!"

Anne blushed. Greg stood up, as it dawned on him that Crawford must have been referring to Polyakov. The bastard who had raped Anne. He could barely hold back from punching the prick.

He was brought back to the present by Brother Peter. "You wouldn't care to offer me a glass of your wine, Greg, like the last time, would you my friend?" The former Piarist camper punctuated this with a cackle.

"Not on your life, Billy." Greg had had enough. "And you had better get the fuck away from us before I call the cops."

He moved in front of the table, remembering that on the one other occasion they had met in the Sacher's bar, the terrorist redhead had poured himself a glass of his wine and spewed it in his face. He certainly wouldn't let that happen again.

"Okay, Greg, have it your way, you unfriendly bastard," Crawford said, turning around in a huff and walking out of the room.

Greg was shaking as he sat down, and the waiter brought the Wienerschnitzel and the Tafelspitzsuppe. But he had lost his appetite and sat there a moment. "Anne, do you have Demeter's emergency number? You had better call him, before this terrorist gets away from us again."

After Anne made the call, she said, "Crawford must have all sorts of aliases and fake passports to be able to get around. It will be difficult to catch him, no doubt."

"He won't be staying at this hotel tonight, that's for sure."

☙☙☙

After dinner, Anne and Greg made their way over to the Revuebar Rasputin. Greg had been a customer there several times before, when he had wanted to meet Julia after Adam's disappearance, and he thought he recognized the spook at the door. As they were led to the long bar at the back of the room, both of them perused the clientele, fully hoping they might see Billy Crawford in one of the dimly lit cubicles.

But there was no sign of his tousled red hair, so they made themselves comfortable at the bar, just as two scantily clad girls were in the throes of a heated performance on stage.

"So this is why you come to these places!" Anne remarked, as the barman sauntered over to take their orders. And looking around at the clientele, she added, "You are all just lecherous old geezers."

Greg recognized the barman from his earlier visits, and when the man brought the bottle of Zweigelt and two glasses, he asked him whether Julia Saparova had been there recently.

"You know, the beautiful Russian blonde. She used to work here a few years ago."

At first, the thug declined to answer, but when Greg plunked a one hundred Euro note on the bar as he poured the wine, the man said, "I know she your friend. I remember. You come here before."

"Good."

"She here a few days ago, Julia. Ask for Kallay. I send her backstage to see big boss."

"So Kallay runs the show now?" Ann asked, but the barman left them without saying another word. So indeed the Kallay impostor, whoever it was, had been here to meet Julia.

Greg and Anne sipped their wine as the two girls on stage finished the feigned sex act, with muted applause coming from the dark nooks of the booths around the walls. In an excited voice, the silver-tuxedoed announcer gave a vividly descriptive rundown of what was to follow the intermission, and turned on some canned music. Greg tried to capture the attention of the barman, who eventually came over, seeing with disdain that their bottle was close to empty.

"Want another?" he asked.

"I need to see Kallay," Greg said, ignoring the question.

"He not here."

"I don't believe you, my friend." Even though he knew the real Kallay was dead. And if the impostor had been Billy, as they had first thought, Greg doubted that he would be anywhere in Vienna any more, let alone near the Rasputin.

"Don't give me no trouble." And this time, the barman glanced over at the thug guarding the door beside the stage who gave a knowing look back before abandoning his post to saunter over their way.

Anne touched Greg on the arm, saying, "Let's just go, Greg. I am tired. I want to go back to the hotel."

"See you later, friend," Greg said as he emptied his glass and placed another hundred Euro note under the bottle to pay for the wine and the cover charge. And to stay in the good graces of the barman. For the next time.

☙☙

"So you saw the terrorist Brother Peter at the Sacher yesterday evening?" John Demeter asked, as Frau Huth placed the steaming *Mélange* she knew Anne loved in front of her to accompany the marzipan-filled croissant they had stopped to pick up from the nearby Aida *Confiserie*. "I am so glad some things never change," Anne had said to Greg when she saw that the bakery was still where she had habitually gone for her morning pastries. "Let's go get some croissants!"

"Yes, I am positive it was he. Billy Crawford, aka. Brother Peter," Greg answered from the other side of the conference table, adding as an afterthought, "And God only knows what else."

"Well, right after you called, Anne—by the way, I was just having my dinner—I got on the hooter with the Austrian police to put out an 'all points' alert. But you know how slow their response can be. I am certain the crook is in Spain by now, or Greece, or wherever, in one of the hiding holes his buddy Polyakov provides for him. We won't catch him any time soon."

"You may be right, John," Greg said, taking a sip of the *kleiner Brauner* Frau Huth had provided for him. "But why would he surface like that just now? And take the risk of being seen at the Sacher? And recognized? After all, he is a wanted terrorist."

"That's just it," Anne took over. "He must be here to buy some more nuclear stuff. So Polyakov and the gang must be planning another heist. And maybe that explains why they captured Julia."

"I don't get it," Demeter said. "Julia works at the

IAEA, and sure, they could try and get her to falsify records or something like what they tried to do with your friend Adam if I remember correctly, but they've done that before. That's old hat. Surely they would think up some new way of getting their hands on some nuclear stuff."

"Well, maybe they think they can coerce her to smuggle some out from Mayak, for example," Greg said. "On the premise that she would probably be searched less thoroughly at the gates."

"Maybe." This from Anne. "That could be the next step, for sure."

"But why come out from hiding? Brother Peter that is?" Greg asked his question again. "And brazenly confront us in the Sacher?"

"Well, he must feel pretty secure. One thought is, that perhaps he has been hiding in Europe all along—somewhere in the Schengen Zone—where, as a Caucasian, he could easily meld in. In spite of all the renewed checks and surveillance. I am sure Interpol and Europol and all the local police are focusing much more on possible terrorists of Middle Eastern or North African background these days. The inevitable racial profiling—"

"But still, Anne." Greg was not satisfied. "He does stand out with his size and red hair and freckles."

"Anne is on the right track, I think. Especially if your Billy was hiding in a place like Ireland, where he would blend in," Demeter added. "In any case, we're actively on the lookout for him and if he raises his ugly head again, the bastard, we will zap it right off, red hair and all, you can be sure of that."

"But why would he confront us like that?" Greg still did not have his answer.

"I see what you are getting at." Anne finally understood where Greg's concern was coming from. "I guess there are two possibilities. One, that Crawford was just as surprised to see us there, in the bar of the Sacher, as we were to see him. And he came up to us because he was sure we had seen him anyway. Or—and this is what worries you I think, Greg—they had him surface to confront us and give us a warning. To let us know that they know of our whereabouts, all our movements. I mean, Polyakov and his gang."

"There is still another possibility, Anne." Greg drained the last drops of coffee from his cup. "An even more worrying one. That they are tempting us to come in search of them, with a view to capturing or killing us when we are on their territory."

"God forbid!" Greg saw that Anne shuddered as she said this.

Chapter 9

Nadia woke to the clanging of the gate of her cage as Ivan opened it. "Come on, you. Get up. It is late. The boss wants you over in the big building with the other girls."

Slowly she rose to her knees—she felt terrible. Her entire body was sore, she wasn't sure whether from the abuse of the evening before or sleeping on the hard wooden floor, or both. And glimpsing what was all around on the walls and hanging from the ceiling, she again cringed with terror.

A desperate, "Oh, no!" escaped her lips, as she buried her face in her hands.

Ivan had to climb inside the cell to get her, and it was only then that she noticed she was still naked.

"You're clothes are over there," the guard said gruffly, pointing to the table.

He waited patiently, but Nadia saw that he couldn't help gawking at her as she put her clothes on. She then turned to rush toward the door to get away from the horrors she saw and imagined in that room.

Outside, crossing the yard that separated the buildings with its carefully groomed grass, flowers and shrubs, for a moment, Nadia delighted in the late afternoon sun. She must have been really exhausted, she thought, to sleep so late. But then again, she had been through a lot, and she was glad, too, to have been able to escape the reality of her situation with a few hours of blessed sleep.

Ivan led Nadia upstairs into the big room in the main building, eyes still red from crying all night, now cold with fright again, and starving since she hadn't been given anything to eat since the meager snack on the airplane. All the other girls who had come with her from Chelyabinsk were there, most of them sitting on the floor in the center, with several separated off in small groups. About twenty or so thugs, wearing black pants and shirts, black boots and baseball caps, batons in hand or in a holder at the waist, pistol on the other side—just like Ivan—stood around the periphery.

She cringed as she saw that Kalinsky was there too. He was sitting at a table, interrogating one of the girls who stood in front of him, head bowed and sobbing. Behind him, leaning against the wall, Nadia thought she recognized the man he had been talking to the night before as she got off the truck. He was balding, square set and quite muscular. When Kalinsky saw Nadia brought in, he quickly finished jotting something on a piece of paper and yelled at a guard to take the girl standing there away and bring Nadia over next.

As she was shoved in front of the creep, she was relieved to see Sasha in one of the smaller groups. It was evident from her eyes that she too, had been crying. So had all the other girls, Nadia ascertained, as she looked around to see if the blonde from the night before was in the big room. But no, she was nowhere to be seen.

Standing there, shuddering as memories of the horrible experience with the man who had abused her and the beautiful blonde overwhelmed her, she heard Kalinsky say to the man behind him, "This is one of the ones who could be useful."

"Good," the square-set man said.

"So, my dear." The pervert leered at her. "Didn't we have fun yesterday evening?" When she did not answer, he added gruffly, "Well, you better get used to it."

"So, your father works as a security guard at Mayak?" The balding man asked. "Where?"

"Yes—Yes." She was not sure why this was relevant.

"Where is he a guard?" Kalinsky repeated the man's question. "Answer the question."

"I don't know. All over, I think."

Kalinsky and the man exchanged glances and then, after a pause, during which he pretended to read the papers in front of him, the creep leered at her. "Have you ever been fucked by a man before?"

Nadia, so shocked by the question that she jumped involuntarily, could barely hold back the tears.

"Come on, honey, you need to tell me whether you are a virgin or not. To be even more specific—is your hymen still intact or not? Tell me. Otherwise, I may just have to do some probing down there myself." Kalinsky let out a raucous laugh at his own disgusting attempt at humor, while the man behind him looked uninterested in his colleague's perverse banter.

"No—I mean yes."

"What is it my dear—virgin or not virgin? And don't even think of lying."

Nadia could barely get the word out: "Virgin."

"Hmm. Very good," Kalinsky replied, visibly pleased. "You go sit over there with those three girls." And as Nadia's eyes followed where he pointed, she saw a small group sitting on the floor in a corner, guarded by two men. She experienced a tiny and mixed feeling of relief when she saw that Sasha was among them. "You will come with us to Vienna," the pervert continued. "I may have some big things in store for you, my dear."

Nadia barely heard the words as her eyes glazed over with tears and a thug came to grab her by the arm and lead her over to her designated group.

⁊⁊⁊

Outside, three guards took the five girls to a large mini-van, and told them to pile in. Nadia managed to squeeze beside Sasha all the way in the back. She looked behind her seat, where any luggage might have been placed, but did not see their suitcases—they had long since disappeared—just two identical black duffel bags, which she presumed must have belonged to the men who climbed in the front. The van quickly took off and exited the compound. Nadia wondered what Vienna would hold for her and her companions.

"Where did they take you last night? I thought you were right behind me."

Nadia was brought back to reality by Sasha's whispered question. The unwanted memories of her ordeal and the beautiful blonde on the bed came flooding back again.

"I—I don't want to talk about it, Sasha. Please. But what about you?"

"They took us downstairs in that main building. There is some kind of dorm room there. No, it's more like a prison. Lots of bare mattresses on a concrete floor. The men ordered us to take our clothes off and forced us into a communal shower. They never let us out of their sight, just insisted on watching, and made lewd remarks. It was terrible. These people are all so weird."

"Did they do anything to you? Did they hurt you?"

"No."

"Phew." Nadia could barely hold back the tears again. "But this is terrible. So…so degrading. What do you think will happen to us? And the others? I am very frightened."

"I heard that guy Kalinsky tell some of the girls that they will take them to Berlin, some others to Paris, or Amsterdam. London too. Some other cities."

"Why, do you think? What are they doing?"

"I have no idea.…"

"Do you think they could be part of some sex ring?" Nadia was hoarse as she gave voice to her suspicion.

"I hope not. Oh, God!"

"Did that Kalinsky ask you whether you are a virgin or not?"

"Yes. The pervert. But I had to tell him—"

"What?"

"That I slept with Pyotr. Just a couple of times."

"So that's not it then."

"What do you mean?"

"I thought maybe they were taking only virgins—"

"Shut up back there. Or I'll make sure you are no longer one by the time you get to Vienna!"

The thug in the passenger seat must have been listening to the conversation all along, Nadia realized.

🙚🙜

They quickly sped through the outskirts of the big city and into the center—was this Vienna? —and in the dusk of evening, Nadia was dazzled by what she saw looking out the window: well-dressed shoppers, expensive cars, boutique windows full of the latest fashions, cafés and restaurants, one after the other. Everything was more exquisite, more beautiful, than she had ever imagined. If only, she thought.

The van pulled up in front of a fancy, early nineteenth century building, in what must have been the heart of the former Imperial capital. A man standing outside a big red door and attired in the same black gear as their two guards came over to greet the driver. After conversing briefly, one of the men opened the sliding door in the back and told the girls to climb out and follow the other thug. Nadia vaguely thought of trying to escape, to get away from these horrible people and this terrifying situation, but she knew she would not stand a chance. In fact, just as these thoughts were running through her mind, the third gangster grabbed her by the arm and propelled her toward the red doors. As she passed through them, she knew that her life would never be the same again.

Chapter 10

It was a balmy spring evening, and Greg and Anne were feeling happy and ready to allow the magic of the city where they had first met completely enthrall them again, and to rediscover their former haunts. So, after dinner at Appiano's with the Labrecques—who, as it turned out, they both found to be a delightful couple—they decided to walk the short distance along Herrengasse back to the Sacher.

They had managed to avoid discussion of Julia's disappearance all night in deference to Marie Christine, but now they could not help but return to the subject that was foremost in their minds.

"You know, Anne, I have been thinking. I doubt that the Kallay impersonator was Billy Crawford. He didn't know Julia at all, and it would have been a real stretch for him to think he could kidnap her and force her to get him some nuclear material."

"Yeah, I see your point. But then why was he in Vienna?"

"Well, maybe, as we were saying, Polyakov is getting set to do another heist, and Billy was just surfacing to pick up the material somewhere. Or to scare the living daylight out of us."

"Hmm. Possible. But then we must be closer to another heist then anybody has thought. In any case it is good that there is a renewed effort to find him."

"Sure. But put that aside for the moment. I also don't think Polyakov would have impersonated Kallay. It just doesn't compute—Polyakov is the head of this huge arms trading operation, and it is not likely that he would stoop to something so…operational."

"So then who?"

"Well, how about Hetzel?" Greg finally voiced the suspicion that had been brewing in his brain since their visit to the Rasputin the night before. "After all, that self-proclaimed friend of Adam had been lusting after Julia all the while, we know that. He must have finally seen his opportunity to get at her, and figured out that the best way was to impersonate Adam and lure her to the Revuebar."

Andreas Hetzel, a supposed friend of Adam Kallay in Vienna, had contacted Greg shortly after Adam's disappearance. He had been on the fringes of the previous heist, and Greg had concluded that he was a friend and ally of Polyakov.

"Hmm. You may be right. Polyakov showed no interest in Julia—" Anne shuddered as she remembered the arms merchant's words in Poti when she and Julia were in his hands that "Russian soldiers don't rape Russian women. "—and as you say, Billy did not even know she existed."

"Hetzel has been on the run. Interpol must have been looking for him after we fingered him as one of those involved in the heist. And knowing that Adam was dead, it would have been easy for him to assume his friend's identity, especially since Adam very probably left his passport and other key documents and credit cards in the car that Hetzel then used to make his getaway in Poti. He must have thought he hit the jackpot. The crook simply appropriated them, when he found them there. In fact, maybe that's when he first got the idea to take on Kallay's identity. Interpol certainly would not be looking for Adam, since they knew he was dead. And signatures are easy to fake. He could easily dye his hair blond to look more like his pictures in the passport and on his driving license."

"Or he could just wear a blond wig, for that matter."

"And of course being Adam would come in very handy for him as a way to lure Julia to come to him. Even though she knew he was dead, she had been very much in love with him, it seems. She would certainly have been curious about his reappearance. It was all just too perfect."

"Yes, good point. Plus it seems that he finally managed to get his hands on the Rasputin, too. Remember, he was trying to acquire it already then."

"Probably with Polyakov's money. Ugh. What a team."

"So that is where he enticed Julia. Impersonating Adam."

"That must be it," Anne agreed. "We're now on the right track, I'm sure."

"Hmm. Come to think of it, Adam did imply when I was with him during the last heist that Hetzel was operating a business trafficking girls from Russia to…I don't know where, but if he—or they—were trying to acquire the Rasputin, that could be part of it all. Maybe a staging point or something…"

"He really is a creep, Hetzel."

They walked in silence, passing through the covered walkway by the Lippizaner stables, and then right after that, crossed over to the Augustiner Kirche side of the street. For Greg, the recollection of being followed by Polyakov's thugs along this very street when he was trying to track Adam, flooded back. But he wanted to erase these thoughts, so he forced himself to think of other, more pleasant memories triggered by the Imperial Capital. So, when they were at the level of the Albertina, he turned to his wife, and leaning against the wall of the museum, pulled her close in to him and gave her a passionate kiss.

"You know, my dear, we have each other now. That is the main thing. I love you, and I am so glad we met. Here, in this wonderful city. Never mind the crazy circumstances—Adam, the heist and all—we should not let work overwhelm our wonderful romantic memories.

Anne kissed back, murmuring "I love you, Greg."

℮ᘓℰᘓ

"You know what, Greg," Anne broke the silence as she was taking her earrings off back in their room at the Sacher. "Tomorrow, I'm going to the Rasputin. To apply for a job—"

"What? Have you lost your mind, Anne?"

"No. Not at all."

"You're not going near that place, my dear. That is a den of…of iniquity. I won't let you."

"Yes, I will, Greg. It's our best chance."

"They don't need waitresses. They're all whores. And the cleaning women are all Serbs or Russians…"

"No." Anne laughed, wrapping her arms around the waist of her husband who had taken his shirt off. "I meant as a stri—as an exotic dancer." Anne started into a sexy little dance, unbuttoning her blouse.

"No bloody way, my dear. You are my wife, and you are not going to be a stripper at the Rasputin!"

"Just think of it, Greg."

"No. No. And no!" He could not help though, imagining Anne up on the Rasputin's stage.

"Hear me out, Greg. Hetzel—if this Kallay impersonator is indeed he, as we now think—does not know me, so he would have nothing to suspect. If I get a job there, I could meet the other women and staff and perhaps learn something. I could check out what happens backstage. It's our best chance to get behind the scenes, you must admit. Our only one, in fact."

"Look, Anne, you would not stand a chance against all those sicko bandits. Hetzel is an alleged human trafficker. And what if Polyakov happens to be there?" Harsh as it was, he knew mention of the arms merchant would give her pause.

"Well…"

"Hetzel and he hang out together, you know that. And he may now be the owner of the Revuebar. Which may be the center of a sex ring. I am not letting you near there."

"But, Greg—"

"Seriously, Anne. I could not bear it if anything would happen to you."

"Hear me out, Greg, I just know I have got to do this."

"Anne, if what we believe is true, these creeps are all part of a major sex trading operation, as well as being arms merchants. You, my dear, are far too beautiful not to be the focus of their attention—you would fetch a very high prize, indeed, on the…the flesh market."

"Come on, Greg, you get me for free," Anne said with a saucy little laugh between kisses, glad that the subject had moved away from the man who had raped her. "All of me, whenever you want. I am yours, always. You know that."

"That's just it, Anne—I want to keep you for myself. I don't want to lose you. These men are real criminals. Rapists and killers."

"Look, Greg. We came back here to try to help find Julia. Who, we now think, may have been kidnapped by Hetzel. Alias Kallay. And our only lead is that he and Julia may have been together at the Rasputin, backstage, a few days ago. We need to go there, question a few people without giving anything away. The only way for one of us to get in there and find out more without blowing everything, is my plan."

"We could have Haffner raid the Revuebar."

"That's just it. Then we will never find Julia. Nor get near the fake Kallay."

Greg's resistance was starting to break down. He too, was becoming convinced that Anne's plan was probably the best step forward. "Well…okay, Anne. I will agree to it, but just if we get Demeter to provide lots of agents as back-up in the Revuebar itself and the surrounds when you are in there. Also, I want you to wear a locator at all times," he said as he climbed on the bed, stretching out, now completely naked.

"Where?" Anne gave her sensual little laugh again, glad that Greg had come around. "Where do you have in mind, my dear, if I am going to be a stripper? Where do you think a tracking device would go unnoticed? Any suggestions?"

"I will let you figure that out for yourself." And then, with a smile, as he propped himself up on a pillow, he added, "What's more, my love, if you want to have any hope of convincing Hetzel and gang that you have a clue about how to strip, you had better get some practice. Now. With me as the audience." And he put another pillow under his shoulders to be more comfortable. "Okay, I am all set for the show."

"You are one lecherous old man, you," Anne said kicking her high heels off. "I always knew it." And she leaned over to give him a passionate kiss. "But I still love you."

Chapter 11

Nadia woke, after a very restless night in the cellar of the Rasputin, to the kick of one of the guards. "Come on, you slut. It's time to get to work. Get your act together, all of you, and go wash up."

She looked around for Sasha as she pulled herself up from the bare mattress on the floor. But her friend was nowhere to be seen. The thug in the van who had told them to shut up had come for her last night just as she was getting ready for bed. He had grabbed her by the arm, and forced her to go with him. Nadia was very worried.

When she and the three other girls were washed and dressed, the guards led them up some rickety stairs, then along a corridor to another windowless room. Here, two older Russian-looking women were standing by a table with lots of loose articles of clothing on it, while three more thugs leaned against the walls, and, over in a corner, near a stand with exotic looking dresses and outfits hanging on it, cowered a pale and forlorn looking Sasha.

"Okay, girls, we're going to find some nice things for you to wear," the brute who had taken Sasha away the night before shouted. "So you better take it all off. What-ever you are wearing. Your panties you can keep on—for now." The jerk laughed before adding, "Or else we'll do it for you." He then reached his hand forward suddenly and started to pull Nadia's T-shirt up her torso. "Like this. Once these ladies have settled on something that looks good on you, we'll make sure it fits."

It was degrading. They had to undress in front of the leering guards, throw the sweaty, soiled clothes they had worn for the last three days in a pile, while the two ba-bushkas eyed them professionally and started to select different articles of clothing for them to try on.

When Sasha did not join in, her keeper went over to her and grabbed her by the chin. "All right, honey, you had better get with it. Just because I showed you some special attention last night doesn't mean you don't obey orders. Take your fucking clothes off now and get over there!"

He shoved the girl toward the center and whacked her on the bottom hard with the baton he was holding in his other hand.

After several tries, all five girls were outfitted with sexy, low-cut, tight-fitting apparel that highlighted their best features. The two attending women then tarted them up with copious make-up. In spite of the terrible peril she suspected she was in, Nadia actually found her image in the mirror remarkably pleasing. She had not thought that she could look so good all made up, although she did re-mark to herself that she looked several years older and that probably her mother would not have approved.

❧❧❧

The girls were led down some stairs to a room at the other side of which was an open door leading to what in the dim shadows Nadia thought might have been a stage jutting out into the middle of a large room with booths and tables and chairs all around. Way over against the back wall, she thought she saw what looked like a bar.

"Don't you all look gorgeous, my lovelies!" Kalinsky bustled through the open door, followed by a black woman in slinky attire. "Nadia, you, in particular, my dear, are sensational." The creep looked her up and down lustfully and touched her naked arm with his sweaty hand, brushing her breasts as he did so. Then, looking from one girl to the next, he said, "Okay, ladies, this is my friend, Ginger," as he pushed the black woman forward to meet the new arrivals. "She is going to teach you how we dance here. In a minute, we will have some music, and Ginger will take you out on the stage one by one. You just need to try to follow her movements. And look sexy, provocative. You had better all try hard, or you will get some more personal training from Ivan or Vlad, my friends here, if I don't like what I see out there." He smiled at the two thugs as he disappeared through the door that led onto the stage.

⌘

When the music stopped after the first three girls had done their dance, the big black woman came backstage one more time with her garments gathered in her hand and beckoned to Nadia. "Okay, honey, it is your turn now. Let's really give it a good effort," she whispered as she temporarily put her clothes back on. "Just do what I do to the music. Ignore everything else. And don't worry. You'll get used to this."

So when the rhythmic tune started up again, Nadia followed Ginger out on stage, and concentrated on trying to copy her antics. She took the kindly stripper's advice and dared not think what the alternative "more personal training with Ivan or Vlad" could comprise. She told herself, no doubt, this was infinitely better to be dancing here with Ginger. Even though much of what she found she was doing was totally new to her, and well beyond her comfort zone.

Up and down the stage they strutted, and Nadia even attacked the floor to ceiling pole with the same feigned lasciviousness she saw Ginger exhibit. She, like her "teacher," shed articles of clothing one after the other, until, as the music came to an end, they both stood there naked, except for Nadia's panties to cover her nether parts, and Ginger's G-string. Nadia did, though, try to hide her breasts—which, compared to the professional stripper's, were not that large—with her bare hands.

As her tears started to flow, Nadia barely heard the clapping and "Brava!" that came her way from one of the booths in the front, although with the bright lights shining in her face, she could at first not make out who her fans were. But, as she followed the black woman to the room behind the stage, she recognized Kalinsky's voice shouting, "Ginger, make sure they shave her and give her a G-string to wear for tonight."

The fear and the terrifying questions came back: was this to be her life from now on? A stripper in Vienna? And what all would that bring?

Oh God, I so want to be back home! I want my mother, my father.

Chapter 12

Anne, dressed to kill in mini skirt, low cut halter-top and stiletto heels, with lots of make-up, appeared from the bathroom.

"Wow! You look no more than twenty, my dear," Greg said, looking up from his laptop and hungrily taking her in with his eyes. "Beautiful! Though a bit slutty, if you don't mind me saying so."

"Well, I am going to try to pawn myself off as a stripper." Anne came close and gave him a peck. "You approved of my act last night, so now I have to look the part."

"I am more concerned that all those perverts will try to paw you." Greg kissed her back. "Good luck, my love. And be careful. I wish I were coming with you." And then, as she disentangled herself, he added, "By the way, did Demeter agree to provide back-up? And have you got the GPS locator on?"

"Yes, and yes. You worry wart. The beeper for it is on the night table. Bye, now." Anne had gone into the Interpol office first thing in the morning to arrange the details of support for this mini-sting operation. "And you don't want to know where the transmitter is," she added in a low voice so Greg would not hear as she closed the door.

And, walking through the lobby of the Sacher, although she did find all the eyes staring at her—lusting men wondering who her lucky last customer might have been—reassuring that she indeed looked the part of an exotic dancer if not a high-class escort, she did feel a pang of fear as to what this next daring adventure would bring.

❧

Anne rang the bell several times at the closed double doors of the Revuebar before a man dressed in black stuck his baseball cap covered head through a crack. Fortunately, it wasn't the same thug as the bouncer at the door the night before.

"What do you want? We are not open yet," he snapped in heavily accented German.

"I came for a job," Anne said, in as sexy a voice as she could muster. "I used to work at the Griffin. In London." On the way over, Anne had remembered her brother talking about the perennial favorite, hoping that the thug might have heard of it. "I know how to dance."

"You a stripper? You want to dance, here, at the club?" The guard looked her over, liked what he saw. "You wait a minute here. I go ask boss."

He was back almost immediately. "Boss say, okay. You in luck. He doing auditions right now. You can show how you dance in a little while. Come. Come with me." He led Anne over to an empty booth, as her eyes adjusted to the gloom. The music was loud and raunchy. On stage a big black dancer was leading a good-looking but rather thin girl—she must have been still in her teens—through a very suggestive set of moves. "You stay here until someone come get you."

As she watched the unfolding dance, Anne wondered whether she might not have gotten in over her head by coming here pretending to look for a job. She did not like what she saw up on stage. The moves that especially the black woman was doing were certainly at the edge of her comfort zone, and she saw that the teenager was trying very hard, but not at all enjoying the act she was seemingly being forced to perform. Was she there against her will? Was this indeed a sex ring that they were stumbling onto? Oh God, and what if Polyakov was here? Anne hoped that she had disguised herself enough with the make-up so that the Russian arms merchant would not recognize her under the lights.

She would have to be very, very careful indeed. *Greg, I wish you were here,* she thought, allowing panic to take over for a second. Anne looked around to see if any of Demeter's men were in the room, but of course, impossible, because the Revuebar was still closed. At best, they would be outside. So she was on her own in here.

∽∾∽

The next dancer that joined the black stripper on stage was even less fit for the job—also a teenager, Anne remarked to herself. This one gave up halfway through, and ran off the stage, crying. The music ground to a halt, and after a few minutes, a man with obviously dyed-blond hair appeared in front of Anne's table.

This must be the boss. Yes, the Kallay impersonator.

"So, Ivan tells me that you are looking for a job."

"Yes, sir. I am a dancer."

"He told me you used to perform at the Griffin."

"Yes, sir. In London." Good. He had heard of the place her brother used to frequent.

"Did you know Aleksandr Petrovsky there?"

"No, sir, I didn't." She looked away, thinking, *I am really in trouble now*.

"Today is your lucky day. That is the right answer. Because Petrovsky manages Stringfellows. That's my favorite club in London. The Griffin was only second best."

"Sorry."

The man eyed her hesitantly for a few seconds, looked her up and down, then glanced at his watch before saying, "Okay, honey. Give us a taste of what you can do. Get up there and perform." And then he yelled to one of the guards loitering nearby, "Ivan, take her backstage. And get Pyotr to do the music one more time."

♥♥♥

Anne gave the performance of a lifetime. She threw everything into it, forcing herself to imagine that she was doing it for Greg, the same strip act, the one she had improvised the night before. When she finished, and was standing there naked under the lights but for the G-string panties she had specially bought that morning, she heard applause from backstage first, and turning around, saw that it was the black stripper who had led the two neophyte teenagers through their act. And then, clapping from out front, and a booming voice, saying, "Very nice, dear. Come down here."

Anne reached down to start to gather the clothes she had shed during the dance, but the voice shouted, "I said come down here. Leave your stuff where you dropped it. Ivan will pick it all up."

Though she felt a wave of panic come over her, she

stood back up and walked in her stilettos toward the steps over on the side and into the comforting darkness of the room below, to approach the table of the man who indeed seemed to be the boss. And Greg was right. It must be Hetzel, alias Kallay, she told herself. Adam had blond hair and a thickset frame, and according to Greg, Hetzel was also rather square. This man was obviously trying to look more like his former friend with this dye job.

"What's your name, honey?"

"Jane. Jane Mortimer."

"Got any ID?"

"No. As you see, I took off everything up there."

"Not everything." The creep looked eerily down at her crotch. "Okay, never mind for now. I want you back here at eight tonight. Ready to do the dance you just did. We may get you involved in other things, too. You are one good stripper, Jane."

Chapter 13

At eight sharp, Anne rang the bell of the Revuebar again, and was ushered in by the same goon who had greeted her in the afternoon. He took her straight backstage, where she was led into a room with about twenty women of different ages and nationalities, most in various states of undress and occupied with putting clothes and make-up on. Five of the younger girls, though, were just sitting around a table over in one corner, downcast, forlorn. The two teenagers she had seen perform earlier were among them.

"Hello. You must be Jane?" The big black woman greeted her. "I loved your dance earlier."

"Thank you. Yours was great too." Anne felt she had to return the compliment.

"You were at the Griffin, Mr. Kallay said."

So the man—this 'Kallay'—definitely was someone masquerading as Adam, probably Hetzel.

"Yes. I danced there a few years back. I quite liked it there," Anne lied again.

"Did you know Jenny? Jenny Svensen? A Swedish blond? Tall, long legs?"

"Yes. But not well." Just another little lie, to spin the story. "Beautiful, and a great dancer."

"Jenny was very popular. She danced here a few times, too. Anyway, welcome to the Revuebar Rasputin."

"Thank you. You are?"

"My name is Ginger." And then she lowered her voice a notch so only Anne could hear. "Jane, let me give you a little advice. Don't ask too many questions around here. Just dance. And keep on the right side of Kallay. He can be a real bastard."

"Thanks, Ginger."

"Sure thing."

"By the way, who are those girls over there?"

"Shh. I said don't ask questions."

"Hey, ladies, we have a couple of new dancers joining us for the show tonight." Just then, the Kallay impersonator bustled into the room, holding a list. "I am posting the order of appearance for tonight. We will have the lovely Nadia replace Mirka as Ginger's partner in the second slot—she did so well earlier—and Jane, who has come to us from the Griffin in London, will do the last solo dance before the intermission. Everything clear?" And then to the thugs who were flanking him, "Ivan, Pyotr. Take these other four girls who arrived yesterday upstairs. They will not be performing on stage tonight. But we will want them up there for sure."

⸞⸞⸟

Greg was very nervous as he arrived in front of the Revuebar with Labrecque promptly at nine p.m., when he knew the doors opened to the public.

"Nicholas, where are your men?"

"Over there." The French Interpol agent pointed out a black BMW SUV across the street with two silhouettes in it. "And several more will join us inside in the next little while, pretending to be customers. No need to worry for your lovely wife, my friend. This is a mission everyone wanted to be in on, you can be sure. Including Demeter himself."

But Greg did worry as the maître d' led them to a booth. He looked around, apprehensive that he would catch sight of Polyakov. That would be the end of the gig, and spell disaster for his wife. The arms merchant—and probably financier of Hetzel's venture—would certainly recognize her. Greg regretted giving in to Anne, and only started to relax a little once he had his first glass of Zweigelt, the lights dimmed, and the music began.

Labrecque and he agreed that the opening performance by a big-breasted and slightly overweight Ukrainian was mediocre, although they both liked the second show. "Yes, that Ginger is fabulous. She was a dancer here already when I used to come to meet up with Julia," Greg told his friend.

"That young Russian was also exquisite. She really has a future in the business, I am sure," Labrecque added. "Even though I hate to wish that on her."

But it was when the silver-tuxedoed presenter announced the last act before the intermission, "…Jane Mortimer, the wild and sexy dancer on loan to us from the famed London club, the Griffin…" and he saw his beautiful wife strut out on stage with a huge smile on her face, waving to the audience, that Greg found himself—against his better judgment—clapping the loudest.

In fact, Labrecque had to say, "Less noise, my friend. We don't want to attract any attention to ourselves, do we now?"

Anne's performance was magnificent. She waltzed around the stage to the *Blue Danube*, swinging on the pole, leaning way back, spreading her legs wide, titillating the audience, and taking her garments off, one by one, until, at the end, she stood there in her naked splendor. Greg sat there in total shock, but also with love and admiration for Anne. Labrecque could not help but remark to him, "You lucky bastard! I can't believe that is your wife out there. Every man in here will be lusting after her."

"That's just what I am afraid of, Nicholas. I would not have agreed to it, had she not convinced me that this was the only way to find Julia." He certainly felt Anne had overplayed the role.

Anne took her third encore, still naked and smiling, then disappeared from the stage.

The floodlights were switched off, the main lights turned up a notch, and canned music replaced the lilting strains of the *Blue Danube*.

It was intermission.

જ⁀જ

Anne strutted off, still smiling, pleased with herself, and grabbed the long, shimmering see-through dress she had shed on stage, handed to her by a fawning helper.

As she slipped it over her head, Ginger approached. "That was very good, Jane. Excellent, in fact. Hats off to you. You really are a pro."

Behind Ginger, Anne saw the black woman's Russian teenage partner sitting uncomfortably by herself in the corner. She went over to the girl. "You were very good, too. What's your name?" Anne wasn't sure if she would understand.

But she did. "Nadia."

"Where are you from, may I ask?"

Nadia hesitated, looking at Anne with her sad eyes,

before she answered. "Ozersk. Chelyabinsk Oblast. In Russia."

Just then the Kallay look-alike rumbled in. "Fantastic, girls. You were all just terrific. Jane and Nadia, you two were first class." And inserting himself between the two, he grabbed each of them by the elbow. "Now I would like you both to come with me. Upstairs. To meet some special guests."

❧❧❧

Anne dislodged herself from the boss's grip, saying, "I need to visit the ladies room," to gain herself some time, as the creep continued on his way with the Russian girl. She did not want to go upstairs with Hetzel—she was sure now that it was he—to meet some "special guests," especially fearing that Polyakov might be among them. She desperately wondered whether there was any way to get word to Greg. He was out there, with Labrecque was the plan, and she had heard his loud cheers and applause, even though she had not been able to see them while performing with all the floodlights shining in her face.

Maybe Ginger would help? No. Impossible. It was just too dangerous even to contemplate. In any case, she was glad for the locator, although dancing with it had been a bit uncomfortable down there.

When Anne came out of the restroom, though, there was no way to escape. The black-attired thug who had handed her the discarded dress after the striptease was there, standing and waiting. He ushered her toward the staircase, saying, "The Boss told you to go with him. Get going. They want you upstairs."

Anne reluctantly took the steps up and, when she got to the top, through the open French doors, was greeted by the sounds and sight of a lavish party in full swing. Waiters were busying themselves carrying platters of champagne, caviar, lobster, cheeses, only the best of everything, while on the dance floor, Arab sheikhs, Russian oligarchs, Chinese politicians and Argentinean *rancheros* danced with scantily dressed nubile women. Including, as Anne noticed, the four glum looking girls who had previously been sitting with Nadia downstairs.

When he saw Anne at the entrance, Hetzel clapped his hands and the music stopped. "Gentlemen. And ladies, of course. Ahem…" He was going to make an announcement. "Let me introduce our two new stars. First, Nadia. Fresh from Russia, beautiful, as you see, a great dancer, and—I am saving the best for last—you will be delighted to hear, still a virgin! Come on, honey, step out there on the floor and show yourself. She is a real treasure, this one." Hetzel gave the Russian girl a little nudge then paused to allow the male audience to view the teenager. Anne looked over to see her blush, on the verge of tears.

"The other new lady in our midst is the exquisite Jane, from England, a fabulous stripper with lots of experience and ahem…I'm sure she's not a virgin. Are you, Jane?" Anne cringed as the creep said this and laughed—what did that have to do with anything? "I'm going to ask the two ladies to give you the same performance they gave downstairs, and then we will see where we go from there."

He grabbed Nadia and pushed her out into the middle of the dance floor, as on cue, the music started up. Her performance—perhaps because she had to do it alone, or because she was nervous after that uncalled for announcement and very afraid as to what it all might mean going forward—was terrible. She clearly was just going through the motions, the poor girl. When it ended,

Hetzel nevertheless thanked her, whacking her on the bottom as she came off the dance floor. He then strutted over to the buffet table and picked up an empty silver ice bucket, saying in a loud voice, "All right, my friends, you can now tell us how much you are willing to pay. Remember, she is young, and a virgin, and she will be all yours to take home if you bid the highest amount." The Kallay impersonator went around to the men sitting or standing around, while each one wrote something on a little piece of paper that he then dropped in the bucket. These oligarchs were obviously used to this bazaar, Anne concluded.

Monstrous! So the fake Kallay and his gang were selling these girls to these rich perverts from all over the world. And she would be next—*Oh God, what did I get myself into!*

৩৩৩

Anne danced, but did not give it her all as before. Her mind was elsewhere. *How can I get out of this mess?* Nevertheless, when she finished, the applause was loud, and she heard murmurs of approval as she slinked off the dance floor.

"Thank you, Jane. Wow! That was excellent, don't you think? Give her a big hand, everyone." Hetzel spoke into the microphone, as he took a glass of champagne from a tray and handed it to her. "You deserve this, my dear. Drink up!"

The creep then went over to the table again to get the silver bucket, pouring its contents out on the table. He took it over to an Arab sheikh and said in a loud voice so everyone could hear, "Offers, gents. Give me your best bid. It had better be good, because otherwise I will keep this one for myself. She would certainly be an asset here at the club. And to me, personally, of course. And my friends, if I want to share."

So she was being auctioned off! Just like Nadia and probably the others.

Or even worse, kept by the creep, for himself and—and his friends.

Including Polyakov?

Where was Greg now? Labrecque, Demeter and Interpol? Would they be able to help? Anne put her glass of champagne down and pulled her dress over her head, shaking herself to get comfortable. Anything, to cover herself from these penetrating eyes, leering at her from all around the room.

Hetzel carried the bucket over to the table and poured its contents out beside the other pile of little folded papers, which he tackled first. After unfolding and looking through them all, he announced, "Okay, gents, Sheikh Al Baradin has the best offer for the lovely little Nadia—fifty thousand dollars. Does anyone care to offer more? Surely, such a rare and beautiful virgin is worth a lot more than that, especially if she can perform the way you saw her dance just now? She will be all yours to take home to your wife." And the fake Kallay laughed his perverted laugh.

Despicable, degrading, unbelievable! And she was next.

A hand shot up in the back. "Sixty." The bidding finally stopped at ninety-five thousand, the diminutive Sheikh not willing to lose his prize. Hetzel seemed pleased, as he dug into the next pile, unfolding and reading the little pieces of paper that would determine Anne's fate.

A few moments later, with an "Ahem!" to clear his throat and get attention, he strutted out onto the dance floor again to announce: "We have been offered eighty thousand for the beautiful Jane in the first round, by Jaime Ramos." One of the Argentinean rancheros, no doubt. "Come on gents, you can surely do better than that! This one brings lots of experience and can make any man happy. At that price, I will keep her for myself."

Heaven forbid, Anne caught herself thinking. Better to go with the Argentinian.

And then from Sheikh al Baradin, who had won the bidding for Nadia, "I'll pay one hundred thousand."

"Much better," Hetzel said with a smug smile. "Our friend Sheikh al Baradin is going for broke. For the harem? Or just a threesome? How delightful, I can just imagine. Are you up to it Sheikh?"

But as the laughter at the sick humor subsided, the bidding opened up: "One hundred ten," from a Chinese official, "one hundred twenty-five" from a Russian looking oligarch, "one hundred and thirty" from an African and so on. It finally stopped at one hundred and sixty-five thousand, which the Chinese politician was willing to pay for Anne.

"Congratulations, Mr. Jiang." Hetzel went over to shake the man's hand. "You will not regret this. I am sure you will get much pleasure out of Ms. Mortimer."

"Thank you very much. Thank you." The winner of the bidding for Anne smiled at her and bowed to Hetzel to show his gratitude.

"We will deliver in three days' time, as usual. Chengdu?"

"Yes. Thank you very much. Thank you."

So she was not this man's first purchase. Her mind wandered: so what happened to the others?

So that was it. If Greg and Interpol did not come through, she would be handed over to this diminutive Chinaman who would own her. To be his chattel. To do with whatever he pleases. To be his sex slave.

So much for trying to help Julia.

Chapter 14

Anne stood there in a daze beside Nadia, sipping the champagne, trying to weigh her options, when suddenly from behind, she was grabbed by two of the black-attired thugs who rapidly ushered her toward the back stairs. Judging from the screams of, "No, no! Leave me alone," she heard behind her, she was sure Nadia was being forced to follow. The assembled guests must have been quite used to this, because none of them lifted a finger to help.

Down to the back entrance, and through it, they were quickly taken along the alley to a waiting truck—Anne noted some slabs of meat and links of sausages painted on the side with the words *Volcker Fleisch und Wurstwaren*—Volcker's Meat and Sausages—in big black letters.

Ironically, very appropriate she thought. Up into the back they were shoved like cattle, but before the guards clamped the doors shut behind them, Anne could see that several other girls were already lying there on the floor, motionless.

Once enveloped by total darkness, she felt around to see if the ones near her were alive. Yes, she ascertained, they were breathing and still had pulses, and stirred somewhat when she touched them.

Could they have been drugged?

"Nadia! Nadia, are you there?" Anne asked first in English, and then when there was no response, in Russian. Fortunately, she was fluent.

"Yes," Anne heard the teenager whimper. "Over here."

The voice came from somewhere on the right.

"Are your friends all here?" She was referring to the four other girls who had not been made to perform on stage. Had they been auctioned off earlier? Anne wondered.

"I think so."

Anne started to scuttle in the direction of the voice. "Where are you?" she asked, groping in the darkness. "Say something."

"Over here, with Sasha, my friend from school. I saw her already in here when we were shoved up."

"I think all these girls must have been given some drugs. Hopefully, nothing else happened."

Then Anne heard Nadia's sobbing right beside her. "Nadia? Oh, there you are." And, finally, touching the Russian teenager, she moved closer and put her arm around her. With her other hand, she felt a face in the Russian girl's lap. "Your friend, Sasha?"

"Yes. She is still out. But she has a pulse, and she's breathing."

"Nadia, you must tell me how you girls got to the Rasputin. That club, where we just were."

Several minutes passed during which Nadia tried to stop her sobbing. "In Ozersk, where my family lives, where my father works, they advertised that they would find good jobs in the West for us—those just finishing school."

"Who? Who advertised?"

"I don't know. Some company. The European Placement Agency, I think they called themselves."

"And your parents agreed?"

"Yes. There is a lot of contamination in the area, you know, from all the nuclear waste. They say it is not healthy to live there."

"Of course."

"My father paid this man—Kalinsky—the boss in the club a lot of money."

So that was the alias he used in Russia. Clearly, a takeoff on Kallay. Adam followed her everywhere, even though, for sure, he was dead.

Anne was getting indignant at the monstrosity of it all. In fact, she now remembered that right after the Kallay affair—that was the nuclear heist—Greg had related that Adam had told him that Hetzel and…what was her name?…Irena Kolchakova, the then Director at Mayak, had a nice little side business going, taking the children of employees at the Mayak nuclear facility to the West for work. Greg's suspicion—that they would then be trafficked as sex slaves—had proved to be right.

They had wrongly thought that with Kolchakova dead—Anne shuddered as she remembered the grisly scene in Poti when the nuclear transaction was being carried out, with the Director's head totally blown away, and brains, bone and blood everywhere—and Adam too, gone, and Hetzel barely getting away alive, that the "nice little business" had come to an end. But no. For sure, Kallay or Kalinsky—this impostor—could be none other than Hetzel.

As she was pondering this in the darkness, Anne suddenly had a revelation. Maybe it was Polyakov who was behind all this evil. Orchestrating it from behind the scenes, out of the limelight. Like he had done with the uranium heist in the Kallay affair. Sergei, the former Russian General, twin brother of Boris, the FSB Deputy Director. For sure, he was well connected in the present day Russian *nomenklatura.*

Polyakov, too, had gotten away in Poti, and, no doubt, had gone back to his empire trading all kinds of illicit things—nuclear material, arms, drugs and women, maybe body parts, for all Anne knew. And for the traffic in women, it looks like he let Hetzel be the front man. Convinced she was right, in the darkness of the rolling truck, Anne was overwhelmed with fear.

"He was supposed to—to—find us good jobs." Anne heard Nadia stutter before she dissolved into sobs again.

"What happened then?"

"They took us to an airplane which flew us west somewhere…Hungary, I think."

"And then?"

"We were driven in a vehicle like this to some kind of compound—and—" Nadia could not go on. "And—" She broke out in tears again. She shifted her leg, and in her lap, Sasha stirred.

"It's all right, dear." Anne put her arms around the teenager. "You don't have to tell me if you don't want to."

"Then that weird guy, Kalinsky separated me from the others and took me to—to an apartment. There was a blonde—a beautiful blonde woman tied up in a bed there." The sobs came now with a vengeance. "And—and he forced me to—to make love to her." Nadia dissolved completely.

"It's all right, dear," Anne, completely shocked, tried to console the girl, but was glad for the pitch darkness.

Could the blonde be Julia? She was on the right track

then. But poor, poor Julia, at the mercy of these vile flesh merchants.

Anne kept her arms around the Russian girl. Eventually, her sobs subsided, and with Sasha's head still resting in her lap, Nadia fell into a light sleep. Anne's mind turned to trying to understand her own situation and to figuring out how she might get out of it. And help these girls.

Her only hope now was that the locator was working. There, down inside her. Ugh. Instinctively, in the darkness she reached down and felt that it was still in place. Just to get some reassurance. That was her only link now to Greg and Labrecque and the entire Interpol team. She hoped that they realized that she was no longer in the Revuebar and were following the truck, wherever it was taking her and these trafficked teenagers.

୧୬୧୬

They had drunk the entire bottle of Zweigelt, so before Intermission was over, Greg ordered another one. The announcer came out to herald the next act—a pair of twins from Thailand, who, he promised, would perform in a way only Asian women could.

As the exotic music began, Labrecque leaned over. "Do you think we will see Anne out there on the stage again?"

"I'm not sure, but I hope she is all right." Greg decided that maybe he should check the receiver. It showed that the target was still in the building. Reassured, he put it back in his jacket pocket, trusting that at the end of the show, it would confirm that Anne was on her way back to the Sacher, where they had agreed to meet after this was all over.

It was midway through the fourth act after the Intermission that the tracking device started to vibrate and beep in Greg's pocket. He quickly grabbed it and looked at the screen. "She is moving away," he said to his companion. "Fast, so no doubt they already have her in a vehicle."

"They must have gone out some back exit," Labrecque answered. "But we had it covered. I am sure our guys are right behind them."

"Let's hope so."

❧❧❧

It seemed like an eternity to Anne, but eventually the truck turned onto a rougher road, and then with a jolt, came to a stop.

It started briefly again, then stopped, and after another interminable pause, she heard the clanging of the bar locking the back being pulled to one side, then the squeaking as the huge doors slowly opened.

Fresh air rushed in, and in the distance, floodlights illuminated a big building. A bright flashlight blinded her. "Okay, girls, everyone out now. Come on, we haven't got all day."

Now that there was a bit of light, Anne looked around in the back of the truck. Some of the girls were stirring and a couple of the guards jumped up into the compartment to hurry them into action, as she helped, first Sasha, and then Nadia, stand up and then clamber down onto terra firma.

"You, you, come with me," one of the thugs grabbed Anne by the arm, separating her from Nadia.

"Anne!" she heard the Russian girl say, "Oh, no! No, no—"

She heard a scream and, looking back, saw another guard tear Nadia away from Sasha, yelling, "You, come too. This way."

Then she saw Sasha's face drop into her hands, as her legs buckled and she went down on her knees, before being roughly pulled back up and jostled along behind the disappearing girls. Nadia was being pushed in the same direction the one guard was roughly shoving Anne, away from her teenager friend and the others. Anne again looked back and saw that all the others were being herded toward the well-lit building, which was in the opposite direction from where she and Nadia were being taken.

Where is this brute taking me? What will they do to me?

And where are you now Greg—and Interpol, who got me into this mess—when I really need you?

Chapter 15

Greg and Labrecque rushed out the front door of the Revuebar Rasputin and saw that the black BMW SUV was still idling just across the street. The French agent waved to his colleagues in the front, as he opened the back door and the two men jumped in.

"Go! Go, go, go," Labrecque yelled at the driver.

"They're heading south," Greg said. "Down Favoritenstrasse. And moving fast."

"South? Hmm—"

"Just turned on to the Gürtel."

Some moments of anxious silence, as the traffic in front slowed. Then the driver speeded up as they passed the Maitzlensdorf Cemetery, and Greg gave directions to turn onto Triester Strasse.

"We'll soon be on the highway, too," the French agent observed, trying to console Greg. "Don't worry, Greg. We'll catch them."

"God, I certainly hope she's okay." Greg was regretting that he had agreed to Anne's harebrained scheme. "I will never forgive myself if something should happen to her."

He should have known that the plodding Interpol would be no match for these ruthless, professional criminals. No doubt many of them were ex-FSB or Russian military, if they were working for Polyakov.

✎✎✎

Twisting her arm brutally behind her back, the thug led Anne over to a smaller side building. As they approached, the door was opened from the inside by another guard.

"Lev, is Kalinsky here already?" the man pushing Anne along asked.

"Yes. He arrived more than twenty minutes ago. But he went over to the office to talk to Polyakov. He said you should just take her upstairs and put her in there with the other one. He'll be along as soon as he can, I am sure."

Oh God, no! Please, no. Just don't let Polyakov near me. Anne was very, very frightened of what could happen next.

Still in the thug's iron grip, Anne was tugged up some stairs and along a long corridor, at the end of which the guard opened a door and shoved her inside before locking it from the outside. She heard scuffling behind her along the hallway, and wondered where they were taking Nadia. When she regained her composure, in the pitch darkness, Anne groped along the wall until she found a light switch.

The single lamp on a small table over on the opposite wall illuminated the room, and Anne saw immediately that there was someone in the king-size bed next to it. A girl's blonde hair spread across the pillow, slender body under rumpled top sheet. It was only when she moved closer, that she recognized her Russian nuclear physicist friend.

"Julia! It's me, Anne. Wake up." As her trained eyes scanned the room for a possible escape route, Anne tried to rouse her friend from what she quickly judged must have been drug-induced sleep. "I need you to wake up."

Then she remembered the conversation downstairs that the man Kalinsky would soon come, and that Polyakov was around too, so she knew she did not have much time. "Come on, Julia, please. Quickly. Wake up."

And then she heard footsteps approaching the door. So, in fact, there was no time at all. In desperation, she cradled her friend's head and whispered in her ear, "Julia, you must not let on that you know me. Remember, you do not know who I am."

Just in time, because the door opened and in strutted the Kallay impostor—or Kalinsky, as he seemed to be known here, who she now was convinced was none other than Hetzel—dressed in a loose fitting sweat suit and flip flops—dangerously waving a pistol. "Well, well, well. What do we have here! Two gorgeous women, being nice and friendly to each other. I like that, really like that."

The brute came over toward Anne, pointing the gun at her. "Now honey, I want you to get undressed. Take it all off for me, just like you did back at the club." And when she did not move, he chuckled to himself. "Well, if that's what you want, I can get my two friends outside to come and rip your clothes off, no problem. Or better still, have them tie you up and do it myself. Like with your little blonde friend here."

And with that he ripped the top sheet off the bed, revealing Julia's beautiful, naked and bruised body, just as the Russian girl was coming to. It was only then that Anne noticed that her friend's one wrist was handcuffed to the bed. Deciding that it was better not to have Hetzel call his men, she slowly started to take her top off. Yes, it was much better odds this way, but she needed to take action soon, find the right moment, before Hetzel did something crazy with that gun.

As Anne took her clothes off, the creep gawked at her with lust in his eyes. Once she was naked, he grabbed her by the hair, and with the gun still at her back, pushed her head down between Julia's legs and told her to make love to her friend. The creep picked up Anne's discarded panties and sniffed them with crazed delight. Then when Julia's moans satisfied him that Anne was carrying out his order, with a little laugh, he put down the pistol on the night table, and started to get undressed. Anne was alert, though, and when his hands were occupied, immediately lashed out with a vicious, well-aimed Karate kick to his crotch. Hetzel collapsed in pain. Anne lunged for the pistol and stuck it in the creep's face.

"Don't try anything, or I will kill you. Or better still, blow your rotten genitalia away," she yelled at Hetzel. "I want to know where you keep the keys for the hand-cuffs—" When Anne aimed the gun point blank at his scrotum, and yelled, "Now, you asshole!" Hetzel, still buckled over in pain, pointed to the drawer of the night table.

Not taking her eyes off the man, Anne opened, and reached into the drawer with her free hand. Finding the keys, she moved toward the bed to unlock Julia's hand-cuffs. In that instance, Hetzel made a move toward her. But Anne's trained reflexes were much better than his, and, as he did so, she fired the pistol at his crotch, graz-ing the inside of his thigh and just missing the genitals. The pervert fell backward with an unearthly scream, bleeding profusely.

As he lay there shrieking, Anne quickly put on her clothes, except for her panties—which were soaked in Hetzel's blood—and her top, which she helped Julia into, along with Hetzel's sweat pants. Just in time, because there was an agitated knock on the door.

"Boss? Are you all right?" Anne heard the guard on the other side, as she went over and put her hand on the latch. She threw open the door, and the thug—not seeing her behind it—entered, as Anne, keeping the gun pointed at him, slammed the door shut.

"Okay, my friend, if you want to stay alive, no funny stuff. Throw me your pistol and baton and any other weapon you have. And get out your cell phone."

The guard's trained eyes surveyed the surreal, horrific scene. Anne had no patience though, and she yelled at the man, who was too shocked to act. "Come on, a-hole, action! Do as I say or you will be spread-eagled there too, with your penis and balls splattered all over the walls, just like this fucking pervert." She hardly ever swore, but she felt it was justified in the situation.

The guard, seeing his naked boss lying there on the floor, moaning in pain, with a bleeding mess between his legs, quickly surmised that this woman did not fool around. He undid the holster at his side and threw down the pistol and truncheon then reached into his pocket, pulling out an iPhone.

"Now, my friend, you are first going to call one-one-two and tell them in English to send an ambulance because there is a man bleeding profusely. If they ask how it happened, you just tell them he shot himself by accident. You will give them our exact location," Anne said calmly, keeping the gun pointed at the thug. "And ask them how long it will take to get here."

The guard did as he was told.

"How long?" She finally had managed to put her shoes back on.

"They said fifteen minutes."

"Cover your boss's repulsive body with your coat.

And put the phone on the bed. Then go over in that corner with your hands above your head and face against the wall," Anne said, waving with the pistol toward the farthest corner of the room. "Any funny stuff and I shoot to kill."

The thug obeyed the orders, while Anne finished helping Julia get dressed. She picked up the iPhone from the bed and dialed Greg's number.

"Where are you? Are you all right?" were his immediate questions.

After she told him everything, and that she was now absolutely sure that Kallay—or Kalinsky, as he seemed to be known by his Russian colleagues—must be Hetzel, they agreed that Julia and she should try to go with the impostor in the ambulance to the hospital.

Having found the walled compound, Greg and Labrecque were waiting at a discrete distance until help arrived. "We will follow the ambulance if the locator says you are in it. Otherwise, we will raid the facilities as soon as the police reinforcements get here."

Anne waited till she heard the wail of the ambulance's siren before she gave the phone back to the guard and, surprising the man, said in Russian, "You're going to call the front gate now and tell them that the boss has had a heart attack and that you have called an ambulance for him. They are to let it through. And no funny stuff. Otherwise this sicko here and you will both die." She waved the gun first at Hetzel then at the guard. "You see, I speak your language!"

The siren got louder and louder, until it was finally turned off, and replaced by commotion downstairs. Just as Anne was retrieving the phone from the bed where she had told the thug to put it, two medics rushed into the room pushing a gurney. Two new guards came in behind them.

"This man had a heart attack as he was loading the gun, and accidentally shot himself," Anne said in English to the Hungarian medics who surveyed the scene.

They looked at her. "We will take care of him," one answered as already the other one of them was bandaging Hetzel's thigh. Anne bent down and whispered in the medic's ear, "We need to come with you in the ambulance. These men were holding us prisoner here when this accident happened. They are human traffickers. Please help us."

The medic finished his work, looked around at the devastation in the room again as if to confirm what Anne had said, and nodded to her. "Okay, you ladies are to come with us. You will need to tell us what happened."

Anne helped push the gurney along the corridor and she and Julia squeezed into the service elevator with it and the medics. One of the guards reached in after Julia to try to pull her back out, but the attendant shoved him aside and the doors closed. As soon as the elevator hit ground floor, the medics rushed the gurney and the girls to the ambulance, and helped them climb in just as the guards who had run down the stairs caught up to them.

"They cannot go. The women stay here," the leader of the group of thugs said.

"If you want us to save the life of your friend here," the one medic said, staving them off, as he pushed the guard aside to close the back doors, "they come with us. We need to know what happened. And you have to make sure that we are not stopped at the gate. If we don't get your buddy to the hospital right away, the man will die. He is losing much blood."

There was a rapid conversation among the guards, as the driver started the engine and took off at speed toward the gate. Fortunately, the barrier was up when they got there, and they sailed through, but Anne only breathed a sigh of relief when the ambulance accelerated on the highway toward the hospital.

Chapter 16

As the ambulance turned onto the highway and picked up speed, Anne hugged Julia. "I'm glad you are safe now. That we're both safe, out of the hands of those depraved human traffickers."

Julia hugged her back, and tears came to her eyes. "Yes, thank you. Thank you, Anne, for rescuing me. It was so awful in there. I was starting to wish I could die."

"Well, we have this monster now." Anne looked over at Hetzel, who was delirious and moaning in pain, in spite of the morphine he had been given. "And for all that you have been through, I am glad you didn't die." She stroked Julia's hair and let her doze off. Her friend needed all the rest she could get.

☙❧

Greg saw the ambulance speed out of the compound, and the tracker immediately registered that Anne was inside and moving fast away from them.

"Okay, go! She's in it. Follow the ambulance," Greg yelled.

The driver had the BMW already accelerating, and, as it passed the gate, it almost collided with a black SUV that turned out onto the road behind the ambulance. Fortunately, the close call caused the other vehicle to veer off the road and come to a full stop in the ditch.

"Those guys know the fake Kallay is in there. And they may also know that Anne and Julia are inside as well. They will no doubt want to make sure that the ladies do not give anything away about the criminal activities they were up to," Labrecque said, looking back at the receding SUV. Then he saw it finally go into reverse, and power out of the ditch, but after hesitating for a moment, instead of racing after them, it turned back into the compound. "Phew. They're not coming after us."

"Hmm. We must have surprised them. They were probably not expecting to be under surveillance."

"Yeah. Either someone got hurt in there, or something is wrong with the vehicle. Or else, they realized they had better clear out all the evidence of their illegal shenanigans at the compound, before we come back with the Hungarian authorities and muster a raid. That would certainly be the smart thing to do."

"They will no doubt figure out other ways to take care of their buddy Hetzel, if they want to—or whoever the hell that is in the ambulance."

Labrecque dialed his Hungarian Interpol counterpart, George Székely, whom he had already alerted on the way from Vienna, and who was now racing there from Budapest, a little over two hours away. "George, we are on our way to the hospital. I think it must be at Vasvàr." He had looked on Google for the nearest town with medical facilities. "Can you meet us there?"

"I am still a little over a half an hour away. But I'll be there as soon as I can."

"Good."

"Must be the Zala County Hospital. I will also get a police officer I know and trust to come there from Szombathely. Lieutenant Péter Körmendi. He'll be able to get us some local help. I expect he'll be there around the same time as me."

"Thanks, George."

Greg called Anne, hoping she would still have the phone she had used to call him.

"How is everything?"

"Boy, we're glad to be out of there, Julia and I. She's not in very good shape, poor girl, and I am a bit rattled, to say the least. But we're hanging in there, I guess."

"Don't worry, love. We're right behind you, and you will soon be in my arms. We have lots of reinforcements coming."

"Good. And Greg, thank God for the tracker. It was a good idea."

"Amen."

∽∾∽

By the time the ambulance arrived at the hospital, Hetzel was sedated with painkillers, his wound thoroughly bandaged and the bleeding staunched. The medics wheeled him in and also insisted that Julia—who was not looking good—be put in a bed and given a thorough examination. Anne had told them the whole story on the way over. They were appalled, and insisted on calling the police, although she told them that matters were in good hands. After all, she had been with Interpol, and her former colleagues were on the case.

Anne did not have to linger long at the emergency entrance before Greg and Labrecque showed up. She ran into her husband's arms, and they hugged for a good minute or two before Greg asked, "Julia? How is she?"

"She's being looked at by the doctors."

"Good. And where is this Kallay impersonator? You are convinced it's Hetzel, no?"

"Absolutely sure."

"Well, I would finally like to meet him, to see for myself. Is the jerk *compus mentis*?"

"I don't know. Let's go and find him."

✁✁✁

A nurse led them to Kallay's room—Anne had registered him with his Hungarian alias—and they all crowded in.

"Hetzel!" Greg immediately recognized the man lying with eyes closed, pale and motionless in bed, who, despite the dyed-blond hair, could be none other to those who had known Adam's Viennese friend.

Hetzel did not respond. He was far away in dreamland, thanks to all the morphine he had been given for the pain.

Anne took the opportunity, while the others consulted the doctors, to excuse herself, and went into the unused en suite bathroom. She needed to relieve herself, and at the same time, wanted to extract the uncomfortable tracker, now that she was safe again. As she finished, she noticed that Hetzel's borrowed jacket was hanging there on a hook, so, on an impulse, she slipped the little gadget into a zippered pocket. "I sure hope I won't need this thing anymore. Although it did save my life. But it may serve some purpose again now with our friend here," she muttered to herself on her way back into the hospital room. "Even if he just goes straight to jail, the bastard."

Since Hetzel was in no state to be questioned yet, they asked to see Julia.

But the doctors were not finished with her, so they

went down to the waiting room and tried to piece together what they knew.

❧

"So Hetzel-Kallay-Kalinsky runs this operation to traffic young women from Russia—and any others he can pick up along the way, it seems. After all, he did capture Julia and me. And abuse us, the creep."

"I'm sure Polyakov is behind it all. Hetzel is just the front man," Greg mused, glancing at Anne, immediately regretting that he had said the Russian's name in front of her when she was in such a fragile state. So he was rather surprised when Anne said, "Well, in fact, Polyakov was there, at the compound. I heard one of the guards say. Fortunately, our paths did not cross. Or else it could have been even a lot worse for me."

Greg was glad to switch focus. "Remember, I told you that Adam recounted to me that Hetzel and Kolchakova had a nice little side business, alongside the obvious main one of stealing and selling nuclear material. Kolchakova would make the referrals of parents with teenage girls who worked for her, and Hetzel would approach them to provide the service of getting their daughters away from that contaminated hellhole of Ozersk. By offering to place them in jobs and with families in the West, but in reality selling them as sex slaves or using them as strippers. A nice little side business, indeed!"

"Yes, they would make money both coming and going—they would rake in an exorbitant sum from the parents, and then sell the girls for a lot in the West. Or else, make them perform as strippers, and more than likely as prostitutes, to earn their keep."

"So the Revuebar Rasputin in Vienna was just some kind of…of vertical integration in this sorry business, and

I guess, a showroom. How clever!" Labrecque was getting the picture.

"It was there, though, that these gangsters did the actual trafficking. At least, that's where they sold the young women to all those perverse rich buyers. Take me, for example. I was sold to some Chinese official there, upstairs. For a good price, supposedly because your friend Hetzel claimed that I was experienced." Anne shuddered at the thought. "And that young Russian girl, Nadia—whom you lecherous old geezers gawked at stripping alongside Ginger at the Revuebar—was sold to a Middle Eastern sheikh. Again, for some very high price, this time though, because she was still a virgin."

"Horrific."

"Yes, it is, isn't it? Nadia was telling me that she and a number of other girls her age were brought by plane from Chelyabinsk to an airstrip in Hungary, and then taken to the compound we were just at. There, they were abused in some fashion or other." Anne paused and took a deep breath, as she remembered that her ordeal had been similar to Nadia's. She did not want to go into the details now with Greg. Or perhaps ever. "Then, some were sent to Vienna, still others to other cities in Europe and elsewhere. To be sold, or used as strippers."

"We will close down the Revuebar. And of course, this compound here in Hungary," Labrecque said indignantly. "We must find all the other clubs around the world that these gangsters use for their despicable business. Now that we have this guy Hetzel in custody—"

"It may not be that easy. This is a very slippery lot," Anne observed. "And we first have to free all those girls they hold captive at the compound."

"Well, at least we have Julia back. And you, of course, my dear." Greg thought to himself that Anne and he had achieved what they had set out to do when asked by Demeter to come back to Vienna.

Time to go home? Not yet. There were still all those girls in the hands of the traffickers, as Anne had said. And the ultimate goal for Interpol, of course, would be to capture Polyakov and destroy his evil trading business.

"Yes, let's go see Julia. Maybe the doctors are finished with her now." Anne jumped up. "Her mother must be worried sick. We need to get her home as quickly as possible."

Chapter 17

It was four p.m., and Mikhail was glad that another workday was done. Today, he had the early shift at the East Gate to Mayak, and there was always a lot of traffic here with officials on their way to the Plutonium Palace—the huge, ultimate storage facility to safeguard highly radioactive material, built largely with American money—just outside the gate. So there was always a lot of checking of vehicles here, to make sure that no uranium or plutonium was leaving the facility illicitly, but at least the work at this post was routine, and Mikhail had a lot of time to think.

And today he had indeed thought a lot, especially about his dear daughter, Nadia, whom he missed greatly since he had entrusted her to the European Placement Agency. He had paid them a lot of money to find work for her in Germany or Austria or somewhere in the European Union. Now, he was hoping to hear from her, after, all, it was already four days since she had left. But Mikhail was in a good mood as he walked over to the locker room in the main building. In spite of his initial misgivings—especially about that guy, Kalinsky—he was generally happy. He had convinced himself that he and Galina had made the right decision to send Nadia off to the capitalist West. His darling daughter would experience new things, the bigger world—things they had never had the chance to live—hopefully, improve her German and English, meet new and interesting people—maybe even a future husband. And most importantly, get away from this godforsaken contaminated place where any grandchildren she might eventually give them were not very likely to be wholesome and healthy.

Inside the changing room, as he opened his locker and took off his holster, his friend, Pavel, who had worked the other side of traffic today, came in and sat down on the bench. He, too, must have been thinking about his daughter, Sasha, for he asked, "Mikhail, have you had any news from Nadia?"

"Not yet. But I hope we hear from her very soon. We really do miss her, Galina and I."

"It's funny. Svetlana and I talk about nothing else. We keep rehashing the decision and convincing ourselves that we did the right thing."

"Yeah. I know what you mean, old friend."

☙❧

They parted as always, by the imposing Kurchatov Statue in Lenin Park, Pavel going left and Mikhail right. Mikhail habitually glanced up at the stern, bearded face of the father of the Soviet atomic bomb with mixed feelings, mindful of the terrible suffering and devastation the nuclear program had caused, but at the same time grateful that he had a good job now despite his lack of higher education. His thoughts returned to his daughter, and he was proud that she would be escaping his lot and have a chance at a better life, perhaps in the capitalist West somewhere. Yes, with a good German husband, Mikhail smiled inwardly, repeating the thought for the second time that day. And maybe—he dared hope—Nadia would even be the ticket for Yuri, Galina and him too, to emigrate.

He was already at the very edge of the park, when he was jolted out of his reverie by a young man on a bike, who pulled up in front of him out of nowhere. "Gospodin Glinkov?" the youth asked.

"Why? Who are you?"

"Never mind, sir. I was told to give you this." The stranger reached a thin envelope toward Mikhail. "Your daughter."

Mikhail was stunned, but he grabbed the packet, as the young man rode away at great speed, back into the park.

For a minute, Mikhail just looked at the envelope, thinking how odd it was that the delivery boy had taken off through Lenin Park, even though riding bicycles there was forbidden. He eventually turned the envelope over, and saw that it was indeed addressed to him, then vehemently tore it open. The only thing inside, was a note saying:

Papa: Please go to the site www.nadiaglinkov.com on our computer for greetings and news from me.
Your loving daughter,
Nadia

Hmm, good, she must have sent this, Mikhail thought relieved and happy, And then: *So, now she even has a website! Well, at least we finally have news of our daughter, and if I am right, we will see her on the computer screen. Talking of her first impressions of the West, and maybe even a little video of her, walking around filming the sights, all just for her parents who have never had the chance to travel. She could not come in person to greet us, no, so she did the next best thing. What a clever girl, she is, my dear Nadia!*

Mikhail picked up the pace, wanting to get home as quickly as possible to view what was on the site Nadia had directed him to open. *Oh, but Galina was not going to be back till later. Tonight was the one night a week she went out with the girls after work.* Well, too bad, he would go ahead and watch it himself. It would not spoil. And he could look at it with her again when she got home. So much the better.

ଏ୬ଏ୬

He ran up the three flights of stairs and lost no time unlocking the door to their apartment. Throwing his bag on a chair as he went straight into the small living room, which served also as dining room and office, Mikhail booted up the computer, and while the machine purred to life, went over to the kitchen to pour himself a celebratory drink from the bottle of Putinka he took down from the cupboard. No, a double vodka. He gulped it down, and poured another one that he took over to the small desk, then sat down and, with eager but shaking hands, typed into Google the site with Nadia's name in it.

The first picture that filled the screen was the one he had given Kalinsky along with the application form. Mikhail smiled at what followed. Nadia waving to them as she boarded the plane—someone must have had a video camera, or maybe just used a cell phone, and given her the video. *Nice touch, that.* Then some music, and lo and behold, Nadia dancing on stage with a black woman. *But what was this?* Mikhail suddenly started to get alarmed—his darling teenage daughter was doing what amounted to a striptease! *This cannot be, no, no, no!* The middle-aged man stood up, banged his fists on the desk, and sat down again, as tears started to flow. "I—I cannot believe it," he muttered, clutching his heart where he felt his angina acting up, just as the take ended with his daughter completely naked— save her panties—on stage, with strangers applauding, laughing and giggling, she about to break into tears while vainly trying to shield her lovely little breasts from those lusting eyes. *Oh God, no, what have I done? This is monstrous!*

But what came next was much, much worse. As an unidentified male voice spoke, pictures of Nadia—being manhandled and made to strip by a pudgy little man whose face was blotted out, then her head shoved brutally between the legs of another woman—flashed on the screen.

Mikhail turned away in despair and disgust, and listened to a deep voice make, in an even tone, the following terrible statement: "Mikhail Petrovich, you must listen carefully, if you ever want to see your daughter alive again. Unless you do exactly as I tell you, she will be sold as a sex slave or made to do things much worse than what you have seen here. Take this as just a taste of what might come if you do not carry out what we ask of you. She has suffered relatively little so far, and if you obey, and if our mission is successful, you will get her back intact. If not, as I said, you will be giving her a future filled with horrors.

"Now, Mikhail Petrovich, you must listen very carefully: we know that you have the day shift this coming Tuesday, May twenty-third, so exactly at four p.m., a white Ford Focus will be driven by a chauffeur to the East Gate where you are scheduled to work. There will be a woman named Julia Saparova in the back seat. You will let this car go through with its passenger and whatever it is carrying, after only a very superficial inspection. If you do this, as I said, your daughter will not be harmed and will be brought back to you. If you do not, or if at any time, you tell the police, your bosses, or anyone else—even your wife—about this approach, as I said earlier, your daughter will suffer the consequences. You need to email us a 'Yes' at info@epctrade.com—I repeat, info@epctrade.com—by tomorrow noon your time if you want your daughter to avoid a fate worse than death."

The sound track ended with Nadia's unearthly screams in the background, as the screen went blank.

Mikhail, sat there unmoving, with his face in his hands. He wanted to kill himself, but he knew that would not help. In his despair, he knew that the only hope for Nadia was if he followed the instructions the voice had given him. He, as a father had no choice. He would never forgive himself if he didn't, even though he realized his decision could have terrible consequences for humanity.

Chapter 18

Julia was surprised and very glad to see Greg in the flesh, just as she had been with Anne back in the compound, albeit under different circumstances. The drugs had worn off, and the hospital rest was doing her a lot of good, although more than anything, it was being free and seeing her friends again that lifted her spirits.

"I am so happy that you found me. I was beginning to wish that I was dead."

Anne stroked the Russian girl's hair. "Yeah. You went through a lot, my dear."

"Well, I'm glad that your boss called you to come help find me. And, that you came. And then you found and rescued me," Julia said with a little laugh. "I can't thank you enough."

"Yes, it was that call from my former boss at Interpol that brought us back to Vienna. Saying you went missing. Dreadful—"

"Just as with Adam," Greg interrupted, "and since we had managed to track him down, Demeter thought we were the obvious ones to find you. You are in a similar position at the IAEA."

"The idea was that it might be the same thugs wanting to steal more uranium," Anne added. "And use you in some way."

"Just like they corrupted Adam to help them."

"Well, they certainly used me."

"But, Julia, did you by any chance overhear any mention of another theft of nuclear material at any point?" Anne asked. "We didn't tell you yet, but in Vienna we bumped into Brother Peter, one of the terrorists who was buying the HEU in Poti from the Polyakov gang. We were wondering if this was all leading up to another heist."

"No, Anne, I certainly did not hear anything nor see any signs that that might be the case."

"On another note, Julia, when we went by your apartment, your mother told us how you came to be at the Revuebar, but we don't know exactly what happened. Nor, after that, how you ended up in that compound here in Hungary. Can you tell us, or would you rather not talk about it?" Anne was wondering how hard she should push her friend just yet. "It may bring back unpleasant memories, so…"

"It would help us understand how these gangsters work. And also, maybe cast a light on how extensive their human trafficking operation is," Labrecque said, as he took a little notebook out of his pocket.

"I will tell you all I know," Julia said, sitting up in the bed. "Maybe it will help put the horrors behind me."

"Thank you." Anne made herself comfortable at Julia's feet. "But stop any time it is too painful."

⁊ↄ⊱

"Tuesday—it was a Tuesday, I think, ten or so days ago. Hmm, what day is it today? I don't even know—I have completely lost track of time."

"Today is Monday."

"So it must have been thirteen days ago. I came home from work, around seven-thirty p.m. I think. My mother—she has been staying with me since the doctors in Russia told her she did not have much longer to live, and I wanted to see if we could find better care for her in Vienna, poor soul—met me at the door, all agitated.

"She said, 'Julia, that nice man—that Hungarian physicist who came to see me in Ozersk—Adam Kallay, your friend, remember? Well, he called. Around six, thinking you might be home. He would like to meet with you tonight at ten p.m. at…here, I have it written down…some bar it was…The Revuebar Rasputin.'

"'The Rasputin?' I perked up, not having thought of my old workplace for quite some time.

"'Yes.' my mother confirmed. 'What an odd name, for a meeting place. Ugh! That Rasputin, was a monk, but an evil one. Hmm. Maybe you should not go, and send a note asking to meet somewhere else.'

"I laughed at the very Russian superstition of my mother, but was surprised. And agitated. It did not seem right. Adam, how could it be? I asked myself. You, Greg, told me in Poti that he was dead."

"Yes, we could not believe it either, when your mother told us that Kallay had called you. He is dead, for sure. I know. I saw him die with my own eyes. I felt for his pulse before I left him, but there was none."

"We believe that someone must be impersonating him," Anne added.

"Well, my first thought was that maybe Adam was not dead after all," Julia countered. "Maybe he had gone into hiding and was now reaching out to me. Maybe he needed help. And he had been so good to me, so kind, that I could not leave him in a lurch. So I resolved to go to the meeting, in spite of my doubts. And my mother's superstition, although, in the end, she did encourage me."

"Of course."

"I got to the Revuebar shortly after ten p.m. The front entrance—not the back where I used to come and go all the time—since I thought Adam would want to meet in one of the dark booths where he would not be seen, and from where he could see the action on stage. He always enjoyed that."

Greg nodded. "Yes, I know."

"I told the guard at the door that a Mr. Kallay was expecting me, so I was surprised when, after letting me in, he directed me with a smile to his colleague guarding the small door that led backstage. I breezed past the podium where my old friend Ginger was doing her solo act, and remembered the times when I was dancing to *Scheherezade*—my exotic dance act up on the stage."

"You were amazing, I remember," Greg could not keep from remarking.

Anne slapped her husband's wrist. "Stop it, now."

"I told this second guard that I was there to see Mr. Kallay, and he led the way through the door, saying 'Come.'

"I followed the man along the dingy corridor I knew so well, from which opened the offices and dressing rooms, past the staircase to an upstairs I had never seen, and all the way to the back door where another guard was standing. The thug leading the way said to his colleague in Russian, 'She come looking for Kallay.'

"They both started to laugh, at the same time grabbing me from front and back, forcing my arms behind me and clasping handcuffs around my wrists. I screamed and yelled 'Let me go!' but no one came to my rescue.

"'Okay, baby, now you go see your friend, Kallay,' the man who had led me to the back door said, giving my breasts a rough fondle.

"Ugh. They pushed me through the door and into the back of a SUV, and a driver and another guard materialized from nowhere. As the first brute closed the seat belt around me, he reached between my legs. 'You're going to have some fun with your dear friend Kallay where you're going. Lucky guy. Such a lovely piece of ass you are!' or something disgusting like that. The vehicle then sped away through Vienna and eventually onto the highway."

"Toward Hungary? The compound?" Anne asked.

"Yes. After several hours, we arrived at that place. I was taken straight to the room where you found me. In fact, to the very bed, Anne, where you first saw me. Here, the guards opened the handcuffs, and released my right wrist replacing it with one of the iron posts at the head of the bed. They then left me fettered to the bedpost."

"God, what creeps." As he said this, Greg wondered how Julia could be so detached in the telling, although, clearly, the experience she had undergone had been emotionally extremely traumatic.

Could it be the drugs she had been given?

"I was left alone in the dark for I don't know how many hours, so I managed to fall into a deep sleep. Eventually, I was woken rudely, by this fat little man, stark naked, without a hair on his body, straddling me and wildly ripping my clothes off. I tried to kick him and beat him off me, but realized that by then my ankles had also been chained to the bed, with my legs spread wide apart. It was only when he looked at me with a wicked scowl that I recognized the face—it was none other than that monster Hetzel. With dyed-blond hair, to look more like the Adam he was trying to impersonate. The same pervert, who had lusted after me back when I was dancing at the Revuebar, now had me in his clutches. Just like that, he had tricked me by pretending he was Adam Kallay.

And I had fallen for it, stupid me." Julia fought to keep back the tears.

"Julia. Julia. It's okay. Are you still all right to talk about this?" Anne asked, now concerned about her friend.

"Yes. I want to tell you everything. This…this… Frankenstein did terrible things with me. The only way I was able to survive it all was to—to remove myself from my body, if you can understand what I am saying."

"Yes, my dear, I can." Anne, who had lived through being raped by Polyakov, fully empathized, with tears coming to her eyes. She held Julia's hand between hers.

"Over the next days, whenever he appeared, the pervert alternated between telling me that he loved me and pleading with me to marry him, saying he would never release me until I agreed, and beating me and abusing me sexually. He took pleasure in hurting me, and—and sodomized me—several times."

Greg had gone white as the hospital's walls. "God! I will kill the bastard."

"He would drug me, and I must admit, I gladly took the pills—they dulled the pain, and allowed me to escape the reality of what was happening to me. He would bring other girls—often young ones, Russians mostly—tell them to strip, beat them and force them to make love to me. As if that would please me, the deranged pervert must have thought. And then, he would push them away and rape me over and over again." At this point, Julia could not hold back the tears any longer. "There was another room, but I don't know—I don't remember—I don't—the drugs—it is all just a horrible haze now."

"Julia, I will not rest until this guy is dead or behind bars for the rest of his life."

"And then, Anne, they brought you," Julia whispered between sobs, cuddling closer with her friend. "And you very cleverly told me not to let on that I knew you. You were so brave to lunge for the pistol and shoot the creep in the groin. Amazing, that you got us out of there in the ambulance. Thank you, thank you."

"Well, I did it also to save myself. Those guys, you don't mess with."

✆✑✆✑

After a moment or two of silence, Greg glanced at his watch, but thought there was maybe enough time to broach the other topic he wanted to discuss with Julia. "Julia, when we were in Vienna, your mother showed us a letter from her father, your grandfather, Efim Pleshkov—who had known my grandfather at Mayak, you may remember. The letter talked about the disappearance of her elder sister, Katerina. Your aunt. Apparently, she was kidnapped by Lavrenti Beria in Ozersk in 1950 and eventually sent to a gulag. I have the letter in my rucksack—Anne, it's over on your side of the bed, by your feet—along with some other letters, Julia, your mother wanted you to have."

"Yes, I know those letters. They were in that old tin box. The one from my grandfather in particular was pretty gruesome, I remember."

"It talked of Katerina's ordeal with Beria, that perverted deputy of Stalin who was the head of the secret police," Anne said.

"Ugh! Now that you mention it, it is similar to what I have been through with this monster Hetzel. My poor aunt didn't have you to help her get away though."

"After Beria abused Katerina—and it would seem, got her pregnant—he wanted her disposed of, but his security chief sent her to some gulag, if I remember correctly," Anne continued, as she pulled out a manila envelope from the rucksack, and then several letters from the package, handing them to Julia.

"Yes, and it was only after Beria died in 1953, six months or so after Stalin, that my grandparents found out which prison camp it was. My grandfather, I think, incorporated the letter that tells this, from a Gospodja Lenkova, into his letter." Julia finally pulled out the yellowing pages from a tattered envelope. "Yes, here it is. She says that her husband, who it seems, was the head of security at Beria's villa in Ozersk—you are right, Anne—took my Aunt Katerina to a corrective labor camp at the Gulag Chelyablag in Chelyabinsk. In defiance of the order from Beria, who wanted her killed. Disposed of—liquidated, as they would say." And she looked up from the letter. "That was still in 1950, sometime in April probably."

"Three years or so before the very same Beria started to dismantle the entire system of the gulags," Greg pointed out.

"It was only after Beria died in the summer of 1953—so after that—that my grandfather felt able to start to look for Katerina. Before then, he was convinced it could have meant the death of all of them, as well as the Lenkov family, since Gospodin Lenkov had disobeyed Beria's command. So he went to Chelyabinsk, made inquiries and searched all over for his daughter and for her child—at grave risk to himself—but found no trace of either. In fact, as he wrote in his letter, the corrective labor camps had been done away with in October of 1951, and any prisoners remaining then would have been transferred somewhere else in the gulag system. And if there were any files, as he said, they would have been taken to Moscow."

"So maybe there is some record of her in the archives of the NKVD or KGB—or their successor, the

FSB—wouldn't you think?" Greg posited.

"Yes, well, just last year, when I was on a business trip to Moscow, I went to visit the State Archives of the Russian Federation—the GARF, as it is known by its Russian acronym—which is where most of the remaining gulag records ended up. But there was nothing about a Katerina Pleshkova in the files on any camp, let alone those on Chelyablag."

"Perhaps they are somewhere else," Anne suggested. "Those records, I mean."

"Or, maybe it is that they have been destroyed. Liquidated, as you say. Just like many Soviet citizens were. Along with their entire life stories. As if they never existed," Labrecque suggested. "We know that happened often there, and in the satellite countries."

"Yes, you are right," Julia agreed. "So maybe we will never be able to find out what happened to my Aunt Katerina. Other than that Lenkov took her to some camp instead of disposing of her. Away from that evil Beria."

"At least that is something," Labrecque said. "In fact, I remember reading somewhere that they found the remains of some of Beria's young female victims in the basement of his villa in Moscow when it was turned into the Tunisian Embassy in 1958. They even discovered an iron door leading to his personal torture chamber. He was a real monster, as you say."

Greg saw Julia wince at this comment from the French Interpol agent.

੭ை੭

Labrecque's phone chirped. It was Székely, downstairs in the lobby.

"We'll be right down."

At the reception, Labrecque went up to two men

lounging by the desk and introduced Anne and Greg, Székely, the Hungarian police officer with him. "Lieutenant Péter Körmendi. Péter and I go back many years. He will work with us to catch these criminals."

"Hello. George told me a little bit of what has been going on. Terrible. I cannot believe these Russian gangsters could operate a sex trafficking ring here, in Hungary. Right under our noses."

"Yeah, pretty brazen of them," Székely agreed.

"Where is this sexual deviant? I will take him into custody immediately," Körmendi asked. "Registered as Adam Kallay, you say?"

As they left the reception area to go back up to the room occupied by Hetzel, Greg glanced at the clock: it was already eight-twenty-three a.m. He had not slept—none of them had—but the adrenaline kept them going. Good, he thought, at least the creep should be awake and finished with breakfast. When Greg entered his room with Anne, the Hungarian police officer and the two men from Interpol, the invalid turned pale and started to shake. He knew the game was up.

"Why, Greg," he whispered, "I never thought I would see you again."

"You have a lot to answer for, you fucking monster." The adjective, for once, was appropriate, Greg thought.

"It's not as it seems, Greg," Hetzel whined.

Körmendi put handcuffs on him. "Okay, my friend, you are under arrest. You're going to stay here until I can talk to the doctors to get you released from hospital and get some men over to take you to jail." He got on his phone and Székely translated for the others: "He's just getting some local officers to come and guard Hetzel here as long as the doctors want him to stay. Then they will take this jerk and put him away. In the meantime, we're going to go over to the compound to free those girls and arrest the other thugs. Péter tells me we will be joined there by some reinforcements."

"We're coming with you."

"Yeah, that would be good."

"Also, it would help if we could take Julia along," Labrecque added. "Since she knows the compound the best, it seems. That is, if she is well enough."

"I'll run and see," Anne said, heading off toward Julia's room.

Chapter 19

They went in two cars, Julia and Anne joining Labrecque and Greg in the black BMW. Székely and the other two Viennese Interpol agents stayed behind at the hospital until the local cops came to guard Hetzel, allowing Körmendi to go and greet the reinforcements and organize the search of the facility.

When they got to the gates of the compound though, there was no one waiting there. Pacing beside his car, the Hungarian police officer called around again, and Greg could see that his frustration level was mounting with each conversation. "They have the warrant, but they are supposedly trying to muster a large force of at least twenty men. That's what's taking so long. I told them to come with however many they have, before it's too late."

In the meantime, Székely arrived at the site with Labrecque's two colleagues from Vienna. Puzzled that they were still just hanging around outside the gate, he asked, "Why don't we go in? There seems to be no one in there. The compound looks totally deserted."

Indeed, the Hungarian Interpol officer was right. No one manned the guard booth at the gate, and there was not a soul visible when they peeked through.

"All right, let's carry on," Körmendi finally agreed. "The back-up should be here momentarily in any case."

ɔɔɛɔ

The place was eerie, disturbingly so. Other than the eight of them, it seemed that there was no one at all in the huge compound, anywhere. At the two ladies' suggestion, they made their way first toward the main building, where neither Julia nor Anne had been, and where they had seen the thugs herd the other girls. It was when they were just breaking in through the front door, that they finally heard the approaching sirens of the local police.

"The reinforcements," Körmendi said. "About bloody time."

They stayed together, Székely, Körmendi, Labrecque, Greg, Anne and Julia, going from room to room in the big building, mostly in silent shock at all the evidence carelessly left behind. It was clear from the smashed computers, destroyed webcams and film cameras, the wall-to-wall mattresses, sex toys, chains and whips, in all the rooms, that there was a major human trafficking ring focused on sex and pornography operating from here. It was also obvious that the gangsters involved had tried to destroy as much of the incriminating proof as they could, but they had been in a great hurry to get away.

When the local Hungarian police finally caught up to them, Anne said to the others, "Okay, I have seen enough now, and in any case, we are just stepping on each other here. There are too many of us now taking stock of the evidence, so I would like to go over to the other building where Julia and I were kept. I am sure there is also stuff there that could be interesting."

"Good idea," Greg agreed.

"That is, if Julia, you are not too traumatized to go back to your chamber of horrors," Anne continued. "Otherwise, Greg can stay outside with you, and I will just go in with my former Interpol colleagues."

Julia did not want to be left out, especially since she knew she could be useful. "Thanks. But no, I will come with you."

"That sounds good," Körmendi agreed. "I will stay and continue on with the local guys, and make sure we get all the evidence here. If we ever catch these creeps, they will spend the rest of their miserable lives in jail. And I, personally, will make sure it is intolerable as hell for them."

☙❧☙

The doors were not locked, so they had no trouble getting into the side building. Székely and Labrecque led the way, with Anne holding Julia's hand and telling them where to go, Greg bringing up the rear. Upstairs, they headed straight for the room at the end of the long corridor where the two women had been held captive and abused. As they approached, Anne's arm went around her friend. "Now, Julia, you really don't have to go in there."

"No, it's okay."

Anne flicked the light on. She knew from her earlier experience where the switch was. The room was exactly as they had left it: soiled and rumpled sheets on the bed, Julia's open handcuffs dangling from the iron bedpost, night table drawer where Anne had found the handcuff keys still open, Anne's blood-soaked underwear halfway under the bed, Hetzel's dried blood all over the floor, wall and furniture, and the disgusting, mingled stale smells of sex, gunpowder and blood in the air.

Labrecque and Székely went around taking finger-prints, snapping pictures and writing notes, while Anne led the others back out into the corridor. "That's enough. There's no need to linger in there. The memories are just too raw."

Anne and Julia walked ahead slowly, with Greg following behind, and they came to the two other doors midway down the hall, one on either side, facing each other. Anne hesitated, then brought them to a halt, saying, "We'll have to look in these rooms too. But let's wait here for Nicholas and George." She felt Julia shudder just a little as she glanced from the right door to the left, and then turned her head away, resting it on Anne's shoulder, with tears streaming down her cheeks.

Spooked a little, the more of them there were to enter through these two doors, the safer somehow Anne knew she would feel.

⌘

Labrecque opened the door on the right. It led to a bedroom: presumably, this was where Hetzel retreated to when he was not molesting the women he brought to the compound. Beside a still made up king-size bed and two chairs, there was a desk in the room with a laptop and a printer on it, a closet to one side of the bed and a door leading to a bathroom on the other.

"Ah! This must have been Hetzel's laptop," Julia said, going straight over to the desk and pointing to an iMac Pro.

"Hmm! Yes, in their big rush to get away, and with Hetzel out of the picture, the thugs must have forgotten about his computer. They clearly didn't come and check in here before leaving. This could be our lucky day!" Labrecque came over to look at the laptop.

"It may be still on," Julia observed, putting her ear close to the machine. "Should we see if we can get in? I am sure there is lots of incriminating evidence on it."

"Don't touch it!" Székely caught Julia's hand just in time. "Let me dust it for fingerprints first."

"But it is a good idea, Julia," Anne, coming over, agreed with the Russian girl. "Let's at least look before those crooks wipe it clean remotely. If they haven't done so already, realizing they had forgotten it."

So while Labrecque and Székely searched the closet, fingerprinted all over and took pictures and notes, Julia, who was the most adept with computers, sat down at the desk, opened up the iMac and got to work. At first she was discouraged, because the laptop needed a password to get in. So she tried a few obvious passwords, starting with Hetzel's names, and when they didn't work, she thought of trying the aliases. First Kallay, then Kalinsky, then Adam Kallay. Different combinations, with caps and without. Spaces and no spaces. No luck. Then, on a whim, she thought of trying her own name: after all the creep seemed to have been obsessed with her. And indeed, when she typed Julia Saparova as the password—freaky as it was—the laptop came alive and she was in!

Within minutes, she had figured out Hetzel's filing system and how to access what was there. With Anne and Greg looking over her shoulders, she quickly surfed from file to file.

"George and Nicholas, you should come take a look. The evidence here is very incriminating," Anne said, beckoning to her colleagues. "These gangsters run a network that extends from Russia and the other countries of the former Soviet Union—where most of the girls are sourced—to many big cities in Europe, where the ring operates through legal strip bars to showcase the women and sell them into slavery or to local pimps. Or just serve time as strippers, maybe prostitutes."

"Yeah, it seems to be a money machine for the guys who run it," Greg said. "With the obvious fringe benefits whenever they desired."

"Unbelievable! Can we print out the list of cities and the names of the bars?" Labrecque asked. "That would make our work at Interpol easier."

"Sure. I'll give it a try." Julia agreed, glad to be of use. She turned on the printer beside the laptop.

"They use an abandoned military base near here to fly the girls in and out of Hungary. And, by the way, Schengen," Anne commented, after reading one of the emails. "It would seem without any obstruction from the authorities."

"I will need to look into how this has been possible here. I need to check with Hungarian Air Traffic Control. And the military," Székely said, seemingly chafed at his countrymen. "No doubt, somebody was paid off."

"Wow! Here I think I have found a list of the names of their major clients," Julia said, excited at her discovery. "These must be all the rich perverts who would come to buy the girls. Hetzel did keep good records."

"Excellent, Julia! Print that out too, please," Labrecque ordered. "We'll pick all of them up, wherever they are, those sexual deviants."

"While Julia and I continue to look through things here and print files, why don't you guys try the door across the hallway? See where that one leads to," Anne suggested, remembering that Julia had shuddered and turned away from that door. Maybe she had some bad memories associated with what was in the room—best not to take her in there, she concluded. But they did need to check it for evidence.

"Good idea, otherwise we'll be here all day." Greg

agreed, conscious of the time. "Those criminals are getting farther and farther away with the girls. We need to get going to hunt them down."

Chapter 20

The door across the hall was locked.

"There must be a key for it. Maybe back in the other room," Székely said.

Labrecque nodded. "Good thinking, George. I'll go look for it."

The French agent was back in no time at all, holding a set of keys. And it did not take them long to find the right one. The door opened with the second key they tried. Pitch dark greeted them.

As the two men from Interpol groped around in the dark on either side of the door for a light switch, Greg was startled by what he thought was a groan coming from the far corner. "Shh! What was that?" he asked.

Before anyone could answer, Labrecque turned on the lights, and Greg was stunned by what greeted his eyes. Over in one corner, a cage, with what appeared to be a human form, lying motionless. On the walls, chains and handcuffs and all sorts of unspeakable implements of torture and pain. A table in the center of the room, speckled with bloodstains. He felt nauseous, as he cast a further glance in the direction of the cage. And there, as he moved closer, he saw that the shape inside was a girl, stark naked, just starting to stir.

At least she is alive, Greg thought, as he saw Labrecque rush over to the structure in the corner.

After trying a few keys from the ring, the Frenchman pulled the cage's entrance open, went in, and knelt beside the young woman. "She is breathing and alive," he said, feeling her pulse, and looking over her body. "I think she's all right—no obvious signs of physical abuse. Just seems to be massively drugged. And, of course, all the trauma she's been through."

"I'll call for an ambulance," George said, already dialing. "We should get her to the hospital ASAP and have her checked out."

"Who are you? Can you tell us your name?" Labrecque whispered in the girl's ear. She moaned again, and muttered something incomprehensible. And when no coherent answer came, he turned to Greg: "Anne. Maybe we should get Anne, don't you think? She might know who this girl is. In any case, I am sure she would probably be better at dealing with this kind of situation."

Within moments, Greg was back with his wife, who looked around and said, "God, this compound is hell on earth." Anne rushed over to the cage, and Labrecque relinquished his place by the girl, who was still lying there on her side.

Anne stroked the teenager's hair. "Nadia! Oh no, what have they done to you?"

"It's all right, I think," Labrecque said. "Just the drugs and the trauma. Do you know her? Who is she?"

"Nadia…Glinkov, I think is her name. One of several girls from Ozersk these gangsters flew here to sell or use for their vile purposes. She was transported from Vienna in the same truck I was. I heard them bring her straight up here right behind me, and was wondering what had happened to her. I guess Hetzel had her put in here while he was dealing with me." Anne shuddered as she said this, before continuing. "For his pleasure later, I am sure. I remember, the pervert was quite taken with her already back at the Rasputin."

Greg had trouble fathoming the depravity of this supposed friend of his former best friend, Adam. "God, what a monster!" Just then, they heard the sirens.

"Let's get some clothing, or at least a blanket, if we can, to cover Nadia," Anne said.

Greg looked around, but could see nothing in the room. "I'll go next door. I'm sure I'll find something there."

When he entered, Julia was still hard at work printing files from the computer. "I'm getting some good material on these criminals here. I have figured out how to access Hetzel's email and there is lots of incriminating stuff there. What are you finding over there?" she asked, her mind completely absorbed by what was on the screen.

"There is a Russian girl. A teenager."

"Is she okay? God, I don't believe it. There is no end to these horrors." She finally looked at Greg, and he could see that she was about to dissolve in tears.

"Yes. Just drugged. And traumatized. Székely called an ambulance for her. But everything seems okay."

"Phew! I feared the worst."

"How are you getting on?"

"I just want to look at the attachments to some recent emails. There might be something in them."

"Good. I think we'll be ready to go as soon as the ambulance arrives for the girl."

"I'll bring the print-outs and the laptop. I'll just be another sec." Julia was engrossed in the file she was opening.

ഢ

Greg heard the medics downstairs as he crossed the corridor. He yelled down, "We're up here!" before entering the chamber of horrors with the blanket he had taken from Hetzel's bed, and announced, "The ambulance is here. I'll just leave the door open so they can hear where we are."

"Great, how is Julia getting on?" Labrecque asked.

"Just about finished, she says."

"Good. I think we're done here too. As soon as the medics take this girl, we'll join up with Körmendi and the local police." Székely was considering the next step already. "Then we've got to figure out where these criminals would have gone with all the other girls."

"Yeah, did Julia find anything that might help us?" Labrecque asked.

"She didn't say. But maybe Körmendi will have come up with something."

"We need to interrogate Hetzel," Anne said, arranging the blanket on Nadia's body. "He'll no doubt be able to give us a clue—"

Just then, the medics burst into the room. Székely explained the situation, and told them that they would come by the hospital a little later, and that hopefully, by then the patient would be able to answer some questions. Although he agreed with Anne, that Hetzel would likely be a better source for where the next chapter of this sorry saga would unfold.

ഢ

"Where's Julia?" Anne asked, as they were getting set to leave the room with the cage.

"Hmm. She must still be over in the bedroom," Greg

answered. "She was just looking at some last email attachments."

"Let's go get her," Anne said, already opening the
door across the hallway.

Julia was at the desk, eyes glued to the screen.
"Come here you guys! You have got to see this! It's a
Russian girl's website. Nadia Glinkov. I found the refer-
ence in an email from Hetzel. I guess it was to Polyakov."

"She's the one the ambulance just took away," Anne
said, as they all gathered around, while Julia opened up a
file. The screen came to life, and a smiling picture of the
pretty teenager they had just seen off to the hospital came
on. This was followed by a shot of Nadia waving to her
parents as she crossed the tarmac toward a waiting plane
somewhere, and—and the clip just deteriorated from
there. Next were some shots of Nadia doing a striptease
with a black girl to which Julia said, "That's Ginger!" as
she recognized the dancer from her days at the Revuebar
Rasputin.

"That was at the Revuebar, just a few minutes before
I went on stage, and we were then taken upstairs to be
sold and brought to this compound," Anne agreed with
her friend. "I was there in the audience. I didn't know
they were filming it. Disgusting."

Then, as the music was replaced with a smooth voice
speaking over the increasingly decadent pictures, and
they came to where they showed Nadia, with her shackled to the bed, Julia, in total shock, uttered the words,
"Oh my God, no!" and sank her face into her hands.
"They made a video of that too, those perverts."

"They made this for Nadia's father, clearly," Anne
interpreted the situation, as she, too, fought hard to keep
calm.

"Yes, it must have been made to coerce him to do

something," Greg said, agreeing with his wife.

And then it became obvious: the voice over wanted Mikhail Glinkov, Nadia's father, to let a chauffeur driven car with Julia, and presumably some highly enriched uranium, through the East Gate of Mayak, in return for not harming, and perhaps releasing, Nadia. Four days hence, next Tuesday, by when presumably, these gangsters had planned to send Julia back to Mayak. Fully under their control, with whatever psychological and physical torture and abuse they would deploy to get her to cooperate.

"So, Julia, it seems that they expected to be able to force you to help them somehow," Anne gave voice to the obvious. "But the video was made before we got you away."

"They might still be planning to carry this heist out," Greg warned. "They may just end up using a Julia look alike. An impostor. They seem to be big on that."

"Julia, can you look at the email address info@epctrade.com?" Anne said, thinking it must be well after noon already in Ozersk. Which was the deadline the voice gave Gospodin Glinkov to respond by.

"I think I saw a message forwarded from that site to Hetzel's email. Just a simple 'Yes,'" Julia answered as she searched again for the email from Glinkov. "Yes, here it is. And his answer is a 'Yes.'"

"So, Nadia's poor father will have been subjected to this grotesque video of his daughter," Labrecque observed. "And it appears that he has agreed to cooperate with them. To try and get his daughter back, not knowing that we have rescued her."

"Have we got anyone in Ozersk or Chelyabinsk?" Anne turned to her former Interpol colleagues, a sense of urgency in her voice. "We need to get to Nadia's father. ASAP. Even though—thank God—Nadia is safe, and Julia is with us, and no longer in their hands. But I think

Greg is right. These gangsters will still want to go through with a heist, now that they have Glinkov playing along."

"I will check with Demeter," Labrecque answered, as he got out his cell phone to make the call.

Anne touched Julia's shoulder, seeing that she was suffering. The mention of her name, and the video—which had replayed the terrible memories of her ordeal—had brought her close to breakdown. She had been through so much the last few days.

"It's okay, Julia." Anne pulled her friend to her feet. "We're going to get you out of this hellish place. Come on." She started leading her toward the door, as Greg, Labrecque and Székely picked up the printouts, closed down the laptop, and followed the two women out the door.

Chapter 21

While Greg waited outside with Julia, the others went to track Körmendi down in the main building. He and his team of local police were still busy photographing the evidence they had managed to uncover there, and putting up police tape all over to prevent any tampering.

"We found a girl. Russian. Locked up in a cage. Like an animal," Székely informed his Hungarian police colleague. "Awful. We sent her off to the County Hospital in Vasvàr."

"Bad shape?"

"She was very traumatized," Anne answered. "And drugged. It seems they wanted to use her to blackmail her father, who is a security guard at a Russian nuclear facility. Probably to help them steal some uranium or plutonium. We're going to go to the hospital to interrogate this Hetzel anyway, so we will see how she is, and maybe ask her a few questions as well."

"Good."

"By the way, Péter, did you find anything that might tell us where these criminals would have gone?" Anne asked the Hungarian police officer. "With the other girls?"

"No. But maybe your man Hetzel can tell us. I will come with you to the hospital. I want to make sure that pervert is properly locked up. And answers all our questions. Even if we have to beat the information out of him, the bastard."

⁙

The six of them went back to the Zala County Hospital in two cars, Labrecque driving Anne, Julia and Greg.

"Any feedback from Demeter?" Anne asked her former colleague from the back seat. "Do we have any Interpol agents near Chelyabinsk?"

"Yes. John said we have no one there. The main office is in Moscow, the closest regional branch in Ekaterinburg."

"We absolutely need to get to Nadia's father. Someone, and in person. Before four p.m. on Tuesday," Anne reminded them. "It is a must, otherwise we will have another major heist of nuclear material on our hands."

"I am not sure how safe it would be to call or email the guys in Moscow. They would have to coordinate everything. We know from experience that the FSB intercepts all our communications. We could try to get them and security at Mayak on our side, but it would be problematic to do it from here."

"Yes, I know," Anne said, not too happy.

"And Polyakov's brother is the Deputy Director at the FSB," Greg reminded them. "He would certainly make sure that the information that we were trying to stop this operation gets to his twin. And they would somehow manage to prevent us from connecting with

Glinkov. This nuclear deal could be too important for these gangsters to miss out on."

"You're right," Labrecque agreed.

"Plus, a bit of under the counter nuclear proliferation to cause problems for the West would no doubt be welcomed by many elements of this rogue ex-FSB run government," Greg added. "Vlad the Impaler included, notwithstanding what he says to our politicians."

"I know. You are right. One of us simply must go to Mayak,"Anne pointed out. "There is no other way."

"The problem though, is getting a visa. It can take days, as you know," Labrecque said. "And we would have to go latest tomorrow to be of any use. I guess from Budapest. Or Vienna might be better."

"Also, even if you do get a visa, the last I checked, you need a permit to go anywhere near Mayak," Greg added. "Not easy."

A few moments of silence, while they pondered how to proceed. Then, from the back seat, Julia said in a grave voice, "I will go. I don't need a visa. I have a Russian passport, plus my job takes me regularly to Mayak. As an IAEA official I have all the necessary papers to go there."

"Julia, are you sure?" Anne asked, surprised and worried about her friend. "You have been through so much."

"I'll be okay. It is my job, after all. And their video did claim that I would be the one taking the nuclear material out illegally from Mayak. Those criminals. I have to make sure I protect my good name."

"I am not happy to have you go, Julia," Greg said, frowning. "We just got you back, for Chrissake. In Mayak, you would be exactly where they want you in the next few days, as we learned. And if they get a hold of you—which will not be difficult for them—we know very well they have the ways to coerce you to do what they want."

"But if I don't go—if we don't get to Nadia's father—they could just use someone to pretend she is me—an impostor—and get the nuclear material out that way. They seem to be good at using other people's identities."

"Well, Nicholas, you really need to find a way to get your colleagues from Moscow to the Mayak area to help Julia if she does go." Greg knew there was no other solution but for Julia to go.

"Sure. I will see what we can do."

"In any case then, Julia, we've got to get you back to Vienna," Greg said. "There will be more flights from there than from Budapest, I am sure, and you can change your clothes and pick up your passport and papers. As soon as we're at the hospital, I will see if I can get reservations for you. For tomorrow."

"I will get my two colleagues to drive you to Vienna," Labrecque said. "And make sure you get on that plane."

A few minutes of silence ensued again, while they all took note of what was happening. Then Anne remarked, "These human traffickers could be anywhere by now with the other girls."

"How many did they have with them?" Greg asked. "Do you know?"

"There were maybe fifteen in the truck that brought me to the compound. Perhaps more, I don't know. Nadia may be able to give us a better fix."

"There might have been others already there, too," Julia observed.

"And how many were they, the traffickers? Do we have any idea?" Labrecque asked.

Anne and Julia looked at each other. "Hmm. At least

fifteen, I would say. Maybe twenty in the whole facility," Anne answered, racking her brains. "More, for all I know."

"I have no notion, really. I was not allowed out of that side building, and only really saw Hetzel—" Julia shuddered at the recollection. "—and a couple of the guards."

"Well, we have our hands full now with tracking them down. Let's hope we will be able to pry out of Hetzel where they have gone," Greg said.

"Yeah, Székely and Körmendi will make sure of that, I'm sure." Labrecque knew from experience that his colleagues would show no mercy with this despicable abuser of women.

Chapter 22

Nadia woke to a hubbub of people arguing outside the door to the hospital room where she had been resting. She was warm and cozy in the bed and felt her energy returning with what already seemed like several hours of rest after her unspeakable ordeal. She had to work hard though to prevent her mind from going there, so she was glad when her door suddenly burst open and the motherly nurse who had been so kind to her earlier entered. But then anxiety took over when she saw that the caregiver looked very upset, and outright fear when the woman was followed immediately by two large men dressed in what Nadia thought were probably Hungarian police uniforms.

"These officers say they have to take you with them," the nurse said to the Russian girl in her passable English. "Even though you just arrived and need some rest and care. They have showed us a warrant to arrest you—"

"What?" Nadia was incredulous.

"For—for prostitution, they claim. Of course, we do not believe it and we have argued with them that you have been abused and you needed to stay here, but they insist to take you with them. I am sorry, but there is not much we can do. They have already forced my boss to sign the release papers."

The policeman who seemed to be in charge gruffly told Nadia in Russian to get dressed, and when she answered that she did not have any clothes, he said, "Okay, you come with us as you are then," which she took to mean that she was to accompany them in her hospital wear.

She gave the nurse a desperate look. "I don't have anything to put on—" whereupon the woman left and, while Nadia went to the bathroom, managed to rustle up some jeans and a T-shirt that more or less fit.

Nadia was ushered outside by the two men and led to the second of two Hungarian police vehicles, which both had their engines running and the blue lights on top flashing. As she passed the car in front, she was horrified to see that the monster who had abused her, Kalinsky, was in the back seat. He was seemingly in some pain, but chatting away with yet another large police officer sitting beside him.

Had they arrested him too? Of course, he deserved to be locked up—but then why were the two men laughing?

The police cars took off, speeding through the town with sirens bleating and blue lights flashing, and finally pulled into a small parking area somewhere in the outskirts on the other side. The front car carrying Kalinsky stopped right beside a big black SUV with two men lounging and smoking around it. Nadia saw the boss get out slowly and, grimacing, limp over to the sports utility vehicle with the help of a cane—he must have gotten a wound or some injury since he abused her, she thought. He then shook hands with these thugs, and beckoned back toward the car she was in. One of the men started making his way over toward the second police car, while the other pulled out a thick envelope from his jacket pocket, which when Kalinsky nodded, he took back and carried over to the boss's earlier police companion who was still waiting in the first car. Nadia saw him hand this officer the envelope, as she obeyed the instructions of the other thug to get out of the police car and climb in the back seat of the SUV. With all these men around her who were obviously in cahoots, there was no way she could even think of disobeying, let alone escaping, so she reluctantly did as she was told.

Then to Nadia's horror, Kalinsky climbed in the back beside her, the man who had handled the pay off in the front passenger seat, while the other crook jumped behind the wheel. The vehicle careened out of the lot and started heading south, Nadia thought, at well over the speed limit. She inched as close to the door as she could, away from Kalinsky, as he plunked his jacket on the seat between them and leered at her, saying, "Well, it's really nice to have you back with us, my dear. You have become such an integral part of the team. We would hate to lose you." She cringed as he placed his hand on her thigh.

What did the creep mean? Nadia wondered, shuddering with fear.

ᘓᗢᘒ

As the SUV sped along the highway, Nadia looked out the window: farms whizzed by and eventually, she saw a sign saying they were on route E74 heading toward some places with difficult names like Zalaegerszeg and Nagykanizsa.

The towns meant nothing to her, but from the position of the sun, she could tell that they were definitely heading south.

The silence was broken by Kalinsky's colleague in the front seat. "Boss, we have the passports. Yours and the girl's. We found them where you said they would be."

"Excellent, Ivan," was Kalinsky's reply.

So that meant that they had been planning to kidnap her. Get her back from her rescuers. Her rescuers—yes, that nice Anne who had befriended her. She remembered seeing her in all that hullabaloo back at the compound. And the blonde, the beautiful blonde she had been forced to—to perform that sex act with. Had she been there too? Lots of men. It was all such a muddle.

But the passports—that meant they were probably going to cross a border. Slovenia? Croatia? Serbia? Those were the countries just to the south of Hungary, Nadia remembered from her geography class. Maybe, just maybe, she hoped, then that the border guards would ask what a young Russian girl from Ozersk was doing with wherever all these men were from. And where were they all going? Where were they taking her?

"Fortunately, I know the local police chief, who led the raid on the compound," Ivan continued. "So it wasn't hard to sneak back in and get what you asked us to find, Boss."

After a few moments of silence, as the driver tried to get around a big truck, Kalinsky asked, "By the way, Ivan, did you see my laptop in my room? It was on the desk."

"Hmm."

"If yes, then somehow we have to get that back too. Maybe you need to call your police chief buddy. Unless the others took it when they evacuated."

"I don't recall seeing a laptop anywhere in the room. Definitely not, Boss."

"Shit! Let's hope the others took it."

"Well—"

"Damn, Ivan, can you call ahead and ask?"

"I will phone Pyotr."

"Thanks. Do it right now, for God's sake." Kalinsky seemed rather nervous as his friend took out his mobile and pressed a few buttons.

As Kalinsky got increasingly agitated, Nadia surmised from the conversation that the man called Pyotr did not have the laptop, and did not know whether any of the others might have taken it when they left the compound. He promised though, to check with the other vehicles in the convoy taking the girls south and call back. Ivan hung up, but kept his cell phone in his hand.

Within minutes, the phone rang. Pyotr again. The two guards talked, and Ivan swore this time as he closed it. "Fuck. They don't know where the laptop is, Boss."

"That's really bad, Ivan. If those assholes from Interpol have got their hands on it—"

Nadia pricked her ears at the mention of Interpol. Maybe, maybe, there was a chance that they might get this monster!

Chapter 23

They pulled up right beside the two Hungarian officers in the hospital's parking lot.

"Let's get this fucking asshole behind bars," Körmendi said, more to himself than the others, after greeting them.

"We want to find out everything he knows first though," Anne said, following him through the glass doors. "At least, about where the other girls and his gangster buddies from the compound are."

"Yeah, I'd love to rough him up a bit to get at all that is in his pea-brain, the jerk. Besides just plain smut, that is." Körmendi was clearly on a warpath as he strutted up to the front desk, Székely following, to ask for the patient Kallay.

The others went over to sit in the waiting area. Greg immediately started to look for a flight for Julia on his phone while Labrecque went off to search for his two Vienna-based Interpol colleagues. When Julia came back from the ladies' room, Greg looked up and said, "I can get you on a plane tonight at five past midnight. It is now just before four p.m., so that should be sufficient for

Nicholas's guys to take you back home, pick up your things and get you back to the airport. Gets into Chelyabinsk at eleven-fifty-five a.m. tomorrow, so, Julia, that should give you enough time to talk to Nadia's father and to line up some extra security to help carry out the operation."

"Good. I think I remember his email address—mglinkov@polymail.ru. I will ask him to meet me after work tomorrow. If I am right, he will have the early shift the whole week, not just Tuesday."

"Look! What's going on over there?" Anne interrupted Julia and her husband, her attention suddenly drawn by an explosion of anger and frustration from the Hungarian officers as they conversed with the two duty nurses: Körmendi banged the desk, and both policemen gesticulated with their voices raised. The conversation dragged on, and it was obvious they were not happy. Finally, a grim Székely came over to them, as his exasperated colleague got on his cell phone.

"Un-fucking-believable!" he said. "Excuse the language, ladies, but that's the only way to describe what has happened. A real fucking mess."

"What do you mean?" This was not going to be good, Anne was sure.

"Hetzel's not here. Do you believe it? Gone. Vanished into thin air!"

"So, he's down at the station, no doubt, then?" Labrecque asked.

"I bloody well hope so. But it doesn't look good, from what those incompetent nurses told us."

"What do you mean?"

"Well, four men, dressed in police uniforms, came just a little more than half an hour ago, saying they were here from the regional office in Szombathely to relieve the two officers Péter had left to guard the jerk. They persisted until they were able to make off with the prisoner, but we don't have a clue where they went. Péter is now calling all over to try to find out who the fuck these men really were, and where they might have taken the asshole."

"Relax, George. Surely our friend will be in Szombathely just as I said. In custody there." This from Labrecque, who had returned with his two Viennese colleagues in tow.

"Bloody well hope so."

"And Nadia?" Anne asked.

"Well, that's what makes us suspect the worst. They took the little Russian girl too, saying she was under arrest for prostitution. For sexual solicitation and lewd behavior, of all things! The leader of the pack waved a warrant under the noses of the doctors and nurses. They, of course, wanted to keep her here. But in the end, they had no choice."

"What, Nadia? For prostitution? You've got to be joking!" Greg exploded.

"Yes, prostitution!"

"The nerve of those bastards. How—how the hell would they even think that she had anything to do willingly with the world's oldest trade?" Labrecque asked. Then, after reflecting a moment, he continued. "They must have known that she was forced into sexual slavery, the sickos. They just painted it as prostitution so they could take her away."

"And how did they even know Nadia was here, I wonder?" Anne gave voice to the disturbing thought that came into her mind.

"Good question," Labrecque complimented her. "It must have come from someone in the hospital. Maybe the medics who brought her here."

"But how would they connect her to Hetzel? And the sex bit?"

"Hmm. I rather think they must have found out from Hetzel himself, or perhaps from whoever locked her up in that room," Greg disagreed. "Hetzel must have surmised that if we found her in that cage, all traumatized and abused, we would bring her here, I am sure."

"Christ! So he must have gotten someone to check to be sure and then arrange for the arrest warrant. One of our corrupt Hungarian police buddies, no doubt." Székely was livid.

"In any case, Julia, you still need to go to Ozersk." Anne turned to her friend, focusing on what she considered the most urgent. "They have Nadia again unless we can get her back by then, but you have got to convince her father not to let these guys leave the Mayak facility with any nuclear material. Under any circumstances. And you need to line up security to capture them if they attempt to do so."

"Yes, you are right," Labrecque agreed with her. "I have already talked to my two colleagues and they are standing by to drive you whenever you're ready."

"Then I best get going."

Just then, Körmendi came over, phone still in hand. "This is not good. Not good at all. I first called my two trusted men from Vasvàr—the ones I left to guard Hetzel—and they said they did not recognize any of the four policemen. Those guys claimed they were there from Szombathely, and were following the orders of the 'boss' for the entire region, although they never gave his name. I then reached Colonel Bartha on his mobile—I report to him, as it happens—and of course, as I guessed, he knows nothing of all this. He never gave any such orders. He was incensed, and will try to find out who is behind it all. But in the meantime, my friends, the golden goose has been stolen right from under our eyes. We are fucked, to put it mildly."

"These sex traffickers are very well organized is all I can say." Labrecque was at a loss. "Better than we are, it seems."

"And the icing on the cake, is that they took that poor Russian girl you guys found locked in some cage, claiming they had a warrant to arrest her for prostitution!" Körmendi continued. "Absolutely ridiculous."

"Of course! We now know that she was one of the keys to their plans," Greg observed, and then turned to Julia. "The other being you, Julia. But, it would seem that you are more easily replaceable in their vile venture."

"Well, if it was them, as it is more than likely, then they are speeding away somewhere this very moment," Székely said. "The only problem is we don't know where. And we have no way to track them."

"I fear for Nadia," Julia said. "I hope they don't do anything nasty to her."

"Yes, poor Nadia," Anne agreed, but her mind was suddenly racing elsewhere. "Greg, do you have the receiver? You know, for that tracker?"

Greg did not see the relevance. "Why? The transmitter is in—on you still, no?"

"Well, that's just it!" Anne said with a little self-satisfied smile. "It was so…so uncomfortable, and it did not serve a purpose any more where it was, so I took it out when we were upstairs in Hetzel's room earlier. I stuck it in the pocket of that jacket the guard had loaned him to come over here. It was hanging right there in the bathroom. So, unless the crooks discarded it, or left it there, we should be able to track where they are going."

Julia was elated. "Wouldn't that be great?"

"Or at least wherever Hetzel's jacket happens to be," Anne added, deflating her own enthusiasm, suddenly thinking that most probably, they would have just left it behind in their great haste.

"I knew Interpol was just not the same without you," Labrecque observed. "I am going to go upstairs to see if that jacket is still there. Or whether they took it with them. I'll also ask a few nurses whether they have seen it."

"I'll run out and get the receiver." Greg, too, was excited. "And turn it on. Let's hope they have the jacket. And that the battery still works on the sucker!"

"What's this?" Székely was stunned, just off his iPhone. "You had a tracker on you, Anne, is that what I am hearing, that you managed to stick into Hetzel's gear? That's terrific!"

"Let's hope it's still there and it works," Anne responded, all in all quite pleased with herself.

☙❧

A few minutes ticked by, and Greg rushed back through the glass doors. "It's still bleeping!" he said with glee, "And it shows them heading south."

"Is that where the airstrip is?" Labrecque asked. "The one they have been using?"

"No. No, that's actually west of here. And a little north, I think," Körmendi answered, consulting an app on his mobile to make sure.

"We still have no idea where they are going," Székely observed. "But at least we now know the direction they are heading in. So we will just have to follow them."

"And the sooner the better. We don't want them to get too far ahead," Labrecque added.

"They already have a good head start." Anne remarked, checking the time on her phone. "A good forty minutes. And the others several hours ahead of them."

"Yeah, and it's already almost four-thirty," Greg added. "So why don't we just have some of your colleagues, pick them up, Péter? And get Nadia back and arrest Hetzel."

"Yeah, easier if those corrupt or fake cops have handed them over to the gang," Körmendi said. "But not so easy if my colleagues are following orders from one of our top commanders. Hmm. One who has been bought by these criminals. They would claim they have jurisdiction. And, of course, the warrant, if it is real."

"I thought of that too, Greg," Anne retorted. "The other problem is that we absolutely need them to lead us to the others.

"Who must be way ahead of them, as you said. We don't know where," Greg added. "And you're right. That is the only chance we have of rescuing all the girls and catching these criminals. But I do fear for Nadia."

"Okay. Greg and Anne, you come with me, if you would like. I have the bigger car," Székely said. "Péter can take Nicholas and follow us, since we will have the tracker. And Julia, goodbye and good luck."

"Thanks," Julia said, and gave kisses all around. "You too, good luck, you guys. Just let me know where you end up so I can join you when I am done in Mayak." And she went out through the glass doors to get in the black BMW waiting outside.

"Hold on a second." Körmendi looked up from his phone. "Let's just think a moment. I think there is something rather fishy going on here. With these strange policemen springing Hetzel and kidnapping that Russian girl from the hospital, I mean. The more I think about it, the more I am convinced that your creepy friend must have had access to someone very high up in the police force here, to be able to get such quick action."

"Hmm. That is certainly what it seems like," Labrecque agreed. "It would also help explain how they got to little Nadia. Unless, of course, they weren't cops, but just crooks dressed up as policemen."

"I thought of that, too, Nicholas, but from just the way those guys apparently acted, and, knowing Hungarian policemen, I think they were real cops. And when I think about it, it must have been someone above Bartha who gave the order, and just used my boss's name to make it all sound legitimate. So the rotten egg could be one or several of four or five officers right at the top of the police hierarchy."

"Well, well," Székely joined in. "That would be a bombshell!"

"In which case, the corrupt guy or guys in the police force," Körmendi continued, "whoever they are, are clearly in the pay of those gangsters, and they may well have put out an alert for all of you. As a precaution, to make sure you cannot give their friends any more trouble. And to try and prevent you following them."

"Good thinking, Péter," Székely agreed. "That is certainly possible."

"Fortunately, Hetzel does not know me," Körmendi continued. "Plus, as a high ranking officer of the Hungarian National Police force, there is very little they can do to prevent me from going about my business. If I am right, and it is these rotten colleagues of mine we are talking about."

"You may be right, Péter," Székely acquiesced. "But as a Hungarian officer of Interpol, they should leave me alone too."

"Yes, but they could slow you down, you know. Hungarian policemen are good at obfuscating, you should know that by now."

"Hmm."

"In any case, what I suggest is that Greg and Anne come with me—that way, if it comes to that, I can use whatever means, including subterfuge, to keep them out of the hands of these rogue elements on our police force. Greg will keep the tracker, and you, George and Nicholas, can follow in your car."

"I see what you're getting at," Labrecque said. "Yes, it does make more sense."

"Okay, let's get going. We'll follow you." Székely was itching to get on the road.

Chapter 24

The two cars left Vasvàr on Györvàri ùt, which soon turned into highway E74 as they sped along, through forest and field, southward toward Zalaegerszeg and Nagykanizsa, following the direction indicated by the receiver communicating with the little tracker still in the zippered pocket of Hetzel's jacket. Körmendi drove fast. He was an excellent driver, and Greg was glad that the Hungarian police officer was at the wheel so he could doze off for a while. None of them had had much sleep during the last couple of days.

He woke with a start, refreshed, just as traffic slowed down when they were approaching Zalaegerszeg.

"Happy to switch off, Péter, if you'd like," he said, rubbing his eyes.

"Thanks, but it's better that I drive," Körmendi answered. "If we're stopped here in my country, it looks bad if the police officer is a passenger in his own car. If our friends continue into Croatia, as it looks, I am sure Nicholas will have you take the wheel at some point. I will turn back from the border and you will all go on in the one car."

Greg checked the receiver again. He had placed it on top of the dashboard. It was still working, indicating that the car carrying Hetzel's jacket was going south, and was now about half an hour ahead of them.

Anne, too, had been napping in the back seat. She stirred. "Boy, I really needed that. Thanks, Péter, for driving while we old fogies sleep."

It was when they were approaching the village of Hahót that they heard the siren, and saw the police car with the flashing blue light come up behind them. "Oh no. What a pity. We'll have to deal with the village idiots now," Körmendi remarked, as he pulled over, and rolled down his window.

A slovenly policeman in his late twenties sauntered over, just as Greg glanced sideways and saw Székely and Labrecque—who had been following at a distance of maybe half a kilometer—pass by, and turn right into the next street. Presumably, to wait and see what happened next.

As Körmendi recounted a few minutes later when he pulled back out onto the highway with a smug smile, the policeman had asked for his papers. Körmendi handed him his driver's license, then the car documents—registered under the police force in Szombathely—and last, his police ID. Seeing the car registration, the policeman asked, "Hmm. You with the police? You don't look like it." But it was when the ragtag junior saw whom he was dealing with—a police major from Szombathely—that the man saluted, clicked his heels, and offered to help in whatever way he could.

Körmendi thought for a moment then told the young officer that they were on a mission to track Russian human traffickers, and they could use a police escort, perhaps as far as the Croatian border. He asked him who his big boss was, and when he said the name of the commander of the outfit in Nagykanizsa, the next big town, Körmendi told him to get the man on his radio.

At this point, Körmendi got out of the car, saying to the two others with a twinkle in his eye, "Just give me a second. I think this is going to be good," and walked over to the police car with the flashing blue light. He came back a few minutes later. "Okay, this joker now has his orders to accompany us to somewhere near Nagykanizsa, where we will be met by two local police cars that will escort us all the way to the Croatian border if need be. We won't be bothered again."

Körmendi then took out his cell phone to call Székely and explained the situation to the two Interpol officers. When he signed off, he said, "Passports. Nicholas asked about your passports. You will need them to get into Croatia, which is not in Schengen."

"I have Anne's and mine," Greg said.

"Good. We shouldn't have any problems then."

✿✿✿

It was just after six when Körmendi pulled over just before the border crossing at Letenye, saying, "Time for you to switch cars. It would be better for me to get back to the office and start trying to figure out who the rogue elements at the top of our police force are. Before they do any more damage."

"Thanks, Péter, for everything," Greg said, taking the still beeping receiver off the dashboard. "You've been great."

They got out and walked back to Labrecque's BMW 225i as it pulled up behind them. After goodbyes, Greg and Anne climbed in the SUV and the French Interpol agent took off as the Hungarian policeman waved and turned around where he could cross the divide to go in the other direction.

Passport control at the Letenye crossing did not take long, and soon they were back on the highway following the signs for Zagreb. After a little over an hour, since they had not eaten a proper meal all day, they stopped for dinner at the Pauza Restaurant in Lucko, just past the capital, for a traditional meal of *Riblji paprikas*, a spicy fish stew.

They were confident that the Hetzel team would also have to take a break, since they too, had to eat and refuel the car at some point.

Indeed, when they resumed the journey with Greg at the wheel, they noted that they were not much further behind than they had been before the stop. The GPS took them toward Split, but then at Hrsina, they took the left fork onto the E65. As they approached Jasenice, the tracker told them that their prey had stopped moving.

"They must have stopped for the night," Anne commented. "They, too, have had a rough day."

"A rough two days and night," Greg added. "And I wonder how Hetzel is surviving the journey. With that serious wound you inflicted on his thigh."

"Yeah, I hope it is getting good and infected." This from Székely.

"I guess we too had better stop soon. We don't want to get much closer to them," Labrecque said.

"Good. I wouldn't mind taking a shower and stretching out for a bit." Anne relished the thought.

"Amen," came the chorus from the others.

They stopped at a nice little Bread & Breakfast just off the road, maybe fifteen minutes behind Hetzel and company. Greg took the receiver inside and kept it on all night, right by his bed. In case the gangsters tried to get away in the dark.

"Probably they won't leave too early," he commented. "My thought is that their destination must be Montenegro, or maybe somewhere further south into Greece, since if their goal had been say Dubrovnik, they would have kept on going. And I am sure the border crossing into Montenegro doesn't stay open all night anyway."

"Yes, you must be right, dear," Anne said, as she slipped out of her jeans and top, ready for that much-desired shower. They may open around six."

"Well, I doubt that they will be there first thing. Since it is another five hours or so from here."

"I think though, they will nevertheless try to leave fairly early. I fear for little Nadia, Greg. I am sure Hetzel will be wanting the stop to change the bandage and to doctor his wound. So he probably needs an inn for that, but I doubt that they would take Nadia into any establishment."

"So what do you think they would do with her?"

"My guess is that one of the guards will stay with her in the car. Maybe both. In some deserted place to park. That's what I am afraid of. Two brutes like that with a beautiful and vulnerable girl."

"I see what you mean. That was why I had thought we should pick them up right away. To get her out of their clutches."

"Yeah, but then we would have no chance of rescuing the others. And putting an end to this criminal gang," Anne said, stepping into the shower.

"So what now, do you think?" Greg asked when she reemerged and started to towel herself down. "My turn."

"Well, come first light, the guards will probably go get Hetzel from his comfortable bed, and they will continue the journey," Anne shouted above the noise of the shower.

"So we had better be ready to continue then too,"

Greg said, drying himself. "It's time to hit the sack."

"Yes, but first there is nothing like a little loving to help us get a good night's sleep," Anne said, as her husband turned the light off and climbed in beside her. "Isn't that so, my dear?"

Chapter 25

Julia was glad the flight from Moscow to Balandino Airport landed on time, and, as she had no baggage, just a few minutes after noon she was already on the M5 heading north toward Ozersk. The drive was uneventful. She had done it on many occasions, but always enjoyed the lush vegetation, each time observing to herself that this extravagant growth must have been at least in part the product of the contamination still lingering in the entire province, from those terrible accidents when Stalin was relentlessly focused on developing the Soviet bomb at any cost. And no doubt, so were the haggard and sickly faces of the local population she saw in the villages the closer she got to Mayak.

By three-thirty she was just passing Lenin Park in Ozersk, which is where she had told Glinkov to meet her. At six p.m. She had just enough time to grab some late lunch and take a bath in her mother's apartment, which was where she always stayed when she spent the night at Mayak. As she pulled up in the parking lot behind the building, she reflected that, in the morning, she would talk to Levinson, the American government representative at Mayak, and Georgy Sukhai, the Deputy Chief of Security, the one person in the security operation who had impressed her the most in the training sessions she had led. But now, her focus had to be on getting to Nadia's father.

She hoped the email message she had sent would be enough to get him to the meeting. It had been brief: "Gospodin Glinkov, I have news of your daughter, Nadia. I will be under the Kurchatov Statue in Lenin Park at six p.m. on Monday, May twenty-second. It is critical you be there. Respectfully, Julia Saparova." She trusted that he would be checking his emails regularly after responding to Hetzel's ugly video message.

ひめひ

Mikhail had butterflies in his stomach as the Mayak shuttle van pulled up at the Lenin Park stop. It was just a few minutes after six, which is exactly how he wanted to play it. He had planned it so that this Julia Saparova—whoever she was—would be there first, so he could observe her for a few minutes before engaging with her. He wanted to make absolutely sure that she matched her picture in the file: the beautiful IAEA representative, responsible for ensuring that nuclear material is not trafficked from Russia. In fact, he and Pavel had remarked on her beauty the times they had caught a glimpse of her as she had passed through the gates where they happened to be standing guard, and he knew from overheard comments in the locker rooms that many of his colleagues lusted after the gorgeous Ms. Saparova.

For Mikhail, as for many others at Mayak, it was hard to believe that such a stunning woman could be a nuclear physicist—she definitely did not match the Russian stereotype of a female scientist. And could it be really true that this very IAEA employee would be working with those gangsters who had kidnapped his darling daughter and were abusing her sexually? Those same perverse beasts who had told him to look the other way while this Julia Saparova smuggled some highly enriched uranium out of Mayak? The whole thing did not add up, but if true, it was monstrous, Glinkov thought. He had half a mind to kill this woman, but he knew he needed to listen to what she had to say. His daughter's life may well depend on it.

Mikhail circled around, and approached the blonde from behind the imposing statue of the father of the Soviet bomb. She was indeed exquisite, standing there in her full splendor—he could not take his eyes off those tanned long legs fully exposed in a mini-skirt—as she glanced down at her watch and then up again toward the main road. And, he observed to himself, rather vulnerable seeming, almost fragile. Could she really have sold out to the gangsters? Very hard to believe.

"Gospodja Saparova?" Mikhail moved toward her.

Julia was startled. Usually the "gospodja" was reserved for her mother. But she recovered quickly, knowing this was her contact. "Gospodin Glinkov? Thank you for coming. Shall we go over to the bench?" She said with a soft smile, pointing toward the one just along the path behind the statue, away from the road.

"Of course."

"Gospodin Glinkov," Julia started the statement she had rehearsed earlier on the flight and then refined in the bath at her mother's, as she sat down and turned to her companion. "We know you have had a horrible shock. Your daughter is in the hands of criminals—human traffickers, and this is terrible for any parent. These gangsters want to use her to get you to do something that would endanger the world but hugely benefit them. Let me tell you that until yesterday, I was a prisoner of these same beasts, and they did things that I do not want to talk about." Julia's voice wavered, and in that second Mikhail connected that in fact it was this woman whom he had seen with Nadia on that depraved video. *Oh my God! And she had been handcuffed!* Yes, clearly it had been she. He had seen her there.

But Julia recovered and continued, "I was rescued by officers of Interpol and other friends. My rescuers sent me here to persuade you not to do what these criminals ask. They are this very minute trying to get your daughter to safety. I work for the International Atomic Energy Agency and we need your help, Gospodin Glinkov, to prevent some nuclear material from getting into the hands of terrorists. Tomorrow, we need you to do a very thorough search of the car that will try to cross through the East Gate at four p.m., with a woman made up to look like me, and using a fake ID in my name. When you find the uranium or plutonium, I will come out of the guard booth with reinforcements and we will arrest these people. I promise your daughter will be safe by then, as Interpol is very close to getting her released right now." Julia knew she was committing to something that might not happen, but she needed to win the security guard over at any cost.

"How do you know all this if you are not working with those crooks?" Mikhail was still not convinced.

"We took Hetzel's—Kalinsky's laptop. And saw the horrific video they put up on your daughter's website. And your answer to their message," Julia answered, hesitating before she added, "also, as you may have gathered, I was the one in the video, handcuffed to the bed, when your daughter was forced to—to—"

Julia stopped, as their eyes met, both experiencing the pain and the distress of the memory, now that it was out in the open between them. Mikhail rallied first, and put it all together. Yes, definitely, he had seen this beautiful creature naked and fettered! On the bed, with Nadia. He jumped right in. "Very well, Gospodja Saparova. You are a brave woman, I can tell. I will follow your instructions. And pray God, your friends can free my Nadia."

"Thank you. Now we had better go our separate ways. We do not want to be seen together if we can avoid it. But I'll be there tomorrow afternoon, at the East Gate, with reinforcements just in case. Good luck, Gospodin Glinkov." And, as she started down the path, she added, in encouragement, "And maybe I will also have good news about your daughter."

"See you then," was Mikhail's glum reply.

ↄↄↄↄↄ

In the morning, Julia went into the office late. She wanted to make sure Charles Levinson was there already. She needed his support with the Deputy Chief of Security: she was a realist, and knew that a middle aged American professional carried much more clout than a young Russian woman—even a smart and beautiful one—in her still very sexist country.

Indeed, Levinson was at his desk, so she poked her head in.

"Julia!" She startled the tall, lanky American. Shirtsleeves rolled up, Levinson sprung to his feet and walked around the furniture. "Boy, we were really worried about you. What happened?"

"Charles, I don't want to go into it now. But we need to talk."

"Okay. Come sit down." And he pulled out the chair on the other side of the desk for her, before going to close the door. "Well, what is it?"

"There isn't much time, but Charles, I need you to come help me persuade Georgy Sukhai to put on extra security this afternoon at the East Gate. It seems that the same arms merchants who got to Kallay and Kolchakova are now at it again. Interpol has clear evidence that this afternoon at four p.m. they will be using someone dressed up like me, armed with a fake ID card in my name, to smuggle out some HEU. Their theory is that normally I would not be given a rigorous check since I am an IAEA employee, but just to make sure, they think they have convinced the guard on duty to let them through without a thorough going over."

"Wow! That is huge."

"I talked to the guard who is supposed to be on duty then—Mikhail Glinkov—yesterday, when I got here and he is willing to work with us. The problem is, I don't know whom else these crooks may have turned. In fact, come to think of it, we had better get security to do more thorough checks everywhere for the next few days at least."

"You know that is very unlikely. Given the poor quality of the guards here."

"Yes, but there is no harm in trying."

"Of course. You are right. In any case, Julia, I am glad to help. Shall we go see Georgy now?" Levinson said, picking up the phone. "I'll see if he is available."

જ⁄જ

Julia and Levinson made sure they were at the East Gate by three-thirty p.m., and listened as over the phone the Deputy Chief of Security finalized the arrangements to position extra guards about half a kilometer down the road, just beyond a curve. In case the smugglers tried to blast their way through the barrier in the event that things went awry with the attempted heist. The three then watched from the guard booth as Mikhail and Pavel, armed with radiation detectors, checked the cars one by one at the East Gate. Just before four p.m., there were ten or eleven vehicles backed up, which was not unusual, but according to the guard in the hut, just a little more traffic than at this time most days. Julia had her eye on the eighth car in line, a nondescript white Ford Focus, with a blonde woman in the back seat, a man sitting beside her and two men in the front. She vaguely wondered to herself what arms they might be carrying, and whether indeed they would use them if things did not go to plan.

She saw the flimsy barrier close behind the car in front after it passed the checkpoint, and the Ford Focus pulled up to the guards. Pavel, standing on the passenger side, asked for their IDs while Mikhail instructed the driver to open the trunk. He walked around to the back, but since the lid did not open, he returned to the driver side as his friend pored over the papers. Julia saw that Mikhail had a heated discussion with the driver, pointing over to the guard station, probably telling him that he would need to go there unless he opened the boot. It seemed this time though it worked, and the trunk flipped open. Mikhail ferreted around inside, taking his time. He went over to Pavel's side, asking to look at the IDs, and then leaned down to talk to those in the vehicle, again gesticulating toward the guard booth. Julia heard the car's engine come on, but instead of turning right toward where they were watching from, the Focus accelerated with a big Vroom and crashed into and through the barrier. To her horror, she heard gun shots add to the cacophony.

As Georgy pulled out his gun and rushed out of the booth, she saw Mikhail go down on his knees clutching his side, and Pavel fall backward. Julia did not hesitate a moment, but ran after Georgy, as a startled Levinson yelled, "Julia, no!"

But she couldn't care less for her own safety. She felt responsible, and she needed to get to Nadia's father as fast as she could.

As she reached Glinkov, Julia saw that Georgy was on his knees behind one of the pillars, shooting at the Ford Focus as it receded. It seemed to her that he had managed to knock out one of the car's back tires, and it careened off the road just before the turn beyond which the extra security forces were hiding. But she had no time to confirm all this. Mikhail was bleeding profusely in the leg. For want of something better, she tore off her cotton T-shirt and tied a tourniquet above the wound, at the same time yelling to Levinson who had just arrived by Pavel's side to call an ambulance.

"There is a false bottom in the trunk, I think," Mikhail whispered between teeth gritted in pain. "The detector indicated there was definitely radioactive matter in there. A very strong signal, for sure. And the woman had an ID card in your name."

"Good work, Gospodin Glinkov," Julia said, as she tried to make him comfortable. "And thank you. Now rest."

"Nadia?"

"No news yet, but she will be safe," Julia lied a little to comfort the man who was bleeding profusely. Hearing the sirens, she tightened the tourniquet. "Hold on, Gospodin Glinkov, the medics will be here very soon." She looked up to see Georgy running toward the car and shooting from the hip, as the security forces in hiding down the road started to close in on the Focus. And then, in a split second, the car went up in flames—Georgy must have hit the fuel tank—and it was all over for the perpetrators of the heist. She was confident though that the nuclear material would have been in a lead case of some sort—nobody in their right mind would have been transporting radioactive substances without this kind of protection.

The ambulances arrived, and the medics quickly placed Mikhail and Pavel on gurneys. Within moments, they were on their way to the hospital. Julia tried to collect herself, wrapping a light cotton blanket—the medics had given her one in exchange for the now bloody top that had served as Glinkov's tourniquet—around her shoulders to cover up a bit as Levinson sauntered over.

"Well, that was way more excitement than I thought we would have," the American said. "Good work on the intel."

"Thanks, but it's Georgy and the two guards we have to thank. They're the ones who stopped these thugs."

"Yes, I'm surprised they were successful."

They walked up the road to where Sukhai had now joined the other security forces by the burning car. "Well done, Georgy," Levinson congratulated the young Russian. "You guys were terrific."

"Yes, thanks," Julia added in appreciation. "Georgy, good shooting. You will recover the nuclear stuff when the fire burns itself out? Glinkov said there must have been a false bottom in the trunk. The detector picked up strong radioactivity, he said."

"I am glad you warned us about this attempt. Often the guards don't bother with the detectors, because just about everything sets them off. There is just so much radioactivity around here. But yes, I will put a guard unit around the car and retrieve the uranium or plutonium when things cool down somewhat."

"It must be in a lead case, I would think," Levinson said.

"We'll see. But I sure hope so."

"Will you make certain Gospodin Glinkov is all right?" Julia asked the Deputy Chief of Security. "I have to get back to Vienna. To report to the IAEA and Interpol."

Actually, she was going to join up with Anne and Greg. But first she would have to find out where they were.

Chapter 26

They did get an early start, fifteen minutes or so after their prey hit the road. With Labrecque at the wheel, they took the A1 most of the way, until they saw signs for Dubrovnik.

Admiring the sights, Greg turned to his wife. "We must come back here, one day, Anne. This is so beautiful!" And indeed it was.

From the famous medieval fortress city, they switched to the coastal road—Highway 8, and it was Greg's turn to drive. They did wonder why their quarry did not take the more direct route, nevertheless, with the tracker poised on the dashboard and continuing to beep, they followed the car carrying Hetzel's jacket and—they hoped—the evil man himself, Nadia and some members of a gang of Russian criminals. But they kept their distance. They wanted to be close, yet out of sight at all times. It would not do, if the human traffickers noticed that a suspicious car with an Austrian license plate was following them so deep inside Croatia.

The sun was close to its zenith, as a little past Gruda they turned onto the smaller but still paved Route 516 that took them through the villages of Plocice and Durinici. And it was already well past noon when they pulled up at the empty border post just before Njivice in Montenegro.

"It seems that Hetzel and co. might be heading for Porto Montenegro," Greg said, consulting Google maps after the friendly Montenegrin border guard had welcomed them to his country with a big smile and the comment, "Hope you have a wonderful time here!"

"Yes, you're probably right, Greg," Anne agreed. "There is a posh seaside resort there, where a lot of Russian oligarchs and wealthy criminals from other countries have bought properties, I remember. It was being built up when I was stationed in Vienna. These crooks would certainly fit in well there."

"So maybe our friends Hetzel and gang have a villa in Porto Montenegro," Labrecque reasoned. "Or two, for that matter. And, talking about oligarchs, Polyakov probably, too."

"That's where they probably intend to hole up with the girls," Greg continued. "And maybe rent them out to their buddies there. I certainly wouldn't put it past these sickos."

Indeed, as they wound their way through the small villages along the Montenegrin coast, they noticed that they were coming closer to their target. The locator had stopped moving.

"They must have arrived at their destination," Greg observed. "But it's not quite Porto Montenegro where they're at, according to the GPS. It is some small town on the coast. Let me see…it is called Lepetane." And then a moment later, he added, "Oh yes, it seems that there is a ferry there. Over to Kamenari. It cuts the distance around the bay by quite a lot."

"Well, let's make sure we don't get on the same boat as they do," Anne said.

"Good point. I'll just check the schedule," Greg said, opening up Google again. And a moment later: "It seems there is a boat every fifteen minutes."

"So, that should be good. They won't get too far ahead of us if we take the following one."

☙❦❧

The next time the tracker stopped, they saw that it was indeed at the luxurious Porto Montenegro Village. Within twenty minutes, Labrecque pulled up in front of the five star Regent Hotel, where Hetzel's borrowed jacket had supposedly landed, with—as Greg and Anne sincerely hoped—the man himself and his entire entourage.

"Okay, this is good," Nicholas said, turning the motor off and taking in the posh surroundings. "Maybe they'll have rooms for us. Let's go see."

They got out, and Labrecque handed the key to the valet, while eager-to-please hotel staff pulled their bags out of the trunk.

"One of us will have to keep an eye out for Hetzel and Nadia at all times," Székely said as they walked through the opulent lobby. "He will want to rejoin the others for sure if they are not here. I don't mind taking the first shift, over there, in that comfortable looking armchair. And I'll order myself a nice little drink and a sandwich."

"I'll keep you company, George. The creep doesn't know me either. But let's check in first," Labrecque said. "Anne and Greg, I am sorry to say, but you had better not show your faces down here in the lobby for now. We'll keep you in the picture if anything happens."

"That sounds just fine," Anne said, flipping through the hotel's brochure at the desk. "It seems that we'll be able to get a room with its own terrace and have a wonderful time relaxing up there. Hope you guys have fun down here, too."

"Nicholas and George, before we part, I was just thinking that we should check if there is a guest registered as Hetzel here," Greg said. "Or someone under one of his aliases. Kallay or Kalinsky. I am just worried about Nadia."

"We could do that," Labrecque answered. "But—"

"I don't know, Greg," Anne joined in, "I doubt that a place like this would give out the names of their guests. And even if we were able to pick Hetzel up here, would he tell us where they have taken the other girls?"

"Hmm. You're probably right, Anne. And it might just arouse suspicion. Who knows who these buggers have paid off here," Labrecque said. "We should stay low for now."

"What we should do Nicholas, is contact our local colleague at Interpol. He would have more leverage here," Székely said. "In fact, we could have him or her come with a warrant to get us into Hetzel/Kalinsky/Kallay's room if there is no movement by then."

"Good idea, George. We will need his help anyway," Labrecque retorted. "I'll do that right away, while you order drinks and a sandwich for us over there."

"That's a deal!"

✂✄

The room Greg and Anne got was indeed luxurious, with a terrace overlooking the Marina. They quickly stripped down to the bare essentials, and while Greg ordered room service lunch for two with a bottle of the local wine, Anne unpacked. They did not waste any time making themselves comfortable outside on the reclining chairs.

A smart waiter brought the delicious seafood platter and Greek salad, which they devoured out on the terrace accompanied by a bottle of the local Krstač white. After lunch, they just continued to lounge out there, soaking up the afternoon sun and, given the ordeals of the last several days, it did not take much for both of them to fall asleep.

ふぶふ

A few hours later, Greg woke with a start to the tune from his cell phone. It was right there under the recliner, so he picked it up immediately.

"Julia! Where are you? How did it go?"

Beside him, Anne sat bolt upright when she heard her Russian friend's name.

"I am on my way to Balandino Airport. Mission accomplished. I will tell you everything when I get there. But where are you?"

"We're in Porto Montenegro. At the Regent. When can you get here?"

"I will look into flights and call you back."

Less than fifteen minutes later, Greg's phone rang again. It was Julia, saying that she managed to get a connection the next morning to Tivat, where the nearest airport was. She would get in at eleven-ten a.m.

"Fabulous! Just take a cab here, and if we're not around, we'll leave a message. We're in Room Twenty-Four. See you then."

ふぶふ

"I wonder what is happening downstairs," Greg said,

checking the receiver. "But the locator says that Hetzel is still holed up in a room here."

"Yeah, and Labrecque and Székely are covering the doors. And they did say they would contact the local Interpol representative. We just have to be patient."

Greg was starting to have his doubts. "Unless he left his jacket in the room."

Twenty minutes later, his phone buzzed, just as he was dozing off again.

"Nicholas here. Hetzel and another man have just stepped out from the elevator. Get down here quickly. But be careful."

Greg and Anne were dressed within five minutes and were downstairs within seven. Labrecque greeted them at the elevators.

"The valet is just getting their car. George has gone to ask for ours."

Greg saw Hetzel's back outside the glass doors, standing on the curb with another man. It took a second for him to recognize who this was: Polyakov. Probably the arms merchant twin, and not the Deputy Director of the FSB, he thought. The valet pulled up with their vehicle, a Porsche Boxster, and handed Polyakov the key. The Russian assisted his injured friend and then got in on the driver's side. Fortunately, another valet drove up with Nicholas' car, just as the convertible pulled out from the drive.

Székely was already behind the wheel when Nicholas, Greg and Anne climbed into the SUV, and he accelerated after the Porsche.

Greg, who had picked up the receiver for the locator as they ran from the room, noted that the transmitter was not on Hetzel.

"We better not lose them. Hetzel left the jacket in the room."

"Don't worry. We won't let these gangsters get away," Székely said speeding after the Porsche but keeping at a safe distance.

Chapter 27

Dusk was gathering already when they saw the Porsche turn off the main road into a dirt driveway that opened through a broken down wire mesh fence, and pull up beside a van and an SUV outside a half finished apartment complex. Székely stayed well back, parking the car behind a bulldozer on the street, just so they could still see if anyone came out of the front door of the building and approached the vehicles.

"Nicholas, maybe you should tell Radomir Borozan where we are, don't you think?" Székely suggested to his colleague. "And find out where the hell he is. It would be good to get our man in Montenegro to show up here soon with some local reinforcements. And a warrant, if possible."

"Definitely. Good idea," the Frenchman responded, pulling out his phone.

⁓ So ⁓

Their wait was not long. Less than half an hour had ticked by, when Polyakov emerged from the derelict building, leading Nadia—the car bringing her and Hetzel all the way from Hungary must have dropped her off here first, Greg surmised—and five other girls, two armed thugs on either side, with a limping Hetzel bringing up the rear. As they made their way over to the van, he could see that the girls were all sexily dressed in just halter-tops and short shorts, the four guards making sure they clambered quickly in the back. After an exchange with one of the thugs, Polyakov helped Hetzel into the Porsche, climbed in again behind the wheel and pulled out of the parking lot with the van following right behind.

"George, maybe one of us should stay to keep an eye on what happens here," Labrecque said. "I have a hunch that all the other girls are being kept in this complex."

"You're probably right," the Hungarian answered. "I will stay."

"Borozan and the reinforcements should be here soon. I suspect they will bring enough muscle to raid the place. Meanwhile, the three of us will follow the Porsche and the van and see where they take these five women. Let's keep each other up to date, okay?"

"Sure thing. See you later." Székely was already out of the car, and was loitering behind the truck in front, as Labrecque started up the engine.

☙☙

Darkness started to settle in, as they followed the two vehicles through Porto Montenegro right to the Marina. The van and the convertible pulled up along Jetty 1, as close as they could get to where the most expensive yachts were moored. Greg, Anne and Labrecque saw Polyakov jump out of the Boxster, run back to the van where he gave instructions to the lead thug, and then clamber across the little walkway and onto what seemed to be the sleekest and most luxurious boat in the harbor. They observed from the BMW parked on the other side of the plaza at the foot of the jetty as one of the other guards helped Hetzel out of the convertible and over to the yacht. The three remaining thugs stood around the van keeping the six girls under close observation as they climbed out of the van.

They saw Nadia look around hesitantly and then obey the orders of the lead guard to follow Hetzel. Polyakov lit a cigarette as he watched the women cross the bridge to the approving stares of the men on the boat. Anne thought she recognized Sasha, but was not sure whether the other four were also Nadia's friends. Not all, she told herself. There was at least one more in this group than the original group of Russian teenagers. They sat there observing the goings on, until the girls were ushered inside through the glass doors at the stern of the yacht, and Polyakov cast one glance back toward the shore to see his convertible driven away by the lead thug and the other three guards climb back into the van and drive away.

Greg broke the silence as all three reflected on what to do next. "We've got to get on there somehow."

"Sure, but first I will call George," Labrecque said, pulling his mobile out from his pocket. "To see how he is getting on and whether the reinforcements have come. And more importantly, if they have arrived, how soon some of them can get here to help us."

Greg pursed his lips. "While you do that, I'll just take a walk to see how we might be able to sneak on the boat."

He got out and sauntered along the jetty on the side farthest from the yacht, then, when he was well past it, crossed over to the side the boat was on, and approached it again. It was a gorgeous, sleek-looking vessel, with the name *Quantum of Love* painted in discrete letters along the stern. Greg was impressed: was this one of those superfast Millennium 140 luxury yachts he had read about? The takeoff on the James Bond theme certainly argued for that. He continued along slowly, hands in his pockets, carefully studying the layout of the yacht. The windows, though, were all tinted so he could not see anything inside. He figured there might be a crew of maybe five needed to run it, and at the most, the same number of probably all male guests on board whom the girls were being taken to entertain.

Greg noted that one of the guards was hanging around near where the little walkway came across, and another one was busying himself for the moment in the front, away from the jetty. There was really only one way onto the boat: via the bridge to the stern over which the recent arrivals had all crossed, although the boat was near enough to shore that he thought an athletic person might be able to jump across. But it would be close, and if a guard were watching the rear, he would certainly see this. In any case, they would be greatly outnumbered. Better to wait till reinforcements arrived, he told himself. Although they shouldn't wait too long, because there was the safety of the girls to consider, and of course, at any moment Polyakov could decide to take his guests out to sea.

Greg climbed back in the front passenger seat. "Any news from George?"

"Well, our Montenegrin friend from Interpol has arrived, but they are still waiting for the local forces to show up to help them raid the derelict building," Labrecque answered. "With a warrant."

"So they probably won't get to us for at least a couple of hours," Anne observed.

Greg shook his head. "We can't wait that long. I am

afraid for the girls. Or for that matter, that they might cast off at any moment."

"Well, what do you propose, Greg?" his wife asked. "After your little stroll to reconnoiter. One thing's for sure: we are grossly outnumbered."

"Our only chance is surprise. There seems to be just the one person out there on the deck now."

"The darkness could help," Labrecque added. "Plus, there are very few people around on shore."

"Okay, here is what I think might work," Anne said, taking charge, since neither of the men had gotten to the point. "I will approach the boat looking…umm…provocative, with a cigarette in my hand, and ask the guard who is loitering there for a light. In Russian."

"Very good," Labrecque interjected. "He will be surprised. Pleasantly, of course, that a beautiful woman would address him in his own language. You need to try and get him to come across the walkway to you, then one or both of us can take him out."

"Better still, I will take him out, since I will be right next to him, and he won't be expecting it."

"How?" a surprised Greg asked.

"A quick knee to his crotch and a chop to the neck. Don't worry. I've done it before."

Greg thought he knew his wife, but this had certainly never come up. He was dubious.

"Then you two rush over and push him in the water," Anne continued.

"Okay, let's go, before they move," Labrecque said. "We all need to be armed."

"We have our Glocks in the back. I'll get them when we get out," Greg said.

Anne quickly looked in the mirror, fluffed up her hair, pulled off the cotton sweater she had on so that she exposed maximum skin in her little camisole top. "Anybody got a cigarette? Or something else to smoke?" she asked coyly.

"You're in luck," Labrecque answered, reaching into the glove compartment. "Marie Christine made me quit, but I carry this pack of Gitanes around for the occasional secret drag. They are foul, though, so watch out."

"Don't worry, I won't inhale."

Anne took one out and squeezed the pack into her pocket, then getting out of the car after Greg, she surreptitiously stuck the Glock he handed her from her suitcase in the back of her jeans, and pulled out her top to hang over it. Greg said, "Good luck! I love you," as he gave his wife a kiss. Closing the trunk of the BMW, he continued to gaze admiringly after Anne.

Labrecque clambered out too, and the two watched as she made her way toward the yacht down the mooring side of the jetty. The walk was provocative, sexy, meant to attract male gawkers, and the one or two who were around did indeed notice her. When she approached the bridge, Greg started down the route he had taken earlier, while Labrecque followed directly in Anne's footsteps.

"Hello, sailor," Anne shouted in Russian at the crewmember pretending to make himself busy on the boat, but obviously charged with keeping guard. "Got a light for a girl wanting a drag?" She grabbed the rope railing and provocatively put one foot up on the walkway, resting her elbow on her knee.

As Labrecque had predicted, the thug was taken aback that this beautiful, sexy woman spoke to him in his native language, here in a foreign country. He sauntered over to the top of the walkway, and pulled out a lighter. "Da. But what you have for me, honey?"

"I see you busy, now," Anne said, pointing the unlit cigarette at him. "But later, maybe. If you think you are up to it. But first, give a me a light."

The crewman came toward Anne. She stood upright, put the cigarette between her lips, and took a step back, inviting him to come off the ramp. As she had promised, she met his approach with a knee in the crotch and a vicious chop to the neck. The man collapsed to the ground, and, in that instant, Labrecque and Greg appeared out of nowhere. Greg was shocked as he saw the Frenchman pull out his pistol with a silencer already attached to it, place the gun barrel on the Russian sailor's forehead, and finish the unconscious man off in cold blood.

"One less thug to worry about later. It's called self-defense."

The two then rolled the body into the water, Greg hoping desperately that no one had heard or seen anything.

Chapter 28

Nadia could not believe the opulence of this yacht, as the girls were herded through the glass doors and into the Main Salon, which opened from the aft deck through a narrow passage with two faux Baroque statues of naked women on either side. Marble and gold everywhere, expensive looking paintings, custom-made furniture—it seemed to have everything that a girl who grew up in post-Communist Russia could not even dream of.

The balding Russian friend of Kalinsky entered behind them, shouting impatiently, "Okay, all of you, follow me upstairs. Come," as he grabbed Nadia by the elbow to show the way. Shoved ahead, Nadia slowly climbed the circular stairs, paranoid of what would come next, as the other girls followed behind the man, with the limping boss of the Revuebar gritting his teeth as he brought up the rear.

The stairs opened into the equally luxurious Sky-lounge, where three bored-looking men were sitting at a long curved bar sipping drinks. The biggest, sporting a shock of disheveled red hair and lots of freckles, greeted them with a distinct southern drawl. "Well, well, it's about time, Maestro. We have been waiting for some hours now for your arrival."

"Sorry. But there was some problem," the square Russian answered testily. "I see, though, that Oleg has looked after you well in the meantime." He nodded to the crewman behind the bar. And then he addressed the girls, who were standing around hesitantly, clinging to each other for solace, and pointed at a sofa and chairs in one of the corners: "You, you lot, go sit over there." But even as he did so, he grabbed Nadia's wrist, twisting it and pulling her toward him. "This one's father didn't do what he was supposed to. What should we do with her now, the little bitch?" He spat the words in her face. "Should we give him a second chance to perform, do you think?"

What had her father not done, Nadia wondered? And what did this man with the freckles want?

"Good idea, Sergei." This from Kalinsky, who was trying to make himself comfortable in one of the armchairs. "What do you think Brother Peter?" The wounded man smirked at the redhead.

"Sure, but first tell me, Sergei, does this mean you didn't get the HEU?"

Sergei was the square Russian friend of Kalinsky, Nadia surmised.

"Yes, unfortunately for you it does. But the deal is still on. We'll get the stuff soon," Sergei answered, shoving Nadia into the armchair opposite Kalinsky. "You, you little slut, you sit right here."

"You guys are jerking me around." The man called Brother Peter—was he really a priest, Nadia wondered—stood up from the barstool to face Sergei. "You get me to come out of hiding, promise me fifty pounds of the stuff, and then don't deliver."

"Listen, Brother Peter." Sergei moved right up

against the big man, but had to look up to meet his eyes. "I am sure you know that getting fifty pounds of uranium is not as easy as buying chewing gum in a convenience store in New York. Don't worry. We'll get it for you as promised. It may just take a little more time. Days, maybe weeks, months even. In the meantime, you can't complain."

"I am not."

"We look after you real well, don't we?" the square Russian continued. "We put you up, you eat our delicious food, drink our expensive alcohol, fuck our beautiful girls. You see, we even got you and our buddies here a fresh lot."

"Yeah, thanks, Sergei."

"You guys can have anyone of those chicks over there." Sergei nodded at the girls cowering in the corner, and then at the two other men who had been sitting silently at the end of the bar, listening to the conversation between Sergei and Brother Peter. "Just not this one. We need Nadia to help teach her father a lesson. That way, you might get your nuclear stuff sooner, Brother Peter. Plus, my friend Andreas has the hots for her, I know," Sergei continued, chuckling to himself as he looked at Kalinsky. "Can't you see, he is literally panting with lust, trying to look up her skirt there? Ahh, the poor guy has been injured so needs all the loving he can get."

Oh no! What did these men have in store for me? Nadia was trembling with fear, on the verge of tears.

"Great!" the redhead said. "Thanks, Sergei."

"Sure thing. So pick one for yourself. You too, Andro and István, go ahead. You guys can use the rooms downstairs. And, Andreas, I know you can't wait. So you can go and have some fun with Nadia first, while I finish up some business here with Brother Peter. Use the Master. Let's save the VIP Guest Room for the holy man—he'll be down in a few minutes. And with your wound, don't do anything to strain yourself, old man. I'll take over with little Nadia when I am done up here. Oleg here—" Sergei nodded in the direction of the barman. "—will take her down there for you and show our friends from the military and the police their rooms, just as soon as he pours us a drink. Champagne, Oleg, for my friend Brother Peter here and me. The Taittinger 2004 will do."

"Thanks again, Sergei," Brother Peter said, as he strolled over to where the other five girls were sitting motionless on the sofa listening with fear to what would come next for them. He looked them over one by one, and to Nadia's horror, pointed at her friend Sasha, "How about this little gem?" And pulling her up by the chin, he asked, "Yes, this is the one I want. What is your name honey?"

"Good. She's all yours."

"Her name is Sasha," Kalinsky answered, since Sasha had dissolved in tears.

"What about you, Andro? István?" The two men at the end of bar—who, Nadia surmised, were the military and police officials Sergei had referred to—got up from their stools to make their choice of partner, the first saying, "This one," as he pointed to a cowering girl on the sofa, and the second, "For me, this gorgeous babe."

"Okay, Oleg," Sergei said, addressing the bartender who had just poured two glasses of champagne. "Take those three down, along with this one for Andreas. Put Nadia in the master. That one there—Sasha—you keep an eye on in the VIP guest room until Brother Peter arrives. Our other two guests can have any of the rooms down there with their chosen sluts." Then as an afterthought, he added, "The two leftovers, there—take them to the master as well, I know Andreas likes to play with more than one at a time. And don't worry, Oleg, you and the rest of the crew can have them all later."

"No, please, no," Nadia screamed, as the barman walked around the end of the bar.

"Come on, honey," the barman said and tried to pull her up from the sofa.

"If she resists, just give her a good whack," Sergei told the thug. "That goes for anyone of them. We won't stand for insubordination. You know that."

Nadia got up as Oleg yelled at the girls to follow him, and the entire retinue descended the circular staircase on the port side of the bar, leaving Sergei and Brother Peter in the Skylounge to conduct their business.

Chapter 29

Within seconds after eliminating the guard at the back of the boat, Greg, Anne, and Labrecque were on either side of the sliding glass doors that led from the aft deck sitting area to the Main Salon. The French Interpol agent touched the sensors to open the doors and they entered to an empty but luxurious living room. Perhaps, Greg thought, Polyakov had let most of the crew have time off, so he and Hetzel and their guests could get up to their nefarious activities undisturbed.

That would be good. There would be fewer thugs to contend with. Plus, he recalled, Labrecque had already eliminated one of them. They moved forward cautiously, pistols with silencers in hand, through the equally extravagant and empty dining room, toward the winding circular staircase, which led, on the one hand, up to the upper deck, from where they heard the low drone of voices, and, on the other, down to the lower deck where presumably some of the bedrooms were.

Labrecque signaled downstairs, and Greg told himself that this made sense. From the conversation, they knew there were probably only two people up top, so best to clear the lower decks first, assuming the others were down there. Crew, or guests, or girls. They tiptoed down the steps, the Frenchman leading, Anne right behind him, and Greg bringing up the rear. Arriving in the lower deck foyer—also laid out elaborately with granite and marble—they saw that three of the four doors were closed. From behind two, they could hear muffled noises.

Labrecque signaled that he would take one of these doors and Anne should take the other, while Greg was to stay in the foyer to cover the other two rooms and the staircase as well as the corridor that led up front to what presumably were the crew's quarters. The two former Interpol colleagues burst through the doors at the same time: as he followed his wife to look through the open door and provide backup if necessary, Greg saw that Anne was greeted by the depraved sight of a very surprised man in the buff standing at the bottom of the bed holding a naked girl face down in front of him. It was not hard to guess what he was about to do.

"Don't move or I will shoot, you creep," Anne shouted, keeping the gun on the man, as she approached the scene of depravity. "Get over there, asshole, against the wall, hands way above your head." She helped the traumatized girl to her feet, saying, "Come on honey, you put this on," as she threw her the dressing gown the man must have been wearing earlier and had shed to force the girl onto the bed to service him in this disgusting manner.

In the room directly across, Greg saw through the open door that Labrecque was untying a naked girl who still had tape on her mouth to gag her screams, with his gun pointed at a man brandishing a whip.

"Okay, buddy, put that down like my friend said," Greg ordered, as he entered and went over to help the Frenchman free the girl.

The two then quickly used the rope to tie the pervert up and wound the tape still on the night table beside the bed tightly around his mouth to gag him.

"Thanks. Here, I am sure Anne can use some of this in the other room," Nicholas said, giving Greg the rest of the roll of tape. "You go see if she needs a hand. I'll just check the other two rooms quickly."

Greg went in the room where he had left his wife, and seeing the scene, yelled at the man who had his hands above his head to sit down in the chair by the desk. When he hesitated, Greg shoved the man into the seat, and wrapped the tape round and round his blubbery flesh so tightly that the prisoner winced and had trouble breathing. When he was finished, he threw the bedcover on top of him to cover his ugly nakedness.

Just then, through the open door, Greg heard a Russian accented voice in the third room, the door of which Labrecque had kicked open, yell, "Drop your gun, or I will kill her."

Greg saw Anne wave at him as she slowly moved in the direction of the door, Glock at the ready. The next thing he heard was Anne shouting, "You drop your gun you asshole and let the girl go. And don't be stupid, there are three of us here from Interpol, and, if you pull that trigger, you are a dead man yourself. Best surrender."

The guard saw that he was outnumbered and outgunned, and it was not worth throwing his life away for his boss. He dropped the gun and released Sasha, who ran to Anne, as Labrecque went over and tied the man to a post.

"Okay, I think these perverts will not give us any more trouble tonight. Let's put the three girls in the other room. We'll tell them to lock the door until we come back, and then let's go check the rest of the boat.

❧

As quietly as they could, they climbed the staircase back up to the main floor and were pleased to hear that the voices coming from the upper deck were still chattering away. Nicholas motioned toward the staircase and, pointing to himself, indicated that he would go first. But all of a sudden, they heard some moaning, mingling with sobbing and laughing from behind the doors that led into the room adjacent to the dining room. So the French Interpol agent changed his mind and pointed at the double doors, indicating to Anne and Greg who were closer to go ahead and break in there, while he covered the two staircases leading up top where they knew at least two of the gangsters were deep in conversation.

Greg kicked the door in as Anne rushed through, Glock moving side to side to find a target. He followed with his gun to the fore and was shocked by the unfolding debauchery in front of his eyes. A man—probably one of the guards, Greg surmised—was brandishing a whip at a girl just in her panties, tied to one of the marble pillars on one side of the king-size bed, with another girl already secured to the pillar on the other side. An undressed Hetzel was sitting on the bottom edge of the bed, with his hands in Nadia's hair, leaning back and pushing her head down between his legs where she was kneeling.

Anne, beside herself with rage, yelled at him, "Get up, you fucking pervert," as Greg covered the thug with the whip.

"You, drop that whip and put your hands up," Greg shouted. He heard Nadia cough, saw her pull away and try to cover herself with her hands, as a whimpering Hetzel slowly got to his feet.

He muttered something that sounded like, "Please, please."

But neither Greg nor Anne had any patience left with these debauched abusers of women.

"Okay, you sicko, spread your legs and swing 'em. Those gonads of yours. And this time, rest assured, I am not going to miss," Greg heard Anne say, and a moment later to his horror, he heard the muffled shot of her pistol, followed a second later by the unearthly scream of the man who had once called himself Adam's friend. Coming out of his shock, Greg, with his pistol still pointing at the guard, rushed over to free the two girls tied to the pillars and then used the rope to secure the thug, as Anne, with an eye on Hetzel, who was lying unconscious on the floor in a rapidly growing pool of blood, kept her gun on the guard.

"Greg, you go after Nicholas. I think I heard him rush up the stairs, when this asshole screamed, to get the guys up there. I will try to stop Hetzel's bleeding and call an ambulance," she said to Greg, who seemed all too shocked by what she had done.

It took him no more than a second to survey the situation and see that, indeed, Anne seemed to have things under control, so he ran out of the room and up the stairs to the lounge on the top deck from where earlier they had heard the voices. There was no one there now, but the door to the cockpit was wide open, so he bolted through it. Then, seeing that it too was empty, he continued through the side door to the exterior walkway that led to the front. Here, Greg surmised that Labrecque and whomever he was chasing would have gone down the outside steps in the front to the lower deck and then out the back, so he followed this route. When he got to the aft deck, a dejected Labrecque was just coming across the walkway back onto the yacht.

"They got away?" Greg asked.

"Yeah, I am quite sure. I got no sight of them. I am

just trying to call George to see whether the reinforce-
ments ever showed up and where the hell they are." Labrecque had taken his phone out and scrolled down, continuing somewhat angrily. "We would have gotten those buggers—whoever they were, talking upstairs—if the local reinforcements had shown up in time."

"Probably Polyakov, since he wasn't here, and we saw him arrive," Anne said.

"Maybe they can still intercept them," Greg said.

"I have no idea of which way to send them."

"Have some of them check at the hotel."

"Good idea. But that's a long shot. Hello, George? Where the hell are you?" A long exchange on the phone between the two Interpol agents followed. "That's great. Good work. We have, I think, six girls here, all pretty traumatized and abused. We need to get them some care. And Hetzel was shot—he's still alive, but for not much longer. Two others taken into custody, plus a couple of guards. One dead. Another two got away, including, we think, Polyakov. Can you or some of the locals with you check at the hotel? And send an 'all points' out for a red Porsche Boxster convertible. What was the license plate, Greg?"

"SX69."

"Yeah, SX69. Easy enough to remember. Will you come soon with the local guys?" Labrecque hung up and looked at Greg. "Well, at least they managed to mop up the situation at that derelict building. Finally. Rescued twenty-three girls, arrested nineteen thugs and five cli-ents. These flesh merchants seem to have another com-plex there, George said, in the basement, like the one in Hungary, except nowhere near as nice."

"Terrific! I think now though we had better go back inside and see how Anne is making out with Hetzel. She really did shoot him in the crotch this time, and he was bleeding like hell. And, yeah, we need to check on how those girls are. Maybe they can tell us something."

"Okay, let's go see what fish we caught here. Besides that pervert Hetzel, may he rot in hell.

⸎

By the time they got back to the master stateroom, Anne had managed to bandage the wounded Hetzel, but he was white as a sheet and had fainted from the loss of blood. "The ambulance is on its way, but they better get here fast, because this creep won't live much longer without drastic medical care," Anne said.

Greg, seeing the three Russian teenagers—who had managed to find enough assorted clothing to get dressed—still cowering in the corner, said, "Let's get all of you together where you can be comfortable. Maybe we can find some food in the kitchen, and then, if you don't mind, we need to ask you some questions. Come. Let's get out of this chamber of horrors." Greg started to lead them through to the kitchen, but added, "Anne, why don't you come, too. We can leave these guys here for now, I am sure." He looked first at Hetzel, and then at the tied up guard to confirm what he had just said. "They can't cause any trouble anymore. And you can look for some food while I get the three ladies from downstairs."

"I will come with you and see to those two perverts in the bedrooms," Labrecque said.

⸎

The ambulance arrived just as Greg came back up to the main deck with the other three girls. Anne directed the medics into the master stateroom, and pulled out some cheese and fruit from the refrigerator, while Greg managed to find some bread and nuts in one of the cupboards. They proceeded to put all this out in front of the girls, hoping they would eat something.

Then Anne addressed them. "Girls, you are safe now, rest assured. My name is Anne and this is my husband Greg Martens. We are here on behalf of Interpol. The other man who went downstairs is an Interpol agent, too. I know Nadia, and I think you are Sasha." Anne nodded in the direction of the girl sitting beside her friend and holding hands with her. "Can the rest of you tell me your names?"

"Magda," the girl next to Sasha volunteered hesitantly.

"Elena."

"Martina."

"Svetlana."

They went around the table.

"We will get you home to your parents in just a few days. As soon as we can. We promise," Anne continued, "but now we need your help in bringing these sick men who did such terrible things to account for their crimes. They are all connected to a gang of human traffickers and arms merchants. Most urgently, we need to find out what we can about the two men who stayed behind upstairs in the lounge. Unfortunately, they got away."

"Yes, can you tell us anything about them?" Greg asked. "Names that others may have used to refer to them, where they were from, what business they were trying to do, accents, anything you might have overheard when they were near you." This was met with silence. Were they afraid, too traumatized to speak up? he asked himself. "Listen, they cannot hurt you, if we put them away. And we will. We will not rest until those crooks are behind bars. Or dead." He would not let it go.

"Andreas." Nadia spoke first, with a voice that trembled. "The man—in the room—the man you shot." She looked straight at Anne. "He was called Andreas by the others. My father introduced him to me as Gospodin Kalinsky. Still in Ozersk. He was the one—"

Here was further confirmation that Kalinsky and Hetzel were one and the same person.

"Thank you, Nadia." Anne was encouraging. "That is exactly what we need."

"Sergei," little dark-haired Magda whispered. "The Russian man who stayed upstairs was called Sergei by the others. He seemed to be the big boss."

"Yes. She is right," Elena, the brunette, agreed.

"That's it. Thank you."

"Polyakov, for sure," Greg said.

"The other man who was up there—" said the tall girl who had identified herself as Svetlana, "—the others called him Brother Peter."

"Yes, Brother Peter," Sasha, close to tears, echoed her. "He was the one who picked me. The big man with red hair. And freckles."

"Brother Peter! Billy Crawford. Here? Well, that explains it! Why he surfaced in Vienna. Probably on his way here," Greg said more to himself than anyone else. And then he added, "Of course! They must have been discussing the next heist."

"The boss—that Sergei—he mentioned something that they needed to teach Nadia's father a lesson," Sasha volunteered hesitantly. "So that Brother Peter could get some nuclear material more quickly. Some HEU, I think, they said."

"Thank you. This is good. It really helps us, girls," Anne said.

Labrecque's head poked up from downstairs, just as they heard the sirens of the approaching police cars.

"Here they are. It's about time," Anne commented.

"Yeah. Great. But wait till you hear this." The French agent could hardly contain himself. "You won't believe it. One of those jerks downstairs is a general in the Montenegrin army, the other, the Deputy Commissioner of Police for all of Hungary. Guests of Polyakov. These guys don't fool around."

"God, no wonder Hetzel had no trouble getting away from the hospital in Vasvár," Greg observed.

"Yeah, a great way to blackmail the important figures you need to control," Labrecque continued.

Within seconds, they heard the police vehicles pull up and the sound of men rushing across the walkway. Székely was first through the glass doors, followed by another man in civilian clothes and several special operations types sporting automatic weapons. The crackling of radios and the stomping of boots punctuated their entrance.

"George, good to see you," Labrecque said, greeting his colleague. "That goes for the rest of you, too. Did you manage to check on the two men who escaped?"

"I sent Radomir with some of the local police to the hotel. So far he hasn't called, though."

"Hetzel's been taken by ambulance to the hospital," the French Interpol agent continued. "Let's send some guys there to guard him, although Anne did such a great job on him that the only place he will be escaping to is the otherworld. No doubt, he has a place reserved in Hell. And we have two others downstairs, all tied up. Pigs too, both of them, abusers of these young ladies."

"I'll have these guys take them in right away," Székely said.

"They're big fish," Labrecque continued. "One is a general in the army here, and the other, the Deputy Commissioner of your country's police, George."

"Goddam! So that's how far up the rottenness

went—no wonder Hetzel was able to escape from that hospital. I will have this Deputy Commissioner extradited, and tried in Hungary."

"Nicholas and George, the other thing is," Anne interjected, glancing at her watch and seeing that it was almost eleven p.m., "that these girls need rest and care. They have had some horrific experiences and it is getting late. I think they are at the breaking point."

"Yes, we need to find a place where they can stay in peace. Then, tomorrow you can question them more in depth," Greg added.

"Well, Radomir found a convent to take the girls from that compound. But as it was, the abbess or whoever, told him that it was going to be very crowded."

"How about the hotel? They would no doubt have space, and Interpol may even be able to get them to put these girls up for free," Anne suggested. "That way they would be near us, and they would not have to go far. We could even walk over now with them. George, maybe give Radomir a call, and if he's still over there, he can arrange it before we get there."

"Good idea," Székely agreed, pulling out his cell and scrolling down. "Nicholas and I can then wrap things up here, while you take them over. And then we can agree to meet up in the morning."

"Excellent."

Chapter 30

Radomir met them at the front desk. After introductions, he looked Anne in the eye. "We have two rooms for the girls, either side of yours."

"That's terrific. Thanks, Radomir."

"We will have a couple of guards in the corridor for the night, and two in front of what we think is Polyakov's suite upstairs. It seems that a company—Adriatica—owns one of the penthouse suites where a square balding Russian is a regular visitor, the manager told me. We will also have some men down here in the lobby at all times, and several outside."

"Speaking of Polyakov. Any news on him? And Brother Peter—that is, Billy Crawford, the other man who got away?" Greg asked, adding as an afterthought, "And by the way, Radomir, did your guys find the Porsche?"

"Well, the Boxster is sitting in the parking lot, out back. We have done a search inside the car and found nothing. Registration says it is also in the name of that company, Adriatica. By the way, my guys have done some digging—Adriatica is a shell, registered in the Sey-chelles."

"Figures."

"More interestingly, I just got one of the guys to check at the airport, you know, over in Tivat," the Montenegrin Interpol agent said, "and apparently, an unmarked private jet—a Gulfstream G-550 to be exact—that came in a couple of days ago and had been sitting there all this time—well, it took off a little more than an hour ago. And I am told it is registered to Adriaticair, if that tells you anything."

"Hmm. I remember Polyakov used to own an Air Miliberia, through his shady trading company, MILEXCO," Anne interjected. "This may be its latest reincarnation, since I think you guys—that is, Interpol tried to get both Air Miliberia and MILEXCO closed down. Could you please do some further checking, Radomir?"

"Already on it, Anne. But listen to this. The pilot of this Gulfstream filed a flight plan to Grozny. You know, in Chechnya."

"That's where our man earned his spurs. He was there with the Russian armed forces in both Chechen wars," Greg said.

"A lot of our visitors here are from Russia, or that part of the world. So we can't necessarily jump to conclusions. But the time of departure would also fit."

"Yeah, you're right," Greg agreed.

"And perhaps they took the other guy's car to the airport."

"Billy's? Hmm. Maybe. Can we check car rental agencies? To see if there were any vehicles returned right around then."

"Good idea, Anne."

"Excellent work, Radomir," Anne said. "I must compliment you. And thank you. I guess the fox has fled the coop for now. But we'll get him, and that Billy or Brother Peter or whatever he calls himself now. No doubt, the two have been plotting another nuclear heist."

"I thought this was a human trafficking investigation."

"That is only one part of it, Radomir. I am sure Nicholas will fill you in." Anne saw that the girls were standing over by the desk, waiting with the two guards.

She went over to join them, as the Montenegrin agent said, "Sure."

"Well, anyway, I am going to say good night now." Greg saw Anne signaling to him, that they were ready to go up. "We'll see you tomorrow. I guess first thing, you will want to interrogate the two men captured on the yacht along with the others you took at the compound."

"Maybe Hetzel, too, if he is well enough."

"He was in pretty bad shape. I'm not so sure he would be up to it."

"Well, if not tomorrow, as soon as he can answer questions."

"Come to think of it, you'll probably need to do a thorough forensic examination back at the boat," Greg added. "And then we will want to look through Polyakov's and Hetzel's rooms here. Anne and I should probably be part of all that because we know both those crooks."

"Sure thing."

"Good night, Radomir. And thanks. It's been a good day."

❧❦❧

They said good night to the girls in the corridor, upstairs.

"You really have nothing to fear now," Anne tried to reassure Nadia, Sasha, and Magda in front of Room

Twenty-Two. "We are right here beside you."

"Yes, and there will be two policemen outside in the corridor guarding our doors," Greg added. "And many more in and around the hotel. So nothing can happen."

"Thank you," Nadia said. "You have been so kind."

"Sleep well." Anne hugged each girl in turn. "And if you need anything, we are in Room Twenty-Four, next door. Oh, yes, order something to eat if you'd like. You must be very hungry. And all of you, feel free to call home and tell them that you are safe."

☙❧☙

Inside, Anne said, "Phew, what a day! I'm going to jump straight into the shower." She started shedding her clothes on the way to the bathroom.

"Good idea, Anne. I will follow you." A shower, not just to wash the body, but also cleanse the soul after the horrors they had encountered during the day.

Hair still wet, and in a fluffy hotel dressing gown, Anne made her way out onto the terrace, under the stars and overlooking the port. Greg, coming out of the bathroom, saw her there looking out at the water, but went over to the mini-bar to pour two glasses of wine for them and to grab some snacks before he went out join his wife. They had missed dinner, and after the tough day, he realized he wanted a drink to settle his nerves. Handing the glass to Anne, he put his arm around her waist as she leaned against the railing.

"Isn't it beautiful out here?" Greg asked. More than anything, he couldn't help but feel how lucky he was to have this competent, beautiful woman as his wife.

"It sure is," was Anne's response, as she took a sip of the wine.

"And it was a good day. Other than Polyakov and

Billy getting away. But we'll get 'em, that's for sure."

"Yes. I am certain. But it may take a while."

"Are you enjoying being back in the field, Anne? Hunting international criminals? It is exciting, I agree."

"I won't say no," Anne replied. "But what makes it particularly fun is that you are here with me, Greg. As my partner in crime. Or against it." She chuckled as she reached up to her husband's neck, gently pulled his face over to hers, and then gave him a kiss. As she did this, the dressing gown fell off her shoulder. Greg reached inside, down her arching naked back, and kissed back with fervor.

"Should we go in?" he asked, aroused, when he came up for air.

"Yes. It is late," Anne answered, taking his hand and leading him toward the bedroom, where, undoing his dressing gown, she pulled him down on top of her in the bed.

Greg could only mutter, "I love you," between kisses, first on the mouth, then her breasts, and then lower down.

Once they finished, it did not take them long to fall asleep after the struggles and stresses of the day.

Chapter 31

Greg and Anne were just getting dressed to go over to the yacht after a leisurely room service breakfast on their terrace, when Anne's cell rang.

"Anne, Nicholas here. You might want to get over here pronto. And bring a laptop if you have one there, and a USB cable—I am sure you can get one of those from the hotel, if you don't have one handy. It'll save me having to go back and get my stuff."

"Why, what's up?"

"We have found some secret video equipment. You know, Polyakov filming his guests."

"God, what a creep." She shuddered with memories of her own terrible experience with the Russian arms merchant. Then Hetzel taping Nadia and Julia. *And dammit, probably Nadia and me too!* Suddenly, the thought froze her.

It took her a moment to recover, before she answered, "Sure. I think between Greg and me we should be able to drum up both, so we'll be there in five."

On the way out, they knocked on the two doors on either side.

Nadia opened up for them at Room Twenty-Two, splendid in the hotel's fluffy dressing gown, hair still wet from showering.

"Good morning, Nadia. I hope you slept well."

"Yes. Thank you. Wonderful!"

"Nadia, we're just going to go over to the yacht for a little while," Greg explained. "We need you to stay in the room. But please feel free to order something to eat from room service. Don't worry, we will make sure the guard out here checks everyone who comes anywhere near your door. We'll see you in a couple of hours."

℘℘℘

The area around the boat was now cordoned off with yellow tape, and several members of the local police force made sure that strolling tourists did not get too curious. Anne asked for Radomir, and one of the policemen went to get him from inside the boat.

"Good that you are here," the Montenegrin Interpol officer said after he greeted them. "Come, come on in. We have found something of interest. I think Nicholas told you. Some filming equipment."

"Yes. We brought the laptop and the cable he asked for. So we can view the videos."

Anne and Greg followed Radomir toward the bow of the boat, past the main salon and the dining room and into the master stateroom. Labrecque and Székely were there already, watching a policeman balancing on a stool extract something from the recessed lighting above the picture on the wall opposite the bed.

"Hi. As I told you, we found some mini video equipment. Downstairs, in all the bedrooms. And now here, too, in the master," Labrecque said after greeting them. "Polyakov could turn it on probably from his cell-phone whenever he wanted, to film his guests in action. Or it seems, himself, for that matter."

"A great way to blackmail anyone he invited to his trysts. God how sick! "

"These are mini spy cameras of sorts," the policeman on the stool said. "They all have a USB port so they can be connected to a computer for viewing or downloading."

"Bring that one down," Radomir said. "We'll look at them all together. Upstairs. In the lounge. That's probably the best place. We can sit around at the bar."

The policeman disconnected the equipment and handed it to Székely, who had four other similar spy cameras on the bed in front of him. The Hungarian gathered them up. "Let's go check out what's on these.

They carted the little machines and the laptop upstairs to the Skylounge, where Nicholas set things up. The first camera they connected showed no activity. "This must be from one of the rooms that wasn't used yesterday," Radomir said.

Labrecque attached the USB cable to the next one. After a moment, they saw the Montenegrin general closing the door, and turning to the girl cowering against the back wall—Anne recognized one of Nadia's friends—he ordered her to get undressed. When she hesitated, he grabbed her, pushed her down on the bed, and started tearing her clothes off. Once he had ripped her panties off, he turned her over on her stomach, and started undressing, even as he was pinning her down with his other hand and a knee. Just when he was naked and had forced the crying girl's legs open, in burst Anne, yelling, "Don't move or I will shoot, you creep!"

"God Almighty! That's enough evidence to put the good General Brankovic away for life, the pervert," Radomir said. "I will personally see to that. I never liked the man."

As Anne said, remembering the scene, "Ugh!" Greg connected the next little camera, and what they saw there was even more shocking: one of the thugs shepherded three very frightened girls—one of whom they recognized as Nadia—into the master stateroom and, at gunpoint told them one by one to strip down to their panties, tearing some of their clothes off at will. He then went over to the tallest, grabbed her frontally by the breasts, twisted her arm behind her back, and tugged her over to a marble pillar on one side of the bed, tying her wrists to it up high. Then he did the same to the second girl, just as Hetzel appeared at the door. They could hear Hetzel say, "Good job, Oleg. You know where the whip is, don't you?"

To which Oleg responded, "Yes, sir, indeed," as he went over to a chest against the wall. He opened one of the drawers and pulled out a horsewhip.

To which Hetzel said, "Yes, that's the one. You can start with either of those bitches," as he struggled out of his shirt and pants.

"Okay, little Nadia, you—you had better get over here, or I will have Oleg whip the shit out of you until you do." And when she didn't move, he yelled, "Now, you little cunt! When I say come, you come!"

They saw Nadia, in tears, just in her undies, move hesitantly to where he was sitting on the edge of his bed holding his flaccid penis in his hand, arm resting on the leg that was not bandaged. They heard him say, "Get down there, baby, and take this in your mouth. Come on, now," as he pushed her down with his hands in her hair, proffering his member. It was at that moment that Anne and Greg burst on the scene, and Anne was so outraged at this depravity, that she blew away most of the man's genitalia.

"God," Greg heard his wife say. "I can't believe

what happened there. I am sorry. I was so angry. But he—he had it coming to him."

Greg embraced her. "It's okay, my love. He did deserve it, that's for sure."

"You did good, Anne," Labrecque said. "That man was the worst. Someone had to put an end to his depravity. The preying on young women."

"Do you think they were making another tape to use with Nadia's father?" Greg, who had been thinking, changed the subject. "Or maybe even to blackmail the families of some of the other girls?"

"Hmm. Good point, Greg," Anne said. "Didn't one of these teenagers—yes, I think it was Nadia's friend, Sasha—say that Polyakov had mentioned that they needed to teach Nadia's father a lesson, so that Brother Peter could get the HEU more quickly? That would certainly point to some intent behind—at the very least—this last video."

"Well, so much the better then that we nipped whatever they were up to in the bud," Labrecque said. "The truth is, they could very well have gotten away with it this time. Another heist, I mean."

"Yeah, with security as lax as it is there at Mayak, no doubt, eventually they are likely to succeed," Greg said. "Despite Interpol's and the IAEA's best efforts."

"We will put these crooks away for good," Székely joined in. "Don't you worry."

"Yes, but the ringleader is still out there. And he knows how to reorganize." Anne, too, was more pessimistic than her former colleagues. "Polyakov. He is the worst of the lot." And then she added with a frown, "And don't I know it."

"Those fanatical Sons of Jesus are still out there, too. That Brother Peter and his gang. As are other terrorist groups, of course," Greg continued. "So if these guys do manage to pull off another heist, the threat of a major nuclear terrorist attack is still very real."

"Well, let's make sure we have all these videos as evidence," Radomir said. "I will take them with me and make sure they are not tampered with. You never know how far Brankovic's corrupt power reaches."

"You know, I was just wondering," Greg would not let up. "Do you think Polyakov might have had a camera filming what was going on up here at the same time? Here in the lounge? As in the bedrooms? If he did, we would know what went on between him and Billy—Brother Peter, I mean."

"Interesting idea, Greg," Labrecque said. "Why didn't I think of that?"

"We will check right away," Radomir said, signaling to one of the two local policemen who had followed them into the lounge, then giving orders to him in Montenegrin.

Within moments, the officer had brought up the ladder and was checking first along the recessed lighting above the bar, where Greg conceded would have been the best place to locate such a video camera. Indeed, it did not take the man more than a few minutes to find the equipment and another several to dismantle and bring it down.

"Good work," Radomir said, connecting the USB cable to it. "All right. Let's see what this item produces."

"Could be interesting," Labrecque said. "A discussion between the chief merchant of evil and the terrorist wanting to buy what he claims he has to sell. Or something like that."

"Okay, I'm ready," Anne said, sitting back in an armchair as the picture came on.

∽∾∽

"Look," Polyakov was saying, as he took a sip of his champagne. "The deal is the same as before. Exactly the same as what you guys paid for the other half. Fifty pounds of HEU for twenty-five million dollars."

"We're okay with that," Billy Crawford acquiesced. "But where is the pickup? Where will you deliver the stuff to? That, as you know, has now become very important."

"Sure."

"The last time, in Poti, we could only get half of what we had contracted for because Interpol and the Georgians found out about the exchange. You had to return the twenty-five million to Khalid, if I remember correctly, and we think that Interpol agent—Anne, whatever the fuck her name is, and her asshole of a husband got their hands on the twenty-five mil I transferred to Kallay. That could have been yours. Not even mentioning the many men, both on your side and ours, who lost their lives. We don't want another cock up like that, Sergei, that's for sure."

Greg had trouble getting over the gall of the man, ever since his brazen appearance in Vienna.

"Okay, okay. Not Georgia, like the last time. Yeah, that was definitely problematic."

They could see on the video that Polyakov was thinking fast, as he stood up and paced in front of the bar.

"And that would have only been the start of our problems," the American said. "We would still have had to get the stuff to where we wanted to use it."

"How about Chechnya? Or here? We could do it here, in Porto Montenegro."

"Not good enough," Brother Peter answered. "As I said, it is too dangerous for me to get nuclear material from here to where I want it."

"And where is that? Need I ask?"

"In the US. And you know that, Sergei, so stop playing games."

"You're crazy. Are you saying that you want us to get the HEU to you in America?"

"Yes. And we would be willing to pay for it, if you do. How about it?"

"What are you talking about? How much more?" Polyakov touched his hand to his chin, tempted and obviously reflecting.

"We'll give you another ten mil—how's that, my friend? If you deliver in the United States."

"Where in the US do you want the stuff delivered?"

"Anywhere in the Northeast—as I said, an extra ten million if we get it there. Plus, for that price, you need to help me get the fifty pounds I already have from the last time there as well."

"Holy shit! Aren't we being demanding."

"Ten million dollars is a lot of money. Total of thirty-five, in your bank account. No questions asked. Half when you show me that you have the stuff, the other half after successful delivery."

"Well, let me think about it."

"No dice. You commit now, my friend, or I go to the Iranians. They would do it for far less, I am sure. They're desperate for the money."

Polyakov thought another moment. "Okay, Brother Peter. You are insistent. You have a deal."

"And, what's more, just to seal the transaction," Billy Crawford said, seemingly certain that he had the upper hand, as he offered his palm for the arms merchant to shake. "I want that little Russian sweetheart thrown in. The one I chose, who's waiting for me downstairs. Plus the other one you claim you need to help you get the stuff out…from wherever. Afterward, of course."

"You've got to be kidding."

"Or merchandise of similar quality," the deputy of the Sons of Jesus terrorists said with a little laugh.

The viewers of the video could see on his face that he knew he had driven the better deal. But Greg wondered whether his last request had in fact been for real. It seemed to be mere icing on the cake, and he thought it would be unlikely that the American terrorist would hold the Russian arms merchant to it. That is if he got his HEU.

But he couldn't be sure. Billy Crawford had always been a strange one.

Chapter 32

Greg and Anne were waiting in the lobby, while Radomir, Labrecque, and Székely were going through the formalities with the hotel manager to have Polyakov's penthouse suite opened up for them, when Greg spotted Julia coming in through the glass doors of the hotel.

"Julia!" he shouted, going over toward her. "Come, we're over here."

After hugs and greetings, their Russian friend quickly told them about her success at foiling the heist attempt at Mayak, and they brought her up to speed on where matters stood in Porto Montenegro.

"Boy, you have been busy!" Julia said. "Too bad Polyakov and that Brother Peter got away again. But how are Nadia and the other girls?"

"We just checked on them," Greg said. "They are resting up here in the hotel for now, and are just grateful to have their ordeal over with."

"We'll have to figure out how to get them back to Ozersk," Anne said, "but we first want to be present when the police tackle Polyakov's place here. Apparently, he owns one of the two penthouse suites, and my former Interpol colleagues are just seeing the manager with the warrant to search it."

"Great, so I got back just in time for that." Julia seemed pleased.

"Here, why don't I come up with you and you can drop your things in our room for the time being?" Anne said, grabbing the handle of her friend's wheeled carry on suitcase. "Until we figure out what happens next. Plus, I am sure you would probably like to freshen up a bit after your trip."

"Thanks. That would be nice."

"I'll tell them to send someone for you," Greg said. "To make sure you can get in up there. Through all the security. Fifteen minutes?"

☙❦❧

Greg was overwhelmed by the opulence of Polyakov's penthouse suite. Exquisitely furnished, the views were magnificent from anywhere in the living or dining rooms, both of which opened onto a wrap-around terrace, as did all three bedrooms and the study.

After quickly checking the other rooms, they concentrated their search on the study and the master bedroom. The Interpol agents did not hesitate in seizing the iMacPro and the iPad on the desk, Labrecque commenting that, "We will have our experts tackle these back in Vienna where we have more resources. I am sure that we will find a lot of incriminating evidence on them."

Greg was looking through the drawers of the desk, when he heard a shout in what, he assumed, was Montenegrin, and, within moments, Radomir appeared in the doorway. "It seems that an officer has found a safe built into the wall behind one of the pictures in the master."

"Excellent! No doubt we'll find some interesting material there," Labrecque said, looking over from his task of checking through a closet.

"Fortunately, one of the policemen we have with us is a specialist safecracker, so with some luck, it won't be impossible for us to open it," Radomir continued. "But it could take a while."

"That's at least something," Anne said, looking at Greg. "Because apart from what might be on the laptop ant the iPad, there doesn't seem to be a lot here."

They all followed the Montenegrin agent into the master and watched as the expert cut away the wall on the side of the safe.

Radomir had no doubt seen this before. "I'll have them call us when they've broken through. I see what he is trying to do—first he drills a small hole on the side of the safe, then he will insert a bore and scope the change keyhole, allowing him to get at the combination. This is what you need to do with such hi-tech safes that have manipulation proof locks and glass re-lockers. We may as well relax and have a drink on the terrace, courtesy of our Russian friend while we wait for results."

They made their way into the living room, where Labrecque went behind the well-stocked bar. Addressing Anne and Julia, he asked, "What would you ladies like? Let's see if there is any champagne in the fridge here to celebrate our success, freeing those girls and capturing all those criminals. Yes, something sparkling would go down well right now, before lunch." The Frenchman opened the refrigerator and saw that it was full of bottles of champagne, white wine and rosé, exotic beers, and vodkas, as well as mixers of all sorts. He leaned down and pulled out a magnum of Roederer Cristal 2004. "Well, well. I haven't had one of these for quite a few years." And he started pulling out flûtes from the glass cabinets and pouring the golden drink into them.

They enjoyed the bubbly on the terrace with a view over the marina and looking out into the bay. After a toast to their success, talk turned to anything but the case at hand. They all relished the chance to dip back into normalcy, away from the depravity and sordidness of this human trafficking and arms trading affair they were trying to untangle.

"I am worried sick about my mother," Julia said. "I hate to leave her even to go to the office, and now it has been more than a week since I've seen her."

"She seemed to be holding up well when we left her in Vienna," Anne tried to reassure her. "Her main concern was for you."

"Well, I need to call her as soon as we finish here."

"Of course."

Just then, a policeman came over and said something to Radomir, who got up, announcing to the others, "He's through. We're about to open the safe. Let's go in there and see."

They all piled in the master suite, as the dusty officer who had stripped down to his T-shirt to cut through the wall and penetrate the safe, waited for Radomir to give the okay.

When the Interpol agent nodded at him, he started turning the dial on the front of the metal box, and, after a couple of changes in direction, the door popped open as if by magic. The safecracker policeman turned to them with a smile, saying something in the local language which Greg surmised must have meant something like "All yours," because Radomir went up to the safe and pushed the door open, allowing everyone to peer inside.

The Montenegrin agent started pulling papers out, as well as stacks and stacks of dollars and euros, passports from different countries—no doubt fake—along with several sets of keys and three chamois bags, all of which he placed on the bed. Lastly, from way in the back, he extracted a somewhat weathered looking cardboard container marked with printed red Cyrillic letters, and tied closed with string.

"That says, 'Top Secret' on it!" Julia was the first one to focus on the old box, as the others were mesmerized by the hundred or so diamonds Radomir was pouring out of the first little sack onto the bed cover. "It looks very official."

Székely stared in stunned disbelief. "God! Those must be worth many millions."

"What would a carton marked 'Top Secret' be doing in the hands of Polyakov, the arms merchant?" Greg was intrigued more by the tarnished old box than the plethora of diamonds. "Wow, it looks like it's from another era."

"I've seen this before—or something like it," Julia said, obviously racking her brains, as Radomir undid the string that tied the second bag, pouring more diamonds onto the bed. She, too, refused to let the jewels distract her.

But Anne asked, "Do we think these are blood diamonds?"

"They could be from Yakutia. In Siberia," Székely opined. "They mine diamonds there too."

"Let's take a look at what's in the box," Anne said, picking it up from the bed. "Julia, you are the only native Russian speaker here. So come, you should be the one who looks through this. That is, if you agree, Radomir, George, and Nicholas." She remembered that she was no longer with Interpol, and the men were officially in charge.

"Of course, that makes sense," Labrecque agreed. "We'll peruse these other papers meanwhile. Most seem to be in English. They seem more recent, too. And probably more relevant as evidence. And we also need to do another more thorough search of the rest of the apartment."

"Anne, actually, let's take the box over to the study," Greg said. "Where we can all sit down, and Julia can take a proper look at what's in there."

☙❧

Anne put the carton down on the desk and undid the string, then stepped aside to let Julia open it. The Russian girl took the lid off gingerly. Inside, there was a stack of browning and fading documents, letters, and files. She picked up the first one, then turned pale and immediately sat down, the hand holding the piece of paper trembling. "Oh God! This is the certificate confirming my Aunt Katerina's handover to officials at Camp Zone Number Three at the Chelyablag Gulag." And then handing it to Anne, she looked up. "Now I know where I have seen this type of box before. At the GARF—the official Archives of the Russian Federation in Moscow. That's where all the gulag documents are supposed to be kept. I told you the ones for Chelyablag were all missing when I went there."

"Amazing. Somehow Polyakov got his hands on these," Greg said. "But how? And why?"

"No wonder I couldn't find anything on Katerina in Moscow!"

"Never mind for now. It doesn't matter how this crook got these files. Let's see what else is in the box. Maybe that will give us some clues." Anne raised her hand. "But hold on a second," she added enthusiastically. "Julia, can you read this signature? Here at the bottom."

Julia took the tattered piece of paper back from her friend and looked at it closely.

"'Aleksandr Ivanovich—' No it can't be! But yes, it says 'Polyakov.'"

"Holy shit!" Greg exclaimed. "Whoever's signature that is, must be related to our friend here."

"What does the rest of the paper say?" Anne asked.

"It says 'This is to confirm that Katerina Efimovna Pleshkova was admitted to Camp Zone Number Three at the Chelyablag Gulag for incarceration for a period of XXX years commencing on the date below. Signed Aleksandr Ivanovich Polyakov, Commander. Dated September 17, 1950.'" Julia displayed no emotion as she was reading this. "The 'XXX' must mean she was to be in there indefinitely," she added in a hoarse whisper.

"So we know now that Lenkov handed Katerina—who, by the way, we think was pregnant, probably with Beria's child—over to an Aleksandr Polyakov, who was Commander of Camp Zone Number Three at the Chelyablag Gulag," Greg summarized as dispassionately as he could. "Let's see what else we can find out."

Julia took the next piece of paper out of the box. It was lined, and obviously torn from a notebook, with both sides filled with writing in a very small hand. She turned it over and searched at the bottom for a signature.

"A letter from my Aunt Katerina!" Turning it back over, she added, "To her parents, Efim and Ludmilla."

"Can you read it for us?" Anne asked.

"I will try, but it is barely legible."

Julia started reading as follows:

"'Dearest Mama and Papa!

"'I know you have been crying a lot for me since I didn't come home that day last May. You probably have found out by now what happened. I do not want to talk about it. I am at peace now, although I have often thought of killing myself. But

I have found kindness here. Gospodja Polyakova, the wife of the commander at this corrective labor camp took care of me when I was close to death. She has gradually restored the will to live in me. It was her unselfish love for me, a stranger, and the thought of the little baby I know I have inside me—who is growing bigger every day—and the hope that I would one day see you again and be able to show the child to you—it was that that has kept me going. I want you to know my baby. I will see you again, I am sure. And I want you to know that I love you. Very much, and think of you every day.

"'Your loving daughter,
"'Katerina.
"'November 22, 1950'"

"God! So it seems that Gospodja Polyakova, the wife of the commander of that corrective labor camp, helped Katerina," Anne commented. "She cared for her and nurtured her."

"So at least there was one good Polyakov in the mix," Greg added. "But the letter was never sent. It stayed in the Gulag. This Aleksandr Polyakov probably thought it too dangerous to let it leave the camp."

Anne urged her friend on. "Let's see what the next piece of paper tells us."

Julia reached into the box for the document on top. She looked at it, and Greg could see tears well up in her eyes. "This is a certificate of death. For Katerina Efimovna Pleshkova. Dated February 27, 1951." She hesitated before continuing, "So she did die in the camp." And then she added in a whisper, "For cause, it says, 'Died in childbirth.'"

Anne sighed. "Terrible! Poor Katerina. Giving birth

in a gulag in the middle of winter, even if the commander's wife is helping to look after you, would have been a real ordeal. Especially after what she had been through. It just proved to be too much for her."

"This, coming after that hopeful letter she wrote earlier," Greg added. "How tragic. Terrible."

"Let's see what else is in here," Julia said, taking another document out of the box. She unfolded two torn and fading pieces of paper. "Wow! A birth certificate," she exclaimed, "No, not one but two. Must be replicas. Here, on this one, it gives Katerina Efimovna Pleshkova as the mother. But the space for father is left blank. It was not filled in. And the name of the child is…Sergei. Amazing!" She looked closer at the document, then felt it in the middle with her index finger. "You won't believe this. The last name is scratched out, and 'Polyakov' is written in the space. Dated February 27, 1951."

The others were stunned. "The same name as this guy here. The bloody arms merchant," Greg said. "Sergei Polyakov."

Looking at the second certificate, Julia continued, "And this one…exactly the same, in all respects, except the child's name is given as…Boris. Last name also erased and replaced by 'Polyakov.' So it is not just a copy."

"Twins! These are the birth certificates of the Polyakov twins," Anne said, but her voice was hoarse. "God, they are Katerina's sons. Sergei and Boris Polyakov." She looked at Julia, who had turned pale. "Difficult to take on board."

"That means—that means—" Julia stuttered in her disbelief, "—that the Polyakov brothers are my cousins, my first cousins." She buried her face in her hands, as the horror of it dawned on her. "And the sons of Katerina and—and Lavrenti Beria—"

Anne and Greg were speechless, as they both embraced the sobbing Russian girl.

"There is one more document here," Greg said, reaching into the box. "It looks like it is a letter, too. In another hand, though, I think." He picked up Katerina's letter to compare, before saying, "Yes, definitely not the same handwriting. But here, Anne, you take it, I can't read the Cyrillic script."

"I'm not too good at it either."

"Here, let me look at it," Julia said, recovering and wiping her eyes. "Maybe this letter will fill in some of the blanks for us."

She took it from Greg, looking at it briefly before turning it over. "It is addressed to Lenkov—the man who took my aunt to the labor camp. But it is not signed, and seems to be unfinished."

"Maybe it's from Polyakov senior," Greg guessed.

"Let me read it."

"'My dear Lenkov!

"'I hope this letter finds you and your lovely wife in good health and spirits in these difficult times for our nation.

"'I am writing to let you know that the young lady you brought last fall to our Camp Zone Number Three, Katerina Efimovna Pleshkova, died in childbirth three days ago. You may remember that when you left her in the camp, she was very weak and traumatized.

My wife, Irena, who had always wanted children but never could have any, took a liking to her and gave her special care, even convincing me to allow her to bring the girl into our home. It was Irena who discovered, very soon after she arrived, that Katerina was pregnant. While she stayed with us, with Irena's love and attention, she grew stronger and even seemed to put behind her the terrible ordeals that she must have been through. But three days ago, as I said, she went into labor during the night, and we called the camp doctor, who delivered her of not one but two healthy sons. Twins.

Unfortunately though, he was not able to save the mother. The poor girl bled to death. We buried her in the common grave here. The boys were destined for an orphanage in Chelyabinsk—which is what we usually do with motherless children in our camp—but Irena begged me to let her keep them, promising to raise them as her own children. Seeing that if I did not grant her request, my wife would forever be unhappy and never forgive me, I agreed to adopt them, against my better judgment. Although now that it is done, and they carry my name, I can see the possible benefits of being a father to the two boys. May they grow up in good health—'"

Here, Julia stopped. "That's it. That's where the writing stopped."

"Perhaps he decided not to finish and send it. It could have been dangerous for him," Greg said. "Beria was still the second most powerful man in the country."

"He never does say outright that he knew that the boys were the sons of Beria, but he hints at it." Anne had been thinking throughout. "He knew that Lenkov was Beria's Chief of Security, and it certainly seemed to be generally known in those circles that Beria was a raving pervert who did whatever he wanted with young women, so when a man in Lenkov's position brought a traumatized pregnant girl to be put away indefinitely in the gulags, it is not difficult to come to the conclusion that it

may have been Beria who knocked her up and now wanted to get rid of the evidence."

"And near the end of the letter, he hints at the possible advantages that saving Beria's sons and raising them
might give him," Greg said, continuing the train of
thought. "On the one hand, if Beria later wanted to
acknowledge his progeny, he would be praised, or on the
other, he had a tool to blackmail Stalin's deputy and head
of the secret services with. Although, no doubt, that
would have been a difficult and dangerous game to play.
But in any case, it would seem that our dear Polyakov
senior was not altogether selfless in agreeing to adopt the
bastard sons of Lavrenti Beria."

"That is maybe the reason why he kept all these documents. In the event he needed them, one way or the other," Anne agreed.

"But how did this Polyakov—Sergei—his son, get
his hands on them?" Greg asked. "They are official documents, that, as you say, Julia, seem to have come from
the state archives."

"Hmm. Good question." Julia did not have an answer.

"Well, maybe it was his brother, Boris, the Deputy
Director of the FSB who absconded with them, and gave
them to Sergei to hide." Anne was thinking out loud.
"After all, being the son of Lavrenti Beria these days
would not be very good for one's career."

"Why wouldn't they just destroy the evidence?"
Greg asked. "No one else had any idea who their real father was."

"The Polyakov brothers have been around too long,"
Anne said. "They have seen a lot. They have experienced
on their own skin that, in Russia, régimes can change,
and what once was a bad pedigree could all of a sudden
become a good one. Or vice versa, as the case may be."

Greg grinned. "Wow, what a story this makes! It is great material for my next book, I can see."

"But first, Julia, you need to take these documents to your mother," Anne said. "So she will have closure on her sister."

"I will, and that reminds me, if we are done here, I need to phone her," Julia said, looking at her watch. "This is a good time, before her afternoon rest."

Anne and Greg left her in the study to make the call and went to find the Interpol agents. They were in the living room, drinking what was left in the Magnum, having finished the search of the apartment.

"Did you find anything else?" Anne asked.

"Yes, indeed," Labrecque answered. "Those documents in the safe were mainly secret contracts of arms sales."

"And we found a lot more money hidden all over the place. Unbelievable!" Székely crowed. "This guy was filthy rich."

"What did you find in the box?" Radomir asked.

"It's a long story," Anne said. "How about it if we tell you over lunch? I bet you guys are hungry, and we do deserve some nourishment."

Chapter 33

They had a delicious lunch of fresh local seafood out in the beautiful Italian Garden Restaurant attached to the hotel, during which Julia related to them in detail how she managed to convince Nadia's father to help her and security at Mayak to foil the most recent attempt to steal some nuclear material. And that, unfortunately, Mikhail Glinov was injured in the action and was now recovering in hospital.

"We'll have to tell Nadia, but gently," Anne commented over coffee.

"You're right," Julia agreed.

"We'll also need to see how many of these poor girls need counseling. Not just now, but longer term," Anne cautioned. "They have been through so much. And no doubt they'll want to get back to their parents as soon as possible." Then, looking at Labrecque, she added: "Of course, once you've had a chance to question them."

"I was thinking that maybe we could use some of the money we found in Polyakov's apartment to pay for any treatment or counseling they may need." Greg had been giving the matter some thought. "And of course, to get them home."

"Excellent idea! I am sure we can justify that as long as we account properly for it all," Radomir agreed.

"Beyond that, maybe once we have it all tallied, we should also think of giving the families some of it," Székely added. "Restitution payments from the criminals to the victims."

"Perhaps we can create a foundation of sorts, to help these girls and other victims of human trafficking," Greg mused. "Of course, depending on how much money there is."

"Not a bad idea," Anne agreed. "Like we did with the money Adam was paid by the terrorists when we defeated their attempt to steal HEU from Mayak earlier." And for the others' benefit, she added, "We created a foundation to help the victims of nuclear contamination from the Soviet program."

"We could also sell the diamonds and add in the proceeds," Greg said, taking it one step further. "That would certainly make for a tidy sum, I'm sure."

"Before you get too far along with your foundation idea, we may need a little to get Hetzel back to Vienna," Labrecque said. "We will definitely want to extradite him and try him there."

"On that point, I was thinking," Greg interjected, "what about sending him—and Polyakov and Brother Peter if we ever catch them—to stand for trial at the International Court of Justice? After all, if I remember correctly, rape and torture are clearly considered to be crimes against humanity, and it could be argued that it would be within their mandate."

"Hmm. You're full of ideas, Greg. And that certainly is an interesting one. We need to look into it. Indeed, I've seen that there have also been some moves recently to try arms merchants in the ICJ," Székely pointed out.

"By the way, do we have a read on how Hetzel is doing?" Anne asked. "He was in a pretty bad way when the ambulance took him."

"Yes, just before lunch, I talked to the officer in charge of the detail that went to guard him at the General Hospital in Melijne where the ambulance took him," Radomir answered. "The patient was resting after a major operation, he said. Ahem…they were working on reconstituting as much of whatever was left of what he had down there, poor bugger. But he is still heavily sedated, and will be for a while."

"He had it coming, the bastard," Anne said. "So don't feel sorry for him."

"He won't be going anywhere soon," Székely commented. "That's for sure."

"But back to the girls," Anne announced, bringing them back to her main concern. "We will need to interview each of them individually with a psychologist present to assess the damage."

"We're already on that," Radomir said. "I have sent one of my colleagues along with a psychologist to start questioning the girls we housed in the nunnery."

"And then I think it would be good if we accompanied them to Russia and helped them ease back into life there," Anne continued. "It may be difficult for some of them to face their families and friends with what they have been through."

"Yes, you are right," Julia agreed. "I will be there to help. But it would be good if Anne, you and Greg would come too."

"The problem is the visa again," Greg said. "And the laissez-passer to get to Ozersk."

"I disagree. I am not so sure it's such a good idea for you two to go," Labrecque said, concern etched on his face. "Even if you had a visa. Polyakov will definitely be on the warpath against you, since this is the second time you helped foil his plans. And with his brother the Deputy Director of the FSB, I would not want to see you set foot in Russia for now. Too dangerous."

"But surely, Julia is in the same boat!" Greg protested. "And she has been through so much already."

"Yes, you are right. But she is Russian, and she was—unfortunate as it is—a victim of their actions, is the way they would see it. Plus, she works for the IAEA. Even the Polyakov brothers would be less inclined to go after someone who works for an international agency like that. So, Julia, if you think you can handle it, it would be best if you go alone. And we will mobilize our colleagues in Russia to stand by, as before."

"Of course, Nicholas," Julia answered. But Greg was not all together sure that he did not detect the slightest hint of fear in her voice. "Certainly, for Nadia and her friends, it makes sense that I go," Julia continued. "For the others, since I don't know them at all, it may be better to send a psychologist, don't you think?"

✂✃✂

After lunch, while Radomir went off to join his colleague who was questioning the girls freed at the compound on the outskirts of Porto Montenegro, and Labrecque and Székely went to interrogate the thugs they had arrested on the boat and in the derelict building, Julia, Anne and Greg decided they should visit Nadia and her friends who were still holed up in their hotel rooms.

"How much do you think I should tell Nadia about her father?" Julia asked Anne as they made their way back into the hotel lobby. "Should I tell her about the video? That these crooks filmed the horrible things that they were putting her through to send to her father so that they could blackmail him into helping them pull off a heist? And as you told me, that they were making a second video since the first heist attempt failed?"

"Hmm. Maybe that's not such a good idea," Anne answered. "That might cause her a lot of stress. It could really do some psychological damage for Nadia to know that her father saw a film of the horrible ordeal she went through. I certainly don't think that would help."

"Yes, I think you're right, Anne," Greg acquiesced. "I guess I would just tell Nadia that her father was a hero trying to help you stop a heist, and that, unfortunately, he was wounded in the process, but is now recovering."

"God! It is unimaginable to me how close these criminals came to abusing these poor girls again in the boat to make more videos to use with their fathers," Anne commented. "And even more scary, for stealing some more uranium."

"Yes, I was just thinking that Nadia's friend, Sasha, may have been next in line to be used for blackmail," Julia said. "Her father was also a guard at Mayak. Mikhail Glinkov's partner."

"Or, they could have just tried with Glinkov again," Greg pointed out. "If we had not rescued Nadia as you had promised him, he would never have trusted you—us again."

"Yes, thanks to you, now they can't do that," Julia said, appreciation for her friends shinning in her eyes. "At least for now."

⁓⁓⁓

Greg knocked on the door of Room Twenty-Two. It was Sasha who opened the door, but just a crack.

"How are you girls doing?" Anne asked them, as the Russian teenager ushered them inside, leading the way to the terrace, and apologizing for what she was wearing. She had been reclining outside on a lounge chair in just her panties, and had grabbed a T-shirt to pull on top on the way.

"Thanks. This is just so great here," Greg heard Sasha answer, followed by something in Russian, which he vaguely deciphered as "Cover Up," since, as they approached, Nadia and Magda, who were also outside sunning themselves, were just grabbing the hotel dressing gowns lying on the ground beside their recliners.

But the Russian girls were happy to see them. All three had come to trust and look up to them. After all, it was they who had rescued them from their terrible ordeal. And Nadia had witnessed the cool manner in which Anne had dealt with her tormentor on the yacht and admired her for it.

"Nadia," Anne started after they pulled up chairs to join the girls outside, "Julia was just in Ozersk, because we managed to get her away earlier, and, despite what she went through with you at the compound in Hungary, she had some very important things to do there. She works for the International Atomic Energy Agency and these criminals were about to steal some nuclear material and sell it to terrorists."

"Yes," Julia said, taking over. "Your father happened to be on duty just then, and he helped stop it. Unfortunately, though, he was shot and injured. Your father, too, Sasha."

"Oh no," Nadia whispered, as she sat up, on the verge of tears.

Sasha covered her face with her hands.

"They are both all right," Anne said. "As far as we know. They are in the hospital, and in good spirits. And really looking forward to seeing you both."

"I am too," came Nadia's reply through the sobs.

"You are sure he is okay, my father?" Sasha wanted more reassurance.

"Yes."

"Well, we'll get you back there as soon as we can," Greg joined in. "But first, to help us catch these gangsters, is there anything more you can tell us about them? Especially anything that would help us understand who they are and how and where they operate from. Did they give any names away that you might remember, for example? Please, please think hard, and later today or tomorrow, if you're up to it, we would like you to talk to Anne's former colleagues at Interpol."

"We are making arrangements for you to go home, that is, if you are ready to see your families," Anne continued. "It will probably be the day after tomorrow. Julia will go with you to help explain everything and to make sure that you have what you need."

"Thank you," came the chorus of gratitude.

ೲೲ

"Julia, I am sure you are keen to see your mother, as soon as possible," Anne said on the way down in the elevator. "So here is what I propose. I don't think we can do anything more here in Porto Montenegro—my former Interpol colleagues are better equipped than we are, for sure, to handle all the interrogation. And really, it is their job to clean all this up. The three of us can fly back to Vienna—maybe even this evening—and you can link up with Nadia and the other girls in Moscow the day after to fly to Chelyabinsk with them."

"That sounds great."

"Yes, that makes a lot of sense," Greg agreed. "I will see what flights are available, Anne, if you can notify Nicholas and Radomir and then pack up."

Chapter 34

It was close to nine p.m. by the time the taxi dropped them at the building where Julia lived on Momsengasse in Vienna's Fourth District.

"I am worried about what I will find," Julia said, after she pressed the button to call the elevator. "I am not sure that my mother would have been able to take care of herself all this time, even though she said she was okay when I called earlier."

"I bet she's asleep," Greg suggested.

And she was. Sitting in front of the TV, Gospodja Pleshkova had dozed off. But when she saw her daughter, she struggled to her feet and embraced her with tears streaming down her cheeks, "Oh my darling! I thought I would never see you again."

"Matushka, me too," came Julia's whispered answer, as she too, started to cry.

"Your daughter has been through a lot these last few days," Anne said. "But so have you, Gospodja Pleshkova."

"The main thing is she is here, and in one piece," the old lady said, holding her daughter's two hands in hers, and not a bit ashamed of the tears that were streaming down her face. "And I get to see her and hold her one more time, my darling, before I go." And then looking at Julia's two friends, she added, "Thank you, Greg and Anne. I knew I could trust you to bring her back to me."

"But, Mama, sit down, we have something to show you."

"What, my love?"

Greg took the old cardboard box marked 'Top Secret' with the red Cyrillic letters out from his suitcase, and placed it on the coffee table in front of Gospodja Pleshkova, who was sitting between Julia and Anne.

"Open it, Matushka," Julia said, untying the string.

The old lady leaned forward and took the lid off with trembling hands. She looked inside and gingerly pulled the top piece of paper out and then stared at it for several minutes without saying anything.

"Oh my God, my sister! Katerina!"

"Yes, Gospodja Pleshkova," Anne said. "These papers tell the story of the last days of your sister."

Julia's mother took out the next sheet from the box. "And this is a letter from Katerina. In her hand, I recognize it after all these years! Julia, read it for me, will you, my love! Oh no, I am about to cry again," Gospodja Pleshkova said, wiping her tears away.

Dispassionately, Julia read the letter from her aunt, written many years ago.

"At least she had some peace and happiness during those last few months," Julia's mother said, breaking the silence that reigned after her daughter finished. "And she was with child, she says! Do you know what happened to the baby?"

During the entire trip from Porto Montenegro, they had agonized over how to answer this question.

"That is the tragedy, Matushka. Both Aunt Katerina

and her unborn child died in childbirth," Julia lied quietly, looking away. "She was just not strong enough, and the conditions in the camp were so terrible. Moreover, it was the middle of winter."

They had decided that the truth that her nephews were the illegitimate sons of Lavrenti Beria, the offspring from the rape of her sister, coupled with all the horrors that the Polyakov twins were accomplices to, would be too much for the old lady. Certainly, they had concluded, there was no reason to traumatize her last days with the facts, terrible as they were.

"That's what these remaining few papers tell us," Julia summed up. "Here, this is the death certificate for Aunt Katerina. See, right here it says, 'Died in Childbirth.'" After showing this document to her mother, she put it back in the box, gathered up the others, and closed it. "There's no need to exhaust yourself by looking at the rest. There is nothing more in them," she lied again.

"My poor, dear sister! What she went through, we will never fully know—" The old lady was crying again. "—but at least now I have had closure. Thank you, for finding this little box and for bringing it to me. And more importantly, thank you again, Greg and Anne, for giving Julia back to me! I will never forget this."

"We're going to go now and leave you with Julia, Gospodja Pleshkova," Greg said. "But we are also happy that this is ending well. You will have your daughter back now to look after you and help restore your health."

"We will just need you, Julia, to come tomorrow to the Interpol offices," Anne said. "And we will have Interpol make the reservations for you to join Nadia and the others to go to Ozersk the day after tomorrow. Afterward, she will be all yours."

છ

They walked down Argentinierstrasse, and Greg was reminded of the time he had walked to the Sacher pulling his roller bag from Adam Kallay's apartment several Februarys ago after his friend had not been there to receive him on his arrival from the USA. And now they were taking this very same sidewalk from Julia's place back to the hotel, as he had when he had been deeply involved in trying to solve the mystery of Adam's sudden disappearance. The snowy night, when he was sure he had seen Kallay under a streetlight and then tried to catch the phantom. He remembered the good times and the bad times with his former best friend and wondered again how the man he had loved could have been tempted over to the dark side.

The fragility of human existence. The fluidity between right and wrong. The ease of slipping into the gray. The basic human penchant to rationalize one's actions.

Probably, it had been the same for Hetzel, Polyakov, Billy, and all the others.

But had they slipped farther?

Were there degrees of evil? Was evil absolute, or was it all subjective?

Greg pondered these questions as he walked in silence with his wife. The route took them through Karlsplatz and Resselpark then down into the Opernpassage, which, he mused, seemed to have been cleaned up since those earlier days. No more homeless people, drug addicts. Certainly, there was less filth now, and the stench was not as pungent.

Passing by the Staatsoper, Greg noted that the next evening, Béla Bartók's masterpiece, *Bluebeard's Castle,* was on the schedule in a double billing with Tschaikovsky's *Iolanta.* Hmm, he had always wanted to see the former, and had also been intrigued by the latter, which was sometimes paired with the Bartók.

At the Sacher, he thought he recognized this door-man, which made him feel right at home. As he ap-proached the front desk, he remembered his first time arriving at the hotel one night too early—because he had planned to stay that first night at Adam's, only to find that his friend had vanished—and being accommodated. So, since they hadn't booked this time, he hoped they would have a free room again. And as the clerk checked through the options on the computer, he wondered whether Crabbe would show up like that time several years back and offer to cover the costs, although Greg reflected, this time their stay would be on Demeter's bill.

Fortunately, they had a room for Herr und Frau Mar-tens, and he was pleasantly surprised that the clerk called him by his name—although, upon reflection, he was quite sure that it was the computer that had recognized him, because when they had stayed a week or so ago, a different clerk had been at the desk—but still, it was a good feeling. As the man handed him the two keycards, Greg asked him whether the hotel could try and get two tickets for them to *Bluebeard's Castle* and *Iolanta* at the Staatsoper for the next evening.

He wanted to surprise Anne, who had been through much lately—and who was standing a bit removed with their bags, so she would not have heard—although he was not quite sure that these operas would be to her lik-ing. As he remembered, they—at least the former—had a rather dark theme. But going to the Staatsoper in Vienna was always a treat, and they would have a nice dinner after at Meinl am Graben, just like the last time.

⁌⁍

"How long do you think we can—or need to—stay

in Vienna?" Greg asked, as they cuddled in the cozy king-size bed.

"Tomorrow we will go to my former office to brief Demeter, and organize the return of Nadia and her friends to their families. And to make sure that Demeter is onside with Julia taking them back to Russia. And that he will mobilize the Interpol men there to stand by in case. I must say, I am worried about her going."

"So am I," Greg agreed. "But I think Nicholas was right about it being much more dangerous for us. I certainly could not bear losing you. Or having you mistreated again."

"Well, we need to make sure Demeter gets the colleagues in Moscow and Ekaterinburg to give Julia some backup. And then, I think we do need to stay here to see this through until Julia gets back from taking the girls home."

"I guess spending a few more days with you in Vienna is not the worst way to pass our time," Greg said.

Anne kissed her husband, murmuring "I love you," and matters simply progressed from there.

Chapter 35

The next morning, after a quick Viennese breakfast in the Sacher Eck, the stylish café attached to the Hotel, Greg and Anne made their way over to the Interpol offices.

There, Greg and Anne briefed Demeter on Julia's recent trip to Mayak and the foiling of the heist attempt and told him of their successes in Porto Montenegro in freeing the girls and capturing most of the gang of human traffickers.

"Yeah, you guys and Nicholas did good," the Interpol chief complimented them. "Nicholas told me that you captured this guy Hetzel and several high ranking clients, including the Deputy Chief of Police for all of Hungary and a Montenegrin general." It seemed that Labrecque had already told him a bit about what had happened in Porto Montenegro and Ozersk, but not really gone into the details. "Those are huge prizes."

"Yeah, it was a pretty slick operation those gangsters ran," Greg said. "Polyakov, along with all his other Mephisthophelean activities, and aided and abetted by that pervert, Hetzel, ran a ring that trafficked girls from Russia and elsewhere, mostly into Europe and the Middle East."

"Yeah, I gathered that," Demeter said.

"The way it would work, John, is that Hetzel would procure the girls, mainly from the contaminated towns near Mayak and the other former Soviet nuclear cities—convincing the parents that those regions were not healthy places to bring children up—while Polyakov had the connections with customers, partly through his arms trading, drug dealing and money laundering."

"Yes, the merchant of evil, Polyakov," Anne interjected, "would handle all the logistics through his various companies, including the flights to a small remote airbase in Hungary, near where they established their central compound. From there, they would send the girls off to strip bars in European capitals and larger cities, which they either owned, or with whose owners they were on good terms."

"Hungary was a good staging point for them, as it is part of Schengen and there are no real border checks between it and many other European countries," Greg continued. "They would showcase the girls in these strip bars, then sell them as sex slaves to rich perverts, or as prostitutes to pimps."

"As a matter of fact, I was sold to a Chinese oligarch," Anne said. "Fortunately, we disrupted the operations before they could hand me over. 'Deliveries'—as they would call them—outside the Schengen zone would be made by Polyakov's planes, flying from the airstrip near the compound. The yacht, the penthouse suite and the warehouse in Montenegro, as well as the compound in Hungary, were all owned by a network of offshore companies that lead to Polyakov. Under the name Adriatica, it would seem."

"And to make matters worse," Greg continued, "we

caught them sexually abusing and torturing one of these teenager girls from Ozersk—the daughter of a guard at Mayak—and making a video of it all, to get her father to look the other way as some stolen HEU was to be taken out of the facility. Julia went to convince him that we would rescue his daughter, but he needed to not do what they wanted him to, and help us prevent the nuclear material from leaving Mayak. And, although we managed to foil this first attempt, they were about to do it again, with another video they were making."

"So that's how they did it," Demeter said.

"We've got to get the monster Polyakov," Anne said. "He is behind it all. Until he is dead or behind bars for life, he will continue to be the source of these problems. Nuclear heists, trafficking, and sexual abuse of women, trade in blood diamonds, as well as arms, and God only knows what else."

"We are trying to track him, you can be sure," Demeter said. "Not easy though. The man is worse than a chameleon."

"He is supposed to have flown from Tivat to Grozny. With Brother Peter," Anne informed her former boss. "Another chameleon."

Demeter shook his head in concern. "We get very little cooperation from the Russians, as you know."

Just then, Frau Huth interrupted. "Ms. Saparova is here."

"Show her in," Demeter said, as Greg and Anne got up to greet their friend.

After introductions, and another thank you to Julia from the Interpol boss for her role in foiling the most recent heist, talk turned to her trip to Ozersk the next day to take Nadia and her friends home. Demeter asked Frau Huth to coordinate with Labrecque so she would be on the same flight from Moscow as the girls coming from Porto Montenegro.

"We're going to mobilize our agents in Ekaterinburg and Moscow to give you support," Demeter said. "I will have them contact you as soon as you land at Balandino. Frau Huth will give you their details."

"Thank you. But I don't think even the FSB would interfere with an official of the IAEA trying to do her job," Julia said.

"Let's hope you're right. In any case, it's not the FSB we're worried about. It's these nasties, Polyakov and crowd, who seem to have a long reach. And we don't know where they will pop up next. But good luck to you, Julia. Be safe!"

❧❧❧

It was over a light lunch of *Wurst mit Brötchen und Sauerkraut* and a Caesar Salad, a carafe of Zweigelt they shared at the Café Central that Greg broke the news to Anne.

"I have tickets for the opera tonight, my dear. And then we'll have dinner at Meinl am Graben, just like the last time."

"That was the evening when you seduced me, you rake. But I couldn't be happier for it," Anne responded, with a little smile, putting her hand on his. "Last time it was Verdi's *Don Carlos*. My favorite, so it will be hard to beat. What will we be seeing this time?"

"It's a double billing—"

"Cav and Pag?" Anne asked, referring to *Cavaliera Rusticana* and *I Pagliacci,* two one act operas usually performed together. "I love those too."

"No. It is more modern. At least, one of them. And a bit out of the ordinary, but something I have always wanted to see, so I am glad it happens to be on at the Staatsoper tonight."

"Well, what is it?"

"Bartók's *Bluebeard's Castle*. It is coupled with Tschaikovsky's *Iolanta*."

"God help us," Anne said, with a smile. "If I remember correctly from reading about it somewhere, the story of the former is pretty horrific. All about obsessive love, no? And the music…well, modern. Bartók. Is it the Hungarian aspect that appeals?"

"I don't know much about *Iolanta*."

"Don't worry. I am looking forward to it, Greg. We will have a great night out. No matter what. Just the two of us. I love you." She took his hands in hers and leaned across the table to kiss him, to emphasize her point.

ℰↈℰↈ

"You are gorgeous, as always!" In the elevator, Greg admired his wife, who just like the last time, was dressed in a simple, low-cut black evening dress with a string of pearls accentuating her delicate neck and features. He drew her to himself and gave her a long, passionate kiss. "I am one lucky man."

"You're not so shabby yourself, Professor," Anne answered, pulling away just as the doors opened, admiring him in his well-tailored navy blue suit, crisp white shirt and striped burgundy tie.

They made their way quickly across Philharmoniker Strasse and arrived inside the Staatsoper just in time for Greg to be able to purchase a program. They found their parterre row ten seats and raced to read about the Bartók opera before curtain time. Anne was delighted to rediscover the little inconspicuous screen on the back of the seat in front where she would be able to follow the libretto in English, since, as Greg had reminded her, *Blue-beard's Castle* would be sung in the original Hungarian version and *Iolanta* in Russian.

As the lights were dimmed, the Bard traditional in Hungarian folk music came out to give the spoken prologue, with its existential questions. But when the slow and spooky introduction started to be played by the orchestra, Anne felt a shiver down her spine and nestled close to her husband. Greg wondered whether it had been a wise choice to take his wife to see this opera, with its heavy symbolism and themes of obsessive love and perverse sexuality, and its violent and graphic score, given what she had just been through.

❧❧❧

"So what did you think of it?" Greg asked as they got up from their seats at intermission, the finale and the applause still ringing in their ears.

"Thrilling," was all Anne could say. "But very dark. Nadja Michael was fabulous as Judith."

"And I loved Petrenko's Bluebeard," Greg said, as they made their way out toward the beautiful Marble Hall reception area, following the noisy crowd. "Here, why don't you just stay here, while I go over to the bar to get us some champagne," he said, as they approached a pillar. It's too crowded over there."

Greg sauntered over to where a queue had already formed. Standing in line, he kept admiring the beauty of his wife, as he reflected on the opera. Despite his concern for Anne, he was glad to have finally seen it. As a music lover, and with his Hungarian roots, it had been on his "bucket list."

He was just about at the head of the line when, out of the crowd, he saw a familiar short, square and balding man approach his Anne, whose expression changed from pleasant idle curiosity to, at first, incredulity, and then horror.

He saw her stiffen as the man greeted her and then said something to her, before glancing over at him and vanishing into the crowd.

Greg grabbed the glasses, forgetting about his change, and rushed back to his wife, who, he could see, had been deeply shaken by the experience.

"Polyakov!" He handed one of the flûtes to his wife, who was pale and still shaking. He grabbed her free hand. "What is he doing here? And what did he say to you?"

"I first thought—but it wasn't—that Polyakov—Sergei, I mean. It was the other one, the Deputy Director of the FSB."

"Boris? What did he say?" Greg took a gulp of his champagne.

"He said that I 'had better watch out,' and not mess with their—he said 'our'—interests. And to keep what I know to myself, because if things got out, it would be all over for me. And, he said, that goes for your 'stupid husband and your friend too.' He probably meant Julia. And that he and his people have a far reach, and that, no doubt, we would not want something like what happened to Litvinenko to happen to me—and you."

"He threatened you—us—right here in the opera?"

"Yes, and he then said that we had better go back to Vermont pronto or else, you and I both would have a fate far worse than that traitor."

"What nerve! You're sure it was not Sergei?"

"How could it be? He's in Chechnya."

"But—"

"Yes, I am sure. I know it wasn't Sergei. But very scary, all the same. Oh, yes, he finished by saying that their reach extends to the darkest corners of the world. Even to Vermont."

"Are you all right, Anne?" Greg asked, putting his arm around his wife, as the bell rang for everyone to go back to their seats.

"Greg, would you mind terribly if we left? I am just too shaken to sit through this...*Iolanta*."

"Of course, my love. No. Let's go. After that—"

As he took the flûtes back, he thought, how fortuitous that it was the Tchaikovsky he was going to miss, and not *Bluebeard's Castle*.

Chapter 36

The next morning, they were at the Interpol office behind the Börse right at nine a.m. with their marzipan filled croissants. Neither had slept well, both trying to think through the ramifications of the approach by Boris Polyakov the evening before. Frau Huth set them up with the usual *Mélange* and *kleiner Brauner* in the conference room while they waited for Demeter.

"The car picked Ms. Saparova up just a few minutes ago, as we requested," Frau Huth said. "Her flight is at ten-thirty a.m. Herr Labrecque should be in too, shortly. He flew in last night."

"Good," Anne said. "It will be good to hear what he has to say."

The Interpol boss showed up within five minutes. "Well, I didn't think I would see you till much later, if at all this morning. But I am grateful for your devotion to the cause."

"John, we came in early because we have something very disturbing to report," Greg said, taking a sip of his coffee.

"What is it now?"

"Greg took me to the opera last night—" Anne started to tell him what had happened.

"By golly, isn't your husband a culture vulture. And such a gentleman!"

"Yes, that too, but John, seriously, at the intermission Greg went over to the bar to get us a couple of glasses of champagne, and as I was standing there by myself, a very spiffily dressed Colonel Boris Polyakov came up to me—"

"That's the twin brother, isn't it? The one who is high up in the FSB?"

"Yes, not Sergei, the arms merchant."

"You're absolutely sure, are you?"

"Rest assured, I would know." Anne had never told Demeter about how the arms merchant and trafficker had raped her in Poti just before the transaction for the Kallay affair was about to take place.

"He told Anne that she had better stop messing with 'their' interests," Greg interjected. "Presumably meaning the interests of the Polyakov brothers. Although it was not clear, because then he went on to say that, otherwise, what happened to Litvinenko or worse could happen to her. To us. You know, Litvinenko was the former Russian agent and journalist who was poisoned with polonium in London by FSB agents supposedly for planning to divulge state secrets and implicate Putin and other higher ups in corruption."

"Well, it is not at all clear that the interests of the Polyakov brothers and the Russian state would not be one and the same," Demeter said. "We know that both the FSB and the GRU—that's military intelligence—are actively involved in transacting with arms merchants, including the Polyakov empire, to sell arms and nuclear material. The standard deal is that thirty percent of the profits go to the 'state,' which you can interpret as the pockets of the Putin gang. And there is no reason that the same deal would not apply to any of the other activities of these 'merchants of evil.' Sex trafficking or whatever."

"Wow, it all sounds very sophisticated and incredibly corrupt. And, downright sick."

"Colonel Polyakov went on to say that we should keep what we know to ourselves. Because, if any if got out…well, we would suffer a fate worse than Litvinenko. Then he literally ordered us to go back to Vermont," Anne continued. "And threatened that they could even get us there, if they wanted. Ugh, it was all very creepy."

"I see."

"We think he meant not just what we know about their activities, but also about their past," Greg said. "That the Polyakov twins are, as we told you, John, the bastard children of Lavrenti Beria."

"Yes, that could be quite detrimental to his career in the FSB right about now, if that got out," Demeter observed. "Although I am sure Putin and some of his friends are admirers of that freak."

"What was really uncanny—" Anne started to say "—was that he seemed to know everything we had been up to. No doubt from his brother. And that he was aware that we were here in Vienna and at the Staatsoper yesterday evening."

"Well, the FSB has a very strong presence here. And we know that Colonel Polyakov likes to come to Vienna a lot," Demeter said, adding with a facetious smile, "Seemingly he has the same taste in opera as you, Greg."

"I guess we had better lay low for the next couple of days," Greg said, ignoring the snide remark.

"No, I think you should get on the next flight back home. You don't mess around with these guys. And as I said, they are all over the place here. Moreover, thank you both, but your mission is finished."

"Not quite," Anne interjected. "We're going to see this through, John, until Julia returns, and everything is back to normal again."

"Well, okay, I see your point. But only if I can put some of my men to watch over you for the next two days, and then you promise you are out of here."

"That's a deal."

"Yeah, I am eager to get you guys off the premises. And the payroll," Demeter acquiesced with a little laugh.

"Well, well, well," Labrecque said, coming through the door. "It's nice to see the beautiful heroine of Porto Montenegro in our humble offices. You guys did a great job. Anne, without that tracker idea of yours, we would have never got these criminals. And the way you castrated that bugger, Hetzel, was real classy. They were certainly not very nice to you, so they deserved everything they got."

"Hello, Nicholas," Anne acknowledged her former colleague with a smile. "Thank you, but the tracker was actually Greg's idea."

"Slipping it in Hetzel's jacket was yours, dear."

"I'm sure Nicholas, you will relate all the gory details in due course," Demeter said. "But tell me now, how did you, George, and Radomir get on with all those thugs and the rest of the girls you guys were able to liberate?"

"Those guards who worked for the Polyakov gang have been jailed in Montenegro for now," Labrecque answered. "They are being charged with being accomplices to sexual trafficking, torture, and a host of other misdeeds. Anne and Greg may have told you that we were considering whether Hetzel should be sent in front of the ICJ—along with Polyakov and Brother Peter if we ever catch them. That is, if the creep survives the damage Anne did to him."

"Well, we've got a huge effort on to catch that Brother Peter," Demeter answered.

"What about the other girls, Nicholas?" Anne asked, concerned.

"Radomir is questioning them one-by-one with a psychologist in tow. They may be able to give us some additional information, but we also want to assess how much damage they have suffered. Greg, you had the idea of some foundation to help all the victims—with all the money and diamonds we managed to recover in Polyakov's apartment. That would go a long way to help these abused women, including the ones Julia is taking home now."

"I think you and Anne have some experience with foundations, Greg," Demeter said. "So I will leave all those arrangements up to you. But I fully support it. And I will get Interpol to back you. Just keep me in the loop."

Chapter 37

The flight to Chelyabinsk had been excruciatingly long, with a five-hour layover in Moscow, where Julia had connected with Nadia, Sasha, and Magda. They finally landed at Balandino Airport in the early morning on Sunday. Fortunately, Julia had boarded in Vienna well rested after sleeping in, and spending the rest of the morning with her mother. She had also managed to catnap on the planes, so she felt up to the one and a half hour drive to Ozersk in the early hours of the morning. Once there, her reasoning was, the four of them could cram into her mother's apartment, sleep a little, wash up, have a good breakfast, and then she could take each of the girls to their families one by one while the others continued to rest. She was eager to get this task over and done with, and to try and return to a normal life—although with what she had been through, she wondered at times whether that would ever be possible.

Now she woke Nadia, who had slept on her mother's bed—while she had dozed in the armchair—to tell her that she had talked to her father in the hospital, and that he and the rest of the family were expecting them there in forty-five minutes. So she needed to get ready.

Mikhail had been pleasantly surprised when he received the call. "Hello, Gospodin Glinkov, this is Julia Saparova. How are you?"

"Gospodja Saparova! Good to hear from you. I am well enough, thank you. Recovering, But I hope you have good news of my daughter."

"Gospodin Glinkov, she is sleeping in the next room. We are in Ozersk, and I will bring her to you within the hour."

"Oh God! How can I ever thank you, Gospodja Saparova. You are an angel of God." She could sense over the phone that the security guard was in tears.

∽∾∽

"Nadia! My darling Nadia," Gospodin Glinkov stretched his arms out from where he was lying in his hospital bed, and his daughter ran to him with a huge smile, the two melding into one in an embrace. "I thought I would never see you again."

"Dear Papa, I was so afraid," Nadia said between her sobs. "I thought I was going to die. But how are you?"

"Never mind me. I am so sorry that I let you go with those awful people. I cannot forgive myself."

"That is all behind us. Now I am here, with you, and I will not leave you and Mama. And Yuri. Ever again."

"I have caused you so much pain and suffering." And then he remembered, in his shame, he had hidden the video from Galina, so it was not a good idea to go into the details with her in the room. "Now darling Nadia, go and hug your mother and brother."

Nadia went over to where her mother had been sitting quietly, weeping tears of joy, waiting her turn, letting Mikhail have his, hoping it would help the recovery from his injury. Although just yesterday, the doctors had given her the devastating news: Mikhail would never walk again. His spinal cord had been damaged in the shooting at the East Gate of Mayak, and he was unable to move his legs.

Nadia hugged her, and Galina, too, was ecstatic to have her back. But what was it that Nadia had been through that Mikhail knew about, but had not told her? What was this pain and suffering that he had caused her? She would find out from him or from Nadia, that was for sure. And this beautiful woman, Julia Saparova, wasn't she the one who was the cause of Mikhail's injuries? And why was it she who was bringing Nadia back? There were a lot of unanswered questions.

Nadia peeled away and took little Yuri's hand. "I am so glad I am back with you. You are my best buddy, Yuri, and I missed you so much." She gave him a hug.

"Come here, my little Nadia, let me hold you again," Mikhail said. "You too, Yuri. I want both my children here by my bedside."

Julia thought this would be a good moment to ask Galina about Mikhail, so she moved closer and asked in a whisper, "Gospodja Glinkova may I ask, how is your husband?"

"Perhaps let's step outside, if you don't mind, Gospodja Saparova."

"Sure." They quietly left the room, closing the door behind them.

There, in the corridor, Galina poured her heart out to Julia: Mikhail would never walk again because of the spinal injuries he had suffered at the East Gate. And she did not know how they would be able to make ends meet. Sure, there would be the small monthly payments from the compensation facility for those injured in the line of work at Mayak, plus whatever meager income she made as a teacher. But that would not be enough for the four of them to live from, especially with the additional costs of having an invalid to look after—even though all Mikhail's medical expenses were supposedly covered by the state. The only way forward now would be for Nadia to stay at home and find a job. There was no question that they could afford for her to go off to the VUZ in Moscow. Absolutely not—they simply could not even contemplate it now.

"Gospodja Glinkova," Julia took the older woman's hand and looked in to her eyes, which had filled with tears as she finished recounting her tale of woe. "We will help you. We—that is Interpol—have confiscated a lot of money from the arms merchants who were the cause of your husband's injuries and your daughter's suffering, and we will be setting up a foundation in the West to help you, and others like you, who have been their victims. So please, please do not worry. Your brave daughter needs to be allowed to pursue her dreams. And we will make that possible, I swear."

Nadia's mother gasped, clasping her hand to her heart and blinking rapidly. Her mouth opened and closed several times before she was able to speak. "Thank you, thank you, Gospodja Saparova."

"Yes, on the flight here, Nadia told me that she is a physics student and she would very much like to attend the Institute of Physics and Technology in Moscow. We will make sure that the financial resources for her to do that will be available for her and her family, rest assured. Moreover, as it happens, I also studied at that institution and still have contacts there, so I will do everything I can to help her get in. Rest assured that I, or my friends, will be in touch with you, shortly and please feel that you and your husband and Nadia can call me at any time. Here is my card. And now, I have other business to attend to, so I will go inside to take my leave of your husband and daughter. Good bye, Gospodja Glinkova."

ℰ✺ℰ

The other girls were easier to hand back to their parents, since she had not grown as emotionally attached to them, and only Sasha's father had suffered an injury like Mikhail. But with these parents too, Julia put forward the offer of help from the foundation that Greg and Anne were setting up with the money confiscated from Polyakov and his gang. After finishing with those families, she popped into her office for a brief chat with Levinson, promising to return at the end of the week, and was back on the road by three p.m., heading toward Chelyabinsk and the airport. She had decided that she would spend the night in the city, but first, on the way, there was something she had to do.

Julia wanted to see if she could find any traces of the corrective labor camp at Gulag Chelyablag, where her Aunt Katerina had spent her last days. She had read in her research that the main gulag had comprised a large land area adjacent to Chelyabinsk, called Pershino, and that it was linked to the then railroad depot at Shagol. It had originally been established to support the war effort in the early forties as the Bakal iron and steel works, which then became known as Chelyabmetallurgstroy, shortened to Chelyablag. After its founding, this first became the primary corrective prison where Volga Germans were sent to work for the Soviet cause. There were three separate 'camp zones' on the main site, and as well, the complex included several satellite lagers and branches, including some as far away as Miass and the coalmines near the cities of Kopeysk and Korkino. Where exactly Camp Zone Number Three, where Katerina had been briefly incarcerated was located, was impossible to tell with the passage of time, but what she thought, based on her research, was that it probably comprised a separate area within the larger main Chelyablag facility.

The huge iron and steel complex—Chelyabinskiy Metallurgicheskiy—that to this day spreads between Shagol and Balandino Airports, she concluded must be the successor to Chelyabmetallurgstroy, the one built by, and for the Gulag inmates. It was in these industrial facilities in and around Chelyabinsk that during the war much of Russia's heavy armor came from—to such an extent that the city became known as 'Tankograd' for its production of the T-34 tank that was the mainstay of Russian heavy armor during World War II. Was her Aunt Katerina made to work on some aspect of this tank, or other armaments, she wondered? Although Julia knew that she would not be able to get into this still important, high security industrial complex, she was convinced that she was on the right track.

Julia had two other clues to follow. One, if she could ever find it, was a memorial to the dead inmates, which was erected in the early 1990s, supposedly on the site of the former cemetery grounds of the camp. Even though the report had said that this monument had been neglected and even vandalized since then, there was a chance that twenty-five or so years later she might still be able to find some traces of it.

Intriguingly, her map showed that just south of the military airport at Shagol and slightly to the east, closer to what was now the M36, was a cemetery called Uspenskoe.

Could this be where the common burial ground for inmates of the gulag where her aunt had been interred, had been located? At least here she could get in, so she could search for that vandalized and neglected memorial. Perhaps some traces of it were still there.

And, according to some of the research she had managed to get her hands on, a street had been named in honor of the Gulag's first and most illustrious Commander, Aleksandr Komarovski, in the part of Chelyabinsk where the original work camp had been located. It was to one of the successors of this man that Aleksandr Polyakov must have reported as head of the corrective labor unit, Camp Zone Number Three.

Julia decided she would make for Komarovski Street, which was in the modern business center of Chelyabinsk. The city must have expanded right over where the Gulag had been, she concluded. As she drove slowly along, taking as much in as she could, she was pleasantly surprised to see a hotel at 9A, the Utes Hotel, and, on the spur of the moment, decided she would stay the night there since her flight was in the morning. At least she would spend this one night very near to where her Aunt Katerina had finished her life.

Fortunately, they had a room. But the girl at the front desk gave her a blank stare when she asked about the Gulag. She knew nothing of a memorial to dead camp prisoners, but when Julia mentioned that she thought that it may have been at Uspenskoe Cemetery, the girl gave her directions how to get there.

Julia told herself that even if this was not where her Aunt Katerina had her resting place, it would give her the peace she was seeking. Just to be here, near where she died, in a place where her aunt may have finally found eternal rest after her short and turbulent life. It would do, given that evil empire's penchant to destroy—to liquidate—not only many of its innocent citizens, but also any vestiges, any memory, of their existence. She was content now that she had done what she could to resuscitate Ka-

terina's kindred spirit. After all, not only were they related, but also, they had suffered similar brutal experiences
at the hands of the monsters who directly ran, or were
allies of the men who ran, this rogue state, then and now.

Julia walked over to the cemetery and spent an hour
strolling through it, finally finding the peace and equilib-
rium that had been denied her since she was kidnapped
by the man Hetzel, alias Kallay. And Kalinsky in Russia.

Chapter 38

Anne's cell phone rang just after they got into the cab. She saw on the screen that it was Julia—the time ten-thirty-seven a.m.

"Julia! Where are you?"

"I just landed in Vienna. I want to meet up with you as soon as possible."

"Great. We are on our way to the Rudolfinerhaus clinic. Labrecque had Hetzel medevaced here to get him better care. We want him to survive so he can face trial at the ICJ. We'll be there in about twenty minutes."

"I'll meet you there. It shouldn't be much longer than that."

"Lovely. We'll wait in the lobby."

෮෮෮

In the elevator on the way up to the Intensive Care Unit, Julia told her friends how joyous the reunion between Nadia and her parents had been. But that it was dampened by the news that Mikhail Glinkov would never walk again because of the injury he suffered to his spinal cord when he helped foil the last heist. She related how Gospodja Glinkova had told her that their family would have a tough time making ends meet, and Nadia would have to go to work.

"Well, that's exactly the kind of thing the money from these crooks will help with," Greg said. "What a tragedy, though, for Glinkov."

"That's what I told them," Julia agreed. "That we would help. But poor man, he was just overjoyed to get his daughter back."

"Good, now let's see how this depraved abuser of women is faring," Anne said as the elevator doors opened.

The head nurse at the desk on the floor informed them that they would only be allowed to see the patient for ten minutes, and that, only because the head of Interpol had specifically instructed the hospital to let them visit with him. And that they should try not to cause the patient any stress.

"Stress?" Greg responded somewhat irately, as the nurse led them to the room. "Do you know what this guy is, Fräulein? A filthy human trafficker. A creep, who abused both these two women, as well as countless others. Young girls. Teenagers."

"*Jawohl, mein Herr. Keine Sorge,*" came the rather bland answer. "Yes, sir. No worries."

Hetzel slowly opened his eyes when they entered the room. His pale and drawn face metamorphosed into a wicked scowl, before he closed his eyelids again, momentarily it seemed, then reopened them, as if wanting to make sure that the three people who appeared before him were for real.

"Hetzel." Greg had thought long and hard about what he would say if he ever saw the man—who was no longer a man—the monster, he corrected himself, alive again. "You did this horrific thing to yourself, by your actions. By abusing my wife, Julia, Nadia, and many others. By corrupting my friend, Adam. By helping Polyakov with these atomic heists." Greg stopped for a moment, discomfited by Hetzel's blank stare at the wall behind him. He wondered whether any of this was penetrating the man's consciousness. Then he composed himself and continued: "You can rest assured that your penance is not over. It will never be, for so long as you live. When you get better, you will be hauled off to court—if we have our way, it will be the International Court of Justice where you will be tried for crimes against humanity. In front of the whole world. Along with some of your evil buddies. Until then, I hope you suffer here both physically and psychologically, in your living hell, you bastard. And may that continue in prison for the rest of your pitiful life."

The two men glowered at each other for a while longer. Greg poured all his hatred for the man into his look. Hetzel's eyes remained blank, showing no remorse, no contrition. After a few moments, he closed them, and Greg, Anne, and Julia left the room.

೧೨೧

"Gospodja Pleshkova," Greg said. "We will be returning home to Vermont tomorrow. Julia is safe, now, and she will look after you."

Julia nodded. "Yes, Matushka, I will not leave you alone again. We will get a nurse to come whenever I have to go away."

"Thank you again, Greg and Anne, for bringing my daughter back to me. And for finding the box of documents that has given me closure on my sister, Katerina's disappearance." The old lady stopped a moment to collect her thoughts before continuing. "But, Greg, there is one other thing I would like you to do. When you visited earlier, we talked about you writing the story of Katerina. You have to promise me that you will do this. So that the world will know what kind of monsters ruled my country, and people will never let such horrible things happen again."

They still rule your country, and it is happening even as we speak, Greg thought before saying, "Of course, Gospodja Pleshkova, I will write the book. But on one condition. Only if you help me. I will have a lot of questions for you as I delve into the life of your sister and of those around her. Also, the whole era of the fifties in the Soviet Union."

"Of course, I will help until I die. In whatever way I can."

"You will stay alive, Mama, well after Greg finishes his book. But this will be your project, with Greg."

"I will be emailing you most days, Gospodja Pleshkova, so you had better stay alive."

It was only in the elevator as they were leaving Julia's apartment, that Anne remarked to Greg, "Well, I hope we will not regret your promise to Julia's mother. Writing that book may end up costing you your life, my dear, if Boris Polyakov's reach extends to Vermont."

"Never mind, Anne. It is something I have to do, in spite of the Polyakovs and the FSB and all the arms traders and flesh merchants of the world."

"Greg, I love you very much," Anne said, pulling her husband to her and kissing him deeply.

∽∾∽

Their last evening in Vienna, as a final thank you, Demeter took Greg, Anne, and Julia to dinner at

Vestibül, the restaurant in the Burgtheater, right on the Ring. They were joined by Labrecque.

After the waiter poured the delicious Frizzante Quin Quin Schloss Eszterházy Demeter had ordered as an *apéritif*, the Interpol boss raised his glass. "Here's to you Anne and Greg, first, for helping us find Julia, and then, at great peril to yourselves, for helping us break open this vile human trafficking trade. And to you, too, Julia, for your special role in that and also for stopping yet another heist."

"Yes, thank you to all of you. And it was great working with you again. We make a great team," Labrecque joined in. "But this will not really be behind us until we capture Polyakov. And that Brother Peter."

"I suspect you're right," Anne concurred. "Especially if what we think is right, that they have at least the tacit support of Russian officials behind them."

"Well, we may need you to come back one more time," Demeter said with a little chuckle. "To help put those buggers behind bars once and for all."

"Or incapacitate them like you did with that pervert Hetzel, Anne," Labrecque added. "That was impressive, and he, at least, will never be the same again."

"So, Nicholas, how much money do you reckon we managed to find on the premises of these criminals?" Greg asked, wanting to change the subject.

"We found just over eight million dollars in notes—both greenbacks and euros," Labrecque answered. "Eight point three, to be exact. In the safe and stashed in various hiding places around the penthouse suite and on the yacht."

"Wow! That's a lot of cash to have hanging around."

"And then there are the diamonds," the French agent continued. "They should be worth another fifteen or so, once we monetize them. Plus the yacht itself—even used—should be worth a cool twenty-five million mini-mum if we sell it. Then there's the penthouse suite—but let's not get greedy. We're looking at say a minimum of fifty million dollars in all. Most, but not all, for your foundation. Contributed involuntarily by these crimi-nals."

"That's fabulous!" Julia exclaimed. "That should go a long way to help Nadia and the others."

"Yes," Greg said, "although some of these girls and their families will need a lot of support for quite a while."

"Well, one thought would be to hold a certain amount back for legal costs," Anne suggested. "As we discussed, to take Polyakov, Billy, and Hetzel before the ICJ once we have all of them in our hands. And demand some real reparations from them—track down all their ill-gotten gains—which could fund both this foundation and the other one we established for the child victims of the Soviet and post-Soviet nuclear program. It would give them a great cushion well into the future."

"Let's not get too far ahead of ourselves," Greg said, not wanting to raise hopes too far.

Epilogue

Greg and Anne settled back into their life in Vermont, but besides his duties as a professor in the English Department at Middlebury, Greg worked on the book with Gospodja Pleshkova over the next four months, keeping her busy with his questions, but letting her rest just enough to recover after each of her sessions of chemotherapy at the Rudolfinerhaus. Her cancer receded, and they were doubly happy when the manuscript, *Katerina, Beria's Slave*, was picked up by a major New York publisher. The executives of the company had such high hopes for the book, that they even flew Julia and her mother over for the book launch.

Anne and Greg completed the arrangements for the foundation, which they named the Katerina Foundation, in honor of Julia's aunt, seeding it with an initial total of twenty-three million dollars, with the prospect that additional funds would be forthcoming from the sale of the yacht and the penthouse suite, as well as further reparations from the Polyakov empire. The foundation's first disbursement was for Nadia's studies at the Institute of Physics and Technology in Moscow, and for her to be able to live in the capital and travel home often to see her parents.

The search continued internationally for Billy and Polyakov, but both the ginger-haired terrorist and the arms merchant continued to elude justice.

In spite of Boris Polyakov's threat, Anne and Greg suffered no Litvinenko-type repercussions in Vermont.

Was this a sign, they wondered, that, as they resumed their activities, the rogue former FSB band around the Polyakov brothers and their evil buddies who ran much of Russia no longer felt threatened by them?

There was no way to tell from where and when the next threat would come, though.

IF YOU ENJOYED

TWISTED TRAFFICK

TURN THE PAGE FOR A
SNEAK PREVIEW
OF THE NEXT BOOK
IN THE SERIES

TWISTED FATES

Summer, 2065

Preface

Andrew put the book down and pulled one dangling leg up underneath him. Staring at Julia for a moment, the gangly fifteen-year-old asked, "Grandma, is it true? Were you really a stripper?"

The two were sitting on the porch of the family house in Vermont overlooking Lake Champlain in one direction and the beautiful Green Mountains in the other: he with one leg still hanging over the side into the flower garden teeming with Bee Bomb and Brown-Eyed Susan, she sitting in a white wicker rocking chair. The late afternoon sun reflected off the pond, bathing the two in its warm, golden glow.

Just then, Anne came through the door. "Mother, can I get you something? Greg is making your favorite drink. The Vermont Vertigo."

"You know what your son asked me just now?" Julia asked, chuckling, instead of answering. "He asked if I really was a stripper in my youth, Anne! Imagine that. Me, his grandmother."

"Andrew!" Anne exclaimed, wanting to scold her son, but not finishing, since she knew that the question was legitimate and she was not sure where she should go with it. Fortunately, she was rescued by the ringing of the phone inside.

"But that's what Grandpa wrote in his book! That you danced and took your clothes off in that…that bar in…Vienna."

"Mom, the phone." Lily, Andrew's sister, appeared in the doorway. "It's for you. The Farmers' Market."

❧❧❧

"Well, Andrew—" Left alone with her grandson, after a long silence Julia launched into an answer to his question. "—when I first came to the West from Russia, that was the only way I could support myself. I was an illegal immigrant in Austria. So yes, I did some exotic dancing, as it was called."

"What's this? Grandma is telling you about her youth? Your grandmother certainly was a beautiful young lady," Greg said with a smile, appearing through the screen door with two glasses of his signature concoction: one part maple syrup, two parts freshly squeezed lime juice, three parts dark rum and lots of crushed ice. "She still is. And she certainly knew how to dance, she did." He handed one of the drinks to Julia, taking a sip from the other. "Hmm. Very good, even if I do say so myself. But more than that, Andrew, she was a very smart lady, your Grandma. And she worked very hard. She's a nuclear physicist after all. The exotic dancing— that she did just to make enough to live on until she got a proper job."

"And there was nothing more to it than that, I can assure you. I had a boyfriend then, you know." And looking lovingly up at her husband, Julia added, "Your grandfather's best friend, as a matter of fact."

"Grandma!" Lily interjected, shocked too, by these revelations. "So, you were a stripper and then you ran off with Grandpa? And left his best friend." It all seemed a little too much for the teenagers.

"Yes. It was my friend from school, Adam Kallay. He was Grandma's boyfriend, way back then. But he…he died well before your grandmother and I got together," Greg said, glancing at Julia. Adam and he had grown up together in Cleveland in Hungarian-American families that had known each other in the old country. They had shared a room at Harvard, fenced together for the college team, and Greg had tried to disentangle his friend from the first sordid nuclear heist affair when he went to visit him in Vienna several years earlier. He hoped the questions would end there.

But they did not. "How did this friend…this Adam Kallay die?" Andrew asked, suspicions aroused.

"He was shot. In a heist. You know, some terrorists wanted to get their hands on some nuclear material." Again, Greg hoped there would be no more questions. "It's all in the book you're reading, Andrew. *Twisted Reasons.* Right toward the end."

"You will see that your Grandpa and some other friends played a very important role in making sure the highly enriched uranium did not get into the wrong hands," Julia explained. "He helped prevent a major atomic blast that could have killed several hundred thousand people. You should be very proud of him."

"And your grandmother, too. She was involved as well."

"I guess I need to finish the story, Grandpa," Andrew said, overwhelmed and sullen, as he buried his head in the book again.

Julia gave Greg a loving smile as he sat down beside her and took her hand in his.

Summer, 2019

Chapter 1

Greg was glad to be back in Vienna. The Imperial Capital was his favorite city: it held fond memories for him, but he also relished its vibrant and changing present. For one, this was where he had met and fallen in love with his beautiful wife, Anne, who was now sitting beside him in the cab from the airport, checking her emails after the two-hour morning flight from London where they had been visiting Anne's brother after a three day stay with her parents in Cornwall.

Vienna was where he had first become entangled in the international intrigue that he had, after that—surprisingly to him—come to thrive on, and now, with his quiet academic life in Vermont, sorely missed. This was all in large part thanks to Anne, who had been working for Interpol at the time. But there were painful memories mixed in: the suspicion of, and disillusionment with his erstwhile best friend, Adam Kallay, had started here. Yes, the messy first attempt by some Russian arms merchants to steal some nuclear material from Mayak—the former secret city where Stalin and Beria had developed the Soviet atomic bomb—that his friend had drawn him into. And that had 'resulted' in Adam's death: Greg had never really told anyone how he had pulled the trigger of the pistol killing his friend as he was taunting him, ready to get away with enough highly enriched uranium for half a bomb.

On the positive side, yes, it was because of Adam that he had met Anne, who had been Kallay's contact at Interpol. And also Julia Saparova, the beautiful physicist who had taken Adam's job at the International Atomic Energy Agency, in charge of monitoring security at the former Soviet nuclear sites. In fact, Anne and he were really looking forward to spending some time with her over the weekend. She was flying back to give a report to the IAEA's top brass, and when she had heard that they would be in Vienna, had made arrangements to stay in town. Although she had said on the phone that she normally liked to get back to Ozersk to spend her free days with her sick mother when work took her there.

Another positive: Vienna had been the source—directly or indirectly—of so much of the material for Greg's writing ever since. In fact, his three most recent successes were all somehow linked to his times in Vienna. First had come the bestseller biography *cum* memoir about his Hungarian grandparents, *András and Lily*. Then *Twisted Reasons*, the story of the 'Adam affair', his second highly acclaimed 'novel' after *Wintertime,* the one he had written straight out of college. And most recently, *Katerina, Beria's Slave*, the true story of Julia's aunt, picked up by a major New York house. Just before leaving on this trip, he had finally finished and sent off to his publisher, *Twisted Traffick,* the next novel in the 'Twisted' trilogy: the story of human trafficking and the second heist attempt by those merchants of evil that he and Anne had helped foil.

Twisted Fates would be the third book in the series,

all of which were basically thrillers based on real life.

Thinking about the past—and really, the reason that he was back in the Imperial Capital this time—brought back another Viennese memory. One that had been unpleasant and nerve-racking then, but with time, had acquired a somewhat humorous patina. It was of that embarrassing moment at the meeting of the Austrian Literary Society, where he had been exposed in the act of impersonating a more famous author with a very similar name, Gareth Martens. And by none other than Billy Crawford, an old acquaintance from summer camp days, who—as he had found out during the 'Kallay Affair'—was now an internationally sought-after terrorist. But that was all now well behind him, and, justifiably, he was proud of the fact that based on his newly acquired renown as a writer, he had been invited back by the Austrian Literary Society to give another lecture. This time, though, since he had written in both genres, he was asked to talk on the continuum between memoir and fiction in modern literature, which he knew he would have no problems with since it had been the topic of many articles he had written. However, this time it was not that busybody imbecile, Crabbe, who had sent Greg the all-expenses-paid invitation, but the newly elected head of the Society, the dowager Frau von Hitzinger whom he vaguely remembered meeting way back then.

Greg returned to the present from his musings about the past just as the taxi pulled up outside the Sacher. He loved to stay in this beautiful hotel, and it helped that, as before, the Society's meeting was to be held here the very next day, Friday. The Hotel Sacher was right across from the Staatsoper, and, as he got out of the cab, Greg resolved to ask the receptionist to get them two tickets to whatever was being performed at the world's most famous opera house. He was an avid lover of the genre, having grown up with it as a child in Cleveland, where, at the insistence of his Hungarian grandmother, Omi, there had always been classical music playing in their home. Fortunately, Anne too, was a keen opera buff, although her tastes were not as eclectic as Greg's and tended toward the more often played romantic pieces.

"Tonight at the Staatsoper, Mr. Martens," the receptionist answered Greg's question, "let me see…there is a new production of *Siegfried*, you know, the third opera in Wagner's Ring Cycle. A great production. Wonderful, I have seen it myself. With Jonas Kauffman and Svetlana Kokova. Tickets are hard to get, but I am sure we can manage. And tomorrow, there is a performance of…let's see…Dmitry Shostakovich's *Lady Macbeth of Mtsensk*. As another possibility, there is also *The Merry Widow* at the Volksoper today and tomorrow. Perhaps that is more to your liking, Mr. Martens?"

Greg glanced over at Anne, who was standing several meters away with the bags, busy looking through a pamphlet on what to do in Vienna that week, then back at the receptionist, and on an impulse, said, "No, please, see if you can get us two tickets for the Wagner for tonight. That would be terrific." He loved the German composer, and although he knew that the Ring wasn't exactly Anne's 'cup of tea', she would certainly prefer it to the Shostakovich. Although he remembered that she had adored Julian Barnes' wonderful little novel about the composer where the opera had been mentioned. He himself had never seen it performed but had always been intrigued by the work, especially since it had caused Shostakovich so many problems with Stalin and his régime. In fact, an article attributed to Stalin himself had dubbed it 'Muddle Instead of Music', he remembered from the book. Also, the complicated story of adultery, scheming and murder spoke to him as an author. He was sorely tempted, but no, Wagner was definitely a better choice, Greg decided. In any case, he knew his wife would be pleased just to go out in their favorite city and make a romantic evening of it, especially with dinner at Julius Meinl after the opera, as on their very first date. Yes, it was indeed something to look forward to. He would break the news to her when they got up to the room.

Why not—maybe that would result in a little loving before we wander out to see the sights, Greg thought, liking his plan very much.

About the Author

Born in Budapest, Geza Tatrallyay escaped with his family from Hungary in 1956, during the Revolution and immigrated to Canada. He has represented Canada as a Rhodes Scholar, as a host in the Ontario Pavilion during World Expo '70 in Osaka, Japan, and as an Olympic fencer in the Montreal 1976 games. He is a graduate of Harvard and Oxford Universities, as well as the London School of Economics.

Twisted Traffick is the second book to be published in the TWISTED trilogy; the first, *Twisted Reasons*, was published by Deux Voiliers Publishing at the end of 2014, and the third will be published in 2018 by Black Opal Books. Tatrallyay has written other thrillers, one of which, *Arctic Meltdown*, was published as an ebook, and is available via Amazon and Smashwords. He has also written two memoirs, one about his family's escape (*For the Children,* Editions Dedicaces, 2015) and a second about his efforts to help three Czechoslovak hostesses at Expo'70 in Japan defect to Canada (*The Expo Affair,* Guernica Editions, 2016). He is currently working on a third memoir about the defection of a Romanian-Hungarian fellow fencer at the Montreal 1976 Olympic Games. *Cello's Tears,* his first collection of poetry, was published by PRA Publishing in mid-2015, with a second, *Sighs and Murmurs* following at the end of 2017.

Tatrallyay is a citizen of both Canada and Hungary and is a green card holder. He and his wife, Marcia Nousanen, divide their time between San Francisco and Barnard, Vermont, with frequent trips back to the many places they have lived, including New York, Boston, Montreal, Toronto, London, Frankfurt, Budapest, Vienna, Bordeaux and Montevideo. They have two children, Alexandra and Nicholas, and two grandsons, Sebastian and Orlando.